Buffalo Lockjaw

Buffalo Lockjaw

GREG AMES

HYPERION
NEW YORK

Library of Congress Cataloging-in-Publication Data is available upon request.

ISBN: 978-1-4013-0980-0

Hyperion books are available for special promotions and premiums. For details contact the HarperCollins Special Markets Department in the New York office at 212-207-7528, fax 212-207-7222, or email spsales@harpercollins.com.

Design by Brian Mulligan

FIRST EDITION

10 9 8 7 6 5 4 3 2 1

For my family

Where you come from is gone, where you thought you were going to was never there, and where you are is no good unless you can get away from it. Where is there a place for you to be? No place. . . . Nothing outside you can give you any place. . . . In yourself right now is all the place you've got.

—Flannery O'Connor, *Wise Blood*

On Vancouver Island, Ruth Benedict tells us, the Indians staged tournaments to measure the greatness of their princes. The rivals competed by destroying their belongings. They threw their canoes, fish oil and salmon eggs on the fire, and from a high promontory, hurled their cloaks and pots into the sea.

Whoever got rid of everything, won.

—Eduardo Galeano, *The Book of Embraces*

Buffalo Lockjaw

GLORY ZYDEL,
small business owner

When twenty-six psychiatric hospitals in New York City were "depopulated"—meaning completely shut down, everybody out!—sometime in the early 1980s, I can't remember the exact year, the released patients were handed one-way bus tickets out of town. The last stop on each ticket was Buffalo. Thousands of mental patients left Manhattan in the middle of the night. They could have gotten off anywhere along the way. In any of those dead upstate towns. They were probably confused, though, and terrified and all doped up. So they just rode for nine hours, staring out the windows, until the drivers parked at the Seneca Street Station and kicked their asses out. "Last stop. Buffalo."

Almost all of them ended up right here on Elmwood Avenue and joined our indigenous population of kooks. In those days, you know, the Reagan years, the insane were out in full force. I don't know if you remember this, James—maybe this was before your time—but they were like a traveling theater troupe. We began to watch for our favorite routines. The Thorazine Lean. The Hermaphrodite's Striptease. . . . Who else? The black-toothed Walking Man. Remember that guy? He wore dirty wool trousers and a dirty sport coat, but he was weirdly handsome when he kept his mouth closed, Native American–looking, strong face, great hair, glossy black hair. He would just stop suddenly on a corner and pose like a runway model, one hand on his jutting hip, grinning his crazy I'm-not-taking-my-meds grin. Sometimes he would flip his sport coat over his shoulder and prance back and forth, his chin held high. I loved watching them. They seemed to know how absurd everything was. They were trying to show us.

I opened this shop twenty-six—no, twenty-eight years ago now. I have sold everything here: animal hides, jewelry, records and tapes, CDs, drug paraphernalia, vintage clothing, you name it. I used to be on the corner of Elmwood and West Utica, but I moved here back in 1986 and I've been here ever since. Maybe it was 1985. . . . Well but anyway, I remember there was a major shift in the aesthetic around that time. All the artists, the true artists, were moving out of town. Some of them landed in Allentown, and that's when Allen Street started to get hip again, but many of them just split. They all went down to the City. All my friends. Jobs were scarce around here, you know? There's a true Buffalo story for you. We basically traded our best young artists for New York's most hopeless rejects. That's pretty sad. But I guess that's more or less every small city's story.

d-unit

I park my rental car outside the Elms and sit without moving, hands resting on the steering wheel, for almost twenty minutes. I'm listening to a CD I made six years ago. In my early twenties I wanted to document the story of my hometown the way Studs Terkel had tackled labor in America, but I abandoned the project, like everything else I ever started, about halfway through.

For two years I carried a digital voice recorder in the back pocket of my jeans. Calling myself an urban ethnographer, I conducted over a hundred interviews with drunks in dive bars, blue-collar kids who grew up near Buffalo's abandoned factories, artists and musicians and athletes who would never become famous and an array of local jokers and knuckleheads. I was not interested in hearing from the winners, I thought. At that time I had a pretty loose definition of what winning meant, but I'm sure it involved easy wealth and unwarranted prestige. I was a reverse snob. If you had earned your victory through hard work and discipline, you were okay by me, but if your whole life had been handed to you and you took your good fortune for granted, I thought you could go to hell. Then I moved to Brooklyn for a better job and have lived in New York City ever since. All I have left of my early ethnographical efforts is a single CD, a greatest-hits compilation of voices that I've spliced together.

I can't sit out here all morning, hiding in the parking lot, so I cut Glory off when she starts talking about zoning laws and trash collection. I pull out the key, slam the door and head for the front entrance. Carrying a potted geranium that I've been assured won't require much attention, I remind myself to be friendly and patient with the staff. I leave my suitcase and my library book, *Assisted Suicide for Dummies*, in the backseat of the car. In the lobby of the Elms, I stamp snow off my boots and sign the guest book with numbed fingers. Then I ride the elevator down to the D-Unit, where I'll find my mother.

Parked in a corner, she seems oblivious to everything going on around her. Her yoga pants are on backward, and she's wearing an orange polyester blouse that definitely belongs to someone else. In honor of today's holiday, one of the staff members has put makeup on her face: blue eyeshadow, pink lipstick, rouge on each cheek. She looks like a drunken clown. Carefully I approach her from the front so she can watch me advance. I don't want to startle her by dropping an alien hand on her shoulder.

"Happy Thanksgiving, Mom," I say, crouching beside her chair.

Wheaten hair, no longer color-treated, sits choppy and deranged over her outraged face. It's a hairstyle she never would have chosen for herself. She opens her eyes and focuses on me through the flecked lenses of her glasses. She stares with inscrutable attention, a ferocious look, before turning her head, lips pursed, as if she has seen nothing at all.

I press her hands together between my palms. "Happy Thanksgiving, Mom." I address her in a spirited, false voice.

She turns her head and smiles at me, as if for the first time. "Jammer," she says happily. She seems to recognize me now. "Janitor," she says.

Her legs are twisted awkwardly, her hips canted to one side. Because she can no longer walk on her own, they use a Hoyer Lift—a sort of crane for human beings—to hoist her out of bed and drop her into her wheelchair. The Elms is considered to have one of the best dementia units in New York State.

Looking away from her, I inspect the geranium's pink flowers. The girl in the flower shop called it a hardy, low-maintenance plant that blooms in minimal light. I hope that's true because she talked me out of the bird of paradise and the zebra plant.

D-Unit is crowded today. Smiling holiday visitors trudge alongside slow-wandering residents. Small hushed groups gather in the cafeteria and in the Common Room. A middle-aged man in a black suit encourages his decrepit father to put his socks back on. "Let's slide these on your feet, Slugger," he says, bending over his dad. "Here we go. One at a time."

A thirty-year-old brunette with pigtails and a bandaged

eyebrow appears beside us. "Mind if I take her in now?" she says to me.

"Not at all. I'll follow you." I gather my coat and stand up, allowing her to pass in front of me. "Is there assigned seating?"

"Oh yeah. Yeah, it's real organized." She wheels my mother into the cafeteria. "This is party central in here."

"Is that a war wound?" I nod at her bandaged eyebrow. "I hope one of the residents didn't . . ." I hope my mother didn't do that to you.

"Oh, this?" She touches her forehead. "No, no, no. We're not allowed to show our piercings during work hours. We have to keep 'em covered up."

"Wait, I think Ellen's in the Nature Room today," says Marianne, a good-looking woman in her mid-forties. She has gray-blue eyes and gray bobbed hair and a youthful face. Marianne looks like a twenty-year-old frozen in ice. If the nursing home is an engine, she is the fuel injector. Everybody moves a little quicker when she's around. She seems to be in perpetual motion, even when she's seated or standing still. On the first day we brought Mom here, Marianne welcomed us and told us to call her directly if we needed anything. "Sorry, Jean, yeah," she says, and looks up from her clipboard. "First table. Nature Room."

Jean swings the chair around in a tight arc and heads for the Nature Room. The muted TV in the corner of the room is tuned to the Macy's parade in New York City. The pale green walls behind the TV are decorated with framed photographs of sycamores and elms. Presumably this is why it is called the Nature Room. On the table nearest the entrance, a small paper plate indicates where I'm expected to sit. "ELLEN + 1 guest" is scrawled in blue ink on the paper plate. "Here you go," says the aide, parking my mother at the foot of the table.

"Thanks, Jean," I say, making an effort to remember her name.

Jean Jelly Bean.

She points at my abandoned geranium. "Want me to bring that down to her room?"

"Would you? That would be great, Jean. Thanks."

"Ellen, I have a drink for you, okay?" says a staff nurse. A plump, lively redhead, she holds a cup of orange juice in her hand. She leans over the chair, one hand on my mom's shoulder. "Here you go, Ellen. Down the hatch."

I push myself up from the chair. "I'm James."

"Pleased to meet you," she says. "Sheila."

We shake hands. *Tequila Sheila*.

Jelly Bean Jean reappears behind the chair and places an enormous bib on my mother's chest. It attaches with Velcro straps behind her neck. It reminds me of the lead chest protector the dentist drapes on a patient before an X-ray, except this thing is made out of cloth. Mom turns her head to see who has just placed this strange thing on her, but the woman has already disappeared.

Perry Como sings, "Empty pockets filled with love."

The D-Unit's boom box has some kind of beige pudding crusted to its speakers.

Marianne wheels a trolley of food into the entrance of the Nature Room. "Okay, let's start with Ellen," she says. "She's a regular, I believe." She examines a slip of paper attached to a plate. "And her son James is her guest today. He gets"—she consults another slip of paper—"a regular, too."

Marianne's son, her helper, carries the trays over. He's a stooped twelve-year-old kid with curly brown hair and amber eyes. His forehead is embroidered with acne. He places a tray before Ellen with great care, making an effort not to look directly at her.

"Go ahead and start when you get your plate," Marianne announces to the room.

I lean over and ask: "Are you ready to eat, Mom?"

She rolls the hem of her bib up her chest. "Snip . . . Snippy did," she says. Then she gazes out the window, shakes her head at this bizarre language, quits, forgets and stares down at the clump of tissues in her fist. The words no longer belong to her. It's so hard to know what she's trying to say, what she means exactly, and it's even harder to ask for clarification. Broken-backed glottals. A jigsaw puzzle of interpretations. Start with the border, the frame, she used to say, then work your way in. Now I am searching for meaning—*snippy did, Snoopy dog, solecism.* The vowels wander off like Grimm children lost in a forest.

I cut the dry white meat on my mother's tray into tiny bites. I lift them to her mouth. She understands what is expected of her. Dutifully she unhinges her jaws and allows the plastic fork tines to enter that contested space. Tasting the food, she learns that she's hungry. After three bites she smiles. She laughs. I feed her lumps of fluorescent orange squash and crusty stuffing and steaming hot mashed potatoes.

With the same fork I eat the food on my tray.

Mom chews each bite thoroughly. I dab her chin with a napkin. She is fifty-six years old. "Good," I say, "good. Take your time. We're in no hurry."

The old woman across the table is calling her own daughter Mama.

"Eat before it turns to ice, Mama," she says to the younger woman feeding her.

"I'm the hostess with the mostest," Marianne calls out.

"Water," says an old man in a ragged voice. He's in a wheelchair at the head of the table. His skeletal left arm is crossed over his right knee, his head jerked to the side. He reminds me of one of Egon Schiele's grotesques.

My mom eats and eats. She likes the buttered bread. She likes the coffee.

"Puh-puh-puh," she says jovially.

"Water," says the man again. He's trying to feed himself, but the food keeps falling off his fork. The seat for his guest is empty. The bald, cadaverous woman parked nearest him is drooling in her sleep.

Nobody has water yet. At the moment there's hot coffee and nothing else. Some folks have finished eating. Some haven't been served yet. Marianne needs more assistance than her son can offer, but the rest of the staff is busy in the cafeteria serving the other residents, or they're feeding the bedridden and infirm their pureed suppers.

"I'll be right back, Mom," I say.

I stand and head over to the tiny kitchen next to the nurses' station. I pour four cups of tap water. The smell of shit and turkey fills the air. Ignore it, I tell myself. I leave one on the table before my mom. I place the second cup near the drooler. I hand off the third to the old woman's "Mama" and bring the fourth to the old man.

"I have water here for you," I tell him in a loud voice.

"Water," the man says sensibly. His hands are folded in his lap, interlocked, beneath his towel-bib. Each resident wears a similar spattered cape, the standard uniform of this coalition of the forsaken.

"Okay." I touch the rim of the cup to his lips. "I have water for you. Are you ready to drink some of this?"

The man nods. I place one hand on the back of his head, on his skull, which feels narrow and delicate, covered in its soft wisps of hair, and I tip a thin trickle of water into his mouth. The parched, pointed tip of the man's white tongue darts forward. He swallows with a shudder of pain. Recoiling, I hold the cup in both hands. I glance around the room. Nobody's watching. The man opens his mouth again. "Water," he rasps. I pour in a little more. The man swallows that. For the most part I'm hoping not to choke him to death. He finishes the contents of the cup.

Meanwhile, down at the other end of the table, Mom has dropped her fork on the floor. An orange splotch of squash clings to her chin. She tugs on her bib and burps gently.

"Lucky we were given two forks," I say, returning to my seat to resume the feeding with a clean utensil.

Marianne is now standing beside our table. She has finally gotten everyone on her trolley served. A few of the aides are carrying trays to other tables. "Ellen, remember when we were talking about the secret ingredient in my stuffing?" she says, her hand resting on my mother's shoulder.

My mother looks up, baffled.

"When I get home, I'm dumping a bottle of wine in the stuffing," Marianne tells me, bringing me up to speed. "I'll let you know how it is tomorrow. We're having a superbig gathering. Oh, here he is now, the master of disaster. Ellen, this is my son Michael."

Michael waves sweetly, a quick swipe of the hand. He glances at Ellen, then lowers his eyes. Evidently he's been taught not to gawk impolitely at oddities like my mother.

"I told your mom that Michael was coming to help out today," Marianne says. "And here he is."

"And this is my friend Lynn," Michael says, indicating the blonde girl with braces who is trying to hide behind him. "She *has* to do volunteer work," Michael says. "I do it 'cause I like it."

"For school?" I ask Lynn.

"Girl Scouts," she whispers, blushing. Her chapped lips close over the glittering braces.

"Well, we appreciate it," I say. "Thanks to both of you."

"It's not so bad," Michael admits, shifting his weight from foot to foot. His hands are shoved deep in the pockets of his rust-colored corduroys. "At first I was scared."

"Me too," I tell him. "I was scared to come here, too."

I press the cup against my mother's hand. "Here's your water, Mom." I don't know. Maybe she wants to do it herself. Presently her eyes are unfocused. She doesn't seem to be looking at anything in particular. It's hard for me to know when she wants help and when she wants to do it on her own. "Are you thirsty?" Her fingers wrap around the cup, and she takes it from my hand. She starts gulping the sploshing water, as if she's trying to please me. An ounce or two dribbles out of her mouth and dampens her second-hand orange blouse. "Good work," I say, watching her. "Jeez, you are thirsty. Everybody's thirsty today."

"Isn't it super to have your son here, Ellen?" Marianne shouts.

Ellen glances in the general direction of the social work-er's alto voice. She holds the cup between forefinger and thumb: it could drop and splash at any moment.

"It . . . yes," my mother manages. The presence of women pleases her. She was a nurse for over thirty years. Her face, I've noticed, becomes more animated when women are around.

All my girlfriends loved her. They called her for advice on dating and medical matters. "Ellen, I've got a swollen foot." Or: "Ellen, this guy I'm seeing . . ." Mara Coursey called my mom for years after our breakup. It was unbeliev-able. I'd walk in and see my mother on the phone, her bare feet under her on the couch, the cord coiled around her wrist. "Oh, that was Mara," she'd say after hanging up. "The weather in Phoenix is over a hundred and ten degrees. Can you imagine?" It didn't strike her as odd that these women I'd dated stayed in touch with her, not with me. They sent her Christmas and birthday gifts. Their affection for Ellen taught me that I had been a fortunate child. I understood this only after I had met their overbearing and maladjusted mothers. My girlfriends showed me that the woman I had for years been rebelling against, the one I was trying to escape, was actually the one person from whom I had the most to learn. "Did you see the ducks are back?" she said, pointing to the backyard.

Now her scalp shines through her thinning hair. Her teeth are clotted with barely chewed food. More than anything I want her to have her mind back, her memory and intelligence. I want her to tell me what to do. But if even a partial recovery is impossible, as I'm told by everyone who has ever studied this disease, then my mother should be allowed to die. And who would argue with me if I decided that it was my responsibility to bring that about?

"You're doing great, Mom," I lie.

"Tribby," she adds, still trying to respond to Marianne's query. She makes a vain attempt at crossing her legs, as if we are all enjoying a nice discussion in somebody's living room. Her left leg hangs suspended in the air for a few seconds, before she lowers it again.

"I'm using white wine," Marianne explains to the oblivious drooler at the end of the table. "You might be tempted to argue for red, but I think I made the right choice." Marianne has grown accustomed to having one-sided conversations. She has perfected the soliloquy. "That's the secret to my stuffing."

I watch with pride as my mother slurps water from her cup. She can still do it herself.

Four years ago, at a diner on Elmwood Avenue, she told me that she was contemplating suicide. "It might be best for all of us," she said, "if I kill myself. Because I've seen where this leads. I've seen it a hundred times before." She sipped her water, watched me over the rim. She wore no makeup or jewelry, other than her wedding ring, and her brown hair hung loose around her shoulders.

Sometimes I regretted that she had become middle-aged in her twenties. She had sacrificed too much, I felt, and might have been better off living like a brat for a few years, partying on the back of someone's speedboat, snorting coke off a compact mirror and flinging her shoes into the ocean. She never allowed herself such indulgences. When she was sixteen years old, she decided to be a registered nurse. It was not a backup plan.

Leaning forward on her elbows, she searched my face with her eyes. "Do you understand why I'm telling you this?" she said. "I should probably do this within the year. Before it gets worse."

I did not understand. I felt betrayed, as every twenty-four-year-old infant would, and after my initial shocked silence, I made an impassioned case against suicide. I argued persuasively and incorrectly that things would turn out fine for her. I had never read any of her writings on the subject of degenerative brain diseases. Still, I took her to school. The results of the MRI had been inconclusive, I reminded her. Suicide was not the solution. Everybody went through hard times. Her confusion and memory lapses were probably attributable to menopause, I suggested, or vitamin deficiencies. I did not go so far as to call it a sin, suicide, but I spoke with the moral rectitude of a man standing in a pulpit.

Listening politely to me, Ellen picked walnuts out of her salad. She seemed dismayed by my speech, as if she didn't recall having mentioned suicide. She had no opinion at all on the topic. "Absolutely," she said, humoring me. "Right, yes, that's very true, Jimmy."

She used a fork to eat her salad. She lifted the food to her mouth without anyone's help. She kept her napkin in her lap.

"You're fine," I told her, and gulped my pint of beer. "Don't worry."

At the time I was working a few nights a week as a bartender. Mom and I lived in the same city—Buffalo—but I saw her infrequently. I liked knowing she was out there, it comforted me, but the actual logistics of providing support and solace were beyond me. I was getting high every night and hanging out with people I found far more interesting than my parents—the artists who made no art, the musicians whose bands never seemed to play anywhere, the stoned philosophers who recycled half-baked thoughts swiped from lyrics sheets. So I think it embarrassed my mom to tell me she was struggling. I recognize now that it was a courageous act. She hadn't told my father. She hadn't told any of her colleagues. And after our unsatisfying discussion, she told nobody else. She was alone with her encroaching dementia.

She retreated from the word "suicide," never spoke it again after our lunch together. That was probably her last chance to save herself, and she let it pass. She took one for the team. Seeing that I was distraught, she tried to joke me out of it. "They shoot horses, don't they?" she said.

Half a year later she was incapable of conceiving a plan to kill herself. The disease had already colonized the frontal lobe of her brain, and she'd completely forgotten what she'd told me. But I haven't forgotten.

My mother stares at me now. She drops the empty cup to the floor. Abruptly she's distracted by a noise that possibly only she can hear. Head cocked, she nods as though somebody is whispering secrets into her ear.

"Thanksgiving is my mom's favorite holiday," I tell Marianne, who's still holding forth on the sagacity of using alcohol as an ingredient. "She woke up before any of us and started cooking while we were still in bed. She wore her Lea and Perrins apron all day. Didn't even bother taking it off when she sat down to eat."

"That's sweet," Marianne says, watching her son Michael and his friend Lynn fool around by the electric organ. "Mike," she calls out.

"And when I woke up on Thanksgiving morning," I continue, inanely, "I smelled the turkey and the pies baking. Coffee brewing. You'd already worked a half day by that point," I say in Mom's direction. "We always hosted Thanksgiving at our house. Everyone she'd ever met, it seemed, was invited. Sometimes thirty people showed up. You never knew who was going to pop up at the table. My kindergarten teacher, Vietnam vets, the mailman."

"Sounds like a lot of fun," Marianne says, distracted.

"It was. She rose to the occasion every Thanksgiving. Didn't you, Mom?"

"You better believe it," says Ellen, abruptly lucid and grinning at me.

I want to jump up and shout. Did everybody hear that? A

perfect sentence. Marianne didn't hear, though. Desperately I want Marianne to hear my mother, to know she's real. "What did you just say?" I touch her wrist. "Say that again, Mom. Tell Marianne what you just said."

She blinks at me and frowns.

MARCY JENKINS,

gift shop worker, Albright-Knox Art Gallery

In my opinion, Clyfford Still was one of the greatest American painters of the twentieth century, definitely the most underrated of all the Abstract Expressionists, but he was very paranoid and notoriously difficult to work with. Hated gallery owners and anybody who brought personal politics into art. He literally tore his paintings off gallery walls in Manhattan if he didn't like how they were hung. . . . Do you know his work? . . . Oh, you should check him out before you leave today.

Gordon Smith was the director here and he made it his personal mission to win Clyfford Still's trust. They wrote a few letters back and forth. We have them on file here if you want to read them. They're pretty fascinating. Still was sort of a recluse, but you can feel him slowly but surely letting his guard down, and finally he allowed Smith to do a rare retrospective of his work in 1959.

It was a huge success and Still was so pleased with the reception when he came—he loved Buffalo—that he donated thirty-one paintings to the gallery. It was a major coup for Smith and the city. But for me that's not the most interesting thing. The rumor I heard is that—I can't remember who told me this. I think it was Oliver, the security guard. Yeah, it was Oliver. . . . No, I'm sorry, it was Don, one of the telemarketers.

In the late fifties, Clyfford Still was feuding with another painter, Barnett Newman. They hated each other. I don't know why. According to Don, they were like oil and water. But Clyfford Still didn't ask for money in exchange for the gold mine of paintings he donated, and he probably could have gotten millions out of Gordon Smith. Instead, the contract his lawyers drew up was amazing. It stipulated that if the Albright-Knox accepted his donation, the gallery could never again hang a Barnett Newman painting on its walls.

Isn't that wild? But Gordon Smith probably loved Newman's work, too—he's a fine painter, a very fine painter—so I imagine it wasn't an easy choice to make, and Don said that Smith waited a few weeks to make the decision, but in the end he cut the deal anyway. . . . No, it was Oliver. Sorry. It was Oliver.

Anyway, it doesn't matter who said it. The fact remains: we have no Barnett Newmans, unfortunately, but the largest collection of Clyfford Stills anywhere in the world.

memory boxes

The nursing home residents are now scattered throughout the D-Unit. Some are asleep in bed. Some are parked in their wheelchairs before the booming TV. Others wander in their food-splotched Bills sweatshirts, reciting *Finnegans Wake* to themselves.

In his bathrobe and slippers Adolf Hitler shuffles into the room, his right arm raised in a rigid Nazi salute. His gray hair is mussed, as if he's just awoken from a nap. A man in his early seventies, a former certified accountant from Batavia, Mr. Myers has somehow fixated on the idea that he is *der Führer*. When Dad and I moved Mom into the Elms, Mr. Myers stood by the door saluting our arrival. I raised some concerns about this with Joanne Syzmanski, the unit coordinator, but I was assured that Mr. Myers was perfectly harmless. A rather extreme case of personality transference, Ms. Syzmanski said, a condition common among those in the early stages of Alzheimer's, but nothing to worry about.

Even though I find Mr. Myers a repellent sight, especially when he attempts to goose-step in front of the TV, he would be even more insufferable if he had a full complement of language at his disposal. As it stands now, he can only muster the words "Achtung" and "Tschüss." When he attempts the latter, saliva bubbles out of his mouth, and the effect is more pitiful than provocative. Generally he spends the entire day lying in bed, his TV tuned to PBS. But when Mr. Myers emerges from his room, his right arm extended, it's considered a notable event, and the aides go on alert. He does not appear to be violent.

According to a textbook I skimmed a few months ago, a person's true character is often magnified by dementia. All the façades and poses are stripped away. Are you a miserable, angry malcontent? That condition will be accentuated in the nursing home. Are you a gentle person, a quiet person? You will most likely become even more so in your decline. Of course this is not true in all cases. I also read stories of peaceful people turning nasty in nursing homes. Residents can get pretty rough with their tapioca pudding.

While Ellen naps, I stroll around the D-Unit. Attached to the wall outside every room is a "memory box"—a wood case with a clear glass front, much like a medicine cabinet with two shelves—decorated with photographs and mementoes. The purpose of the box is threefold: residents can peer in and recall their past lives, though they rarely do; family members can arrange a photo montage honoring their dying loved one; and new aides can look at the photos to double-check who is supposed to sleep where. To most residents, the beds are communal property. Ownership is a concept they no longer understand.

Some of these boxes tell fascinating tales. You lean forward and peer into a display, and a hearty young soldier in uniform or a handsome athlete with pomaded hair looks back at you, almost challenging you to doubt his authenticity.

He glows with the confidence of youth. Can this graceful young man in a basketball uniform really be the same human being as that feeble codger in the diaper now seated on the carpeted floor, struggling with his own socks while his middle-aged son looks on in dismay? I should approach them and put my hand on the middle-aged son's shoulder. I should say, "Can I do anything for you?" but I know there's nothing. The son will only smile and shake his head. In truth, that's not the type of thing I would do anyway. Not only am I reluctant to intrude, but I worry that the man might say, "Yes. Help me." And then what am I supposed to do for him?

I detour into my mother's room. I'm on a mission here: stay focused. We need lip balm and moisturizer and nail clippers. Maintenance work is best done while she's sleeping.

Using all my patience and stealth, I manage to trim the fingernails on her right hand before she awakens with a murderous face and clenches her left fist. Guiltily I slide the nail clippers into the front pocket of my jeans. "Sorry," I say. "No more of that." Luckily the assault will soon be forgotten, and in a few minutes I'll just be that friendly young man again, the one who sits beside her. One manicured hand is better than none. And the right hand is the one that scratches unsuspecting passersby. Later in the week my father can work on the left hand.

Testing my luck, I put a dollop of lotion on my fingertip and show it to her. "Lotion," I say.

In response Mom yawns and shuts her eyes.

"There we go." I rub lotion into her dry flaking forehead. "Doesn't this feel good?"

Silence. It's nap time again.

Folding my hands behind my head, I lean back in my chair and try to remember if there are any women in town that I can call. I've lost touch with all my old contacts in Buffalo. . . . Shannon Brodie? Does she still live in Allentown? The last time I saw Shannon she was bartending at a martini bar on Chippewa. And she played soccer on Sundays in Delaware Park. Maybe I'll give her a call. "Still playing footie, Shannon?" But didn't she get married last summer? No. Yes. That's right. She married Bill Hogan. They have a kid now. A boy. Fine. No problem. Good luck with that. There's also Monica Swados with her pierced tongue and amazing— No. She got married, too.

A minute passes. Time to stretch my legs. I stand and reach my arms high above my head. Bending at the waist, I tap my toes with my fingers: left hand to right foot, right hand to left foot. This kills half a minute or so.

Where can I find beauty in this situation? I read somewhere that this is a good exercise for cynics. It sounds ridiculous, but I've been doing it anyway. When things get ugly, I ask myself: Where can I find beauty here? Right now I'm finding it a challenge to answer this. I guess my recollections can comfort me when I'm bored or distraught. A thin reed, but better than nothing. Few people my age consider the importance of memory. Without it, I'd have nothing. I wouldn't know how to rise from this chair. There would be no continuity. How did I get here? Why am I here? What is a toilet? How do my hands and mouth work? Relating to the world in any logical way would be an impossible task.

My memory keeps me tethered to sanity.

Every part of me demands escape right now, but I promised I'd hang out here until the rest of my family arrived. In the meantime, I pull out my notepad and begin working on greeting card ideas.

I WISH YOU A MERRY SYPHILIS AND A HAPPY GONOR-RHEA.

Not bad.

Can't use it, though. It's a line stolen from a Graham Greene novel.

The D-Unit door opens, and my sister, Kate, walks in with her girlfriend, Allison. Standing side by side, arms around each other's waists, they stop and read the bulletin board together: the daily menu; the calendar of upcoming events; the Resident of the Month Award.

Mom hasn't won the coveted ROMA yet.

I remind myself not to mention that I'm sober, or "dry" in the common parlance, and only to reveal it to my sister if it comes up organically in our conversation. That's humility. That's emotional growth, buddy.

"Hey, you," Kate says when she sees me. "Are you staying out of trouble?"

First words out of her mouth. I could be the president of the United States with hundreds of people rushing forward to shake my hand, thanking me for universal health care and worldwide peace and prosperity, and my sister would stand back from the crowd, shouting through a megaphone: "But. Are. You. Staying. Out. Of. Trouble?"

"Yeah," I say. "I'm trying to."

"Good."

Once again I'm struck by the amplitude of Kate's presence. Despite her diminutiveness, there really is something grand about her. Maybe her poise is the result of so many hours spent onstage, singing in musicals and acting in plays. Her face just glows. Shining black hair, shining smile. Men and women both stare at her in public. One of us must be illegitimate. If so, Mom's taking her dark secrets to the grave with her. Today Kate's dressed down in a black leather coat, old jeans and black boots, nothing special, but she still looks terrific. People often remember her as much taller than she really is, causing them to say, "But you're so tiny!" when they see her again. She's barely five feet tall.

Laughing, she cups my cheeks between her frigid hands. "Look at this beard! You look like a trucker. Or a caveman."

"I've been meaning to shave."

"No, no, it suits you," she says, appraising my face. "You look good. Healthy."

I can't resist. "That's because I'm sober!"

Kate doesn't respond. She just stares at me and nods.

Normal people don't blurt things like this, I realize, but I've set the bar so low for myself that abstinence seems like a worthy accomplishment.

I haven't had a drink in eight days.

"Good to see you again, James," Allison says, stepping around Kate. A half foot taller than my sister, she's an attorney in her late thirties. She's wearing a black wool trench coat and gray pleated slacks. "Kate's right. You look much better than the last time we saw you." She winks at me.

"Do you even remember that?" Kate asks me. "You almost burned the house down."

Cannot let them goad me this early. Amateur move to retaliate. Yes, the last time I visited, I took a brief siesta on their couch while making a stockpot of beans and rice. Yes, the pot was destroyed. But a culinary artist should never respond to his critics. A good sport like me? Not a chance. I haven't had a drop of alcohol in eight days. I feel like Amerigo Vespucci, a stout, intrepid man exploring undiscovered lands.

"Let's not dwell on the past, ladies," I say. "Today is Thanksgiving, after all."

My sister is not cocky or brash. She simply believes in herself. But that's not what I find so maddening. It irritates me that Kate assumes that life should be this easy for everybody. Her smile radiates not only her own confidence but also her confidence in *me*. She gives me consoling looks that seem to imply: *Hey, I know you will find yourself someday*. I can see it in her face whenever she speaks to me: the serene, pitying eyes that say, *I understand. Life is hard for you*. I instinctively want to say, *No, you don't fucking understand*. And she will tilt her head tolerantly and maybe even touch my forearm, as if to say: *I understand your desire to say, 'No, you don't fucking understand,' but someday you'll be comfortable in your own skin*.

"James," Kate says. "Did you put makeup on Mom?"

"I did not do that. She was like that when I got here."

"Electric blue eyeshadow," Allison says. "Wow."

"Trust me," I say to her, "if I had done that, I would have at least gone with a peach or apricot. Something to complement that crazy blouse she's wearing."

Allison nods. "It does look a little big on her."

"It would look big on a pavilion. Somebody around here is wearing one of her sweaters."

Kate hugs Mom. Then Allison leans down and squeezes Mom's hands and wishes her a happy happy Thanksgiving. Ellen smiles and giggles and falls asleep. She has no idea that one of her family members will end her life.

alive

My father wants us all to share one last family holiday together before he sells the house. Though he's not a sentimental man and never has been, Rodney even offered to buy airline tickets for my sister and me. We both agreed to come home, and we both refused to let him pay for our tickets.

Lately I've been too busy and too broke to fly to Buffalo. I come back when I can, maybe twice a year. Last week, in fact, I ignored the invitation to my ten-year high school reunion. It was an easy decision. Who wants to stand around in a hotel ballroom with former classmates reminiscing about the teachers we feared or laughing about how much hair we've lost or comparing the weight we've gained? No, thanks. Maybe forty years from now I'll be ready for something like that.

Not that I'm embarrassed. For the past three years, I've made a decent living at Sensitive Sentiments, one of the biggest greeting card companies in America. When I was twenty-five, I started in their Birthday division. Four days a week I brainstormed concepts with a weed-smoking nihilist named Cal. We ate jelly doughnuts, drank gallons of coffee and tried to make each other laugh with our bullshit. One of my best cards began like this: "Son, though I may not have the words to say it . . . ," and I had to resist the urge to add "or the time, or the patience, or frankly the desire." When I finished the card, Cal made a gesture of approval by tasting the imaginary vomit in his mouth, which was his equivalent of a thumbs-up. It surprised neither of us when "Son, No Words for Love" was approved by the board.

Last year, though, I was moved to the Laffs division on 53rd Street in Manhattan, when Sensitive Sentiments became part of Kwality Kards. "I'm out," Cal said. "No más." He became a waiter in Dumbo. But I've put up with much worse jobs in Buffalo, so I packed up my *Rodale's Synonym Finder* and my pink FUCKING THE BOSS coffee mug, and I relocated to Kwality Kards.

Eight of us congregate in a windowless office with torn couches, a ten-year-old desktop PC and a microwave. I am probably the youngest and least jaded person in the room, but I fear that I am gaining on my colleagues. We are required, as a group, to produce one completed mock-up per week. If we reach this weekly goal, we are awarded a small bonus in our paychecks. This is the vaunted incentives package that our company is known for in the industry. But if we screw around all week and get nothing done, which is always a distinct possibility, our weekly pay is docked the same amount. A goose egg is frowned upon by corporate. Unproductive workers have been asked to leave the "family."

My latest kill—our term for a successful concept—was a card that has since become popular with secretaries and other office workers. On the cover, a muscular, bare-chested man leans against a tree, smiling. HAVE I GOT A DONG FOR YOU, reads the caption. On the inside of the card, he's fully dressed and ringing a bell. DING-DONG! IT'S YOUR BIRTH-DAY!!!!!

We drink a lot of beer to dull the sorrow.

My father arrives fifteen minutes after Kate and Allison. His manner is brisk and military when he enters a room. He's on a mission. Focused. A tall, bald man with a clean-shaven face, Rodney carries himself with the upright posture of one who believes that carriage reveals character. A retired Senior Office Manager for TidyPro Industries, a commercial cleaning contractor, he's efficient and professional in all things. He wears a white shirt, a blue-and-red-striped tie and slate gray slacks.

"James," he says.

"Dad."

"Good to see you." He extends his hand. "Happy Thanksgiving."

Our greetings are always a stiff dance, formal and awkward, two tin men in need of an oilcan. We will loosen up soon. I give his hand a good strong clench before releasing. "Happy Thanksgiving to you," I say. "How was Mass?"

"Oh, hell, I didn't think we'd ever get out of there." His eyes soften to match his sardonic smile. Beneath the armor is a stunted funnyman. "There was a baptism, a coronation, lion tamers. The homily was at least half an hour long. Father Brian set a world record today, I think. The theme was 'The Joy of Giving,' but all he gave me was a headache." He glances down at Mom. "Did she eat?"

"Oh yeah," I say. "She ate everything. She really chowed down."

He lowers his voice. "Let me ask you a question. What happened to her face?"

"It wasn't me," I say. "I think one of the aides did that. Apparently she used a house painting brush."

Rodney leans down and hugs her. "Happy Thanksgiving, hon."

Ellen's hand reaches up unsteadily, pats the back of his head. She burps into his ear. Rodney straightens up, shoots his cuffs and smiles at me.

"She liked the turkey," I say to him.

"Clearly."

"And for dessert she had—"

"Hi, Earl," my father says to a decrepit old man inching toward us. "Happy Thanksgiving."

Rodney knows the names of all the residents. He visits the D-Unit every day.

"Th-th-thank you," says Earl, a man whose sparse side whiskers connect with his mustache, like a pugilist in a daguerreotype, "s-s-same . . ."

He can't complete the sentence.

"Got some snow on the ground out there," Rodney says to him. "Gotta get the chains on your tires, Earl. Winter's here."

Earl is cashed out. He lifts his hands and holds them up in the air, fingers knotty and useless. Like most of the people here, he's at least two decades older than my mother. "Th-thanks," he manages again with his caved-in voice.

At times like this, I try to believe that I am learning

some great lesson from this experience. There must be something required of me here, some act of service or kindness, but I have no idea what it could be, other than just showing up and pretending that we're okay.

A burst of gunfire erupts from the big-screen TV in the Nature Room. We pause to watch it. A handsome man with a dirt-streaked face, an actor whose name eludes me at the moment, falls to his knees in an alley. Blood is geysering out of him, a champagne spray of red. He dies. Nobody cares. During a battery commercial, Rodney leans over and says, "You know, *Consumer Reports* says that all batteries are the same, so you might as well buy the cheapest ones on the shelves and not pay any attention to this advertising. Keep that in mind the next time you're in Walgreens."

"Okay."

Our old animosity is blurred and almost hard to remember, like graffiti scrubbed from a brick wall: the fights over my clothes and hair; his hatred for my hooligan friends; his strict punishments that only provoked further rebellions, which resulted in still harsher penalties. How foreign it all seems now, like the history of another family that had nothing really to worry about.

When Mom stumbled and fell on the battlefield, Rodney and I realized, maybe for the first time, that we were allies and our ranks had dwindled considerably. We needed to come together. In some ways we have done this, but we are only just now learning how to talk to each other.

Motioning to Mom, he asks: "She share any of her food with you?"

"I had my own plate."

"That's good," he says. "So how are things down in the Big Apple?"

"Same old grind," I say, steering the conversation away from any openings for mockery. I quit bartending years ago, but I'm making even less money now as a greeting card scribe. Late twenties. Single. Living with two roommates. Not a world-beater by any means but I am a guy who shows up to work every day. I like to think of myself as a late bloomer, a tortoise rather than a hare, but I haven't advanced very far in life, and I know this disappoints Rodney. He climbed higher than his own father. He expects me to do the same. But in my father and sister's presence I seem to regress and become a petulant delinquent again, the jerky kid who spots hypocrisy everywhere, enjoys nothing and won't reveal himself. Nobody likes that asswipe, including me. "And how are things with you?" I say.

"Can't complain," my father says. "My headaches are back but I've got a new prescription that seems to be working out."

"That's good."

Silence ensues.

"Snowing out there?" I say.

"Not too bad. Nothing's sticking."

More silence. We nod and smile at each other, rock on our heels.

FATHER, YOUR MANY WORDS OF ENCOURAGEMENT . . .

Kate and Allison return from the ladies' room, holding hands. A smile bursts onto Rodney's face when he spots them approaching. "Here they are," he sings in a rumbling basso profundo, "Misses America."

"Dad," Kate says.

When we were in school, if my sister and I had activities on the same night—a rare but occasional occurrence—Mom always attended mine, while Dad went to Kate's. We all knew that Mom was getting shortchanged in the deal—she had to sit in a cramped gymnasium for two hours to watch her son, "the sixth man," play about eight minutes of a basketball game—but it was harder still to imagine that Dad would miss any of Kate's performances in school plays. His devotion to her, his favorite child, never really concerned me because I always had Mom, champion of the underdogs, in my corner.

This is a rarely acknowledged truth of families. Alliances are formed early.

But unlike my sister, who lived to make my parents happy, I longed for a debauched life. I wanted drugs and sex and close calls with death. By the time I was twelve years old, I knew my sister's path was unacceptable to me. When I was kicked out of public middle school for trying to sell oregano joints to unwitting sixth-graders, Rodney exiled me to one Catholic school after another, each of which was more strict than the last, each less willing to tolerate my unique brand of subversive humor. One summer Rodney even sent me to a sleep-away camp in Maine in the hopes that I'd shape up. I didn't. I learned how to blow smoke rings and burp the national anthem. The following two schools didn't appreciate my act either, and both asked me not to return in the fall. That's when Rodney played his trump card: he sent me to St. Aloysius' School for Boys. Stern-faced Jesuit priests patrolled the halls. Detention was called JUG: "Justice Under God." I wore a sport coat and tie every day. Father Joseph made me cut my hair and shave off the downy mustache I was cultivating.

By then I had become a rogue element occupying a back bedroom in my parents' house. I snuck out almost every night. No amount of punishment tempered my zeal for exploring the streets after dark. My associates and I met behind a gas station, where we smoked and philosophized about girls, ice hockey and vehicular maintenance. Meanwhile, Kate was constructing an impressive résumé, brick by brick. Piano lessons. Gymnastics practices. A private French tutor on Saturday mornings. Church choir practice on Saturday nights. Nobody forced her to do these things. She received a form letter from President Bush *père* congratulating her on being one of the outstanding high school students in the country. She was driven by some inner motor to succeed. She attended Duke on a scholarship and graduated summa cum laude. On the Friday morning after graduation, she moved to Portland, Oregon, where a job awaited her. She had her pick of cities, and moved as far away from Buffalo as she could.

"You guys want to get a bite to eat?" Rodney checks his watch. "There are a few restaurants open today. Or we could go to the Greenfield Club tonight. They'll give us whatever we want." He smiles at me. "But I doubt anything could match the banquet you've already enjoyed, James."

Kate says, "I was thinking I'd take Allison for a quick tour around town. Show her some of the sights and sounds."

Anxious to escape, I say: "Actually I need to run a few errands myself. I came here straight from the airport."

"Go ahead," Rodney says and waves us off. "We'll meet back at the house at six. Is that clear, everybody? James? Six o'clock."

The elevator doors close in front of me, protecting me. Leaving D-Unit, I feel lighter. Tomorrow I'll return, or the next day, but right now I'm alive and clearheaded. I can remember my home address, my Social Security number and my second-grade teacher's name. Mrs. Brewer. And I'm leaving behind the squalor of "the top-rated nursing home in Erie County," according to a plaque in the lobby.

An attractive girl is seated at the reception desk, pulling her long hair back and tying it in a knot behind her head. "Have a nice day," she says to me, her head tilted to the side as she ties her hair up.

"Thanks. You too." I stop at the desk. Mr. Casual. Mom's dying down in the D-Unit, sure, we all have our problems, but— "Are you new here?"

Indigo silk blouse, the two top buttons undone.

"I've been here a little over a month." She has a magazine open in front of her. "Five weeks, I guess."

Ringless fingers, no nail polish.

Casually I lean my hand against the counter. "How is it so far? Do you like it?"

"I don't do much. Answer the phone . . ."

"Smile at people."

"Yep. Smile at people when they come in. Say 'Have a

nice day' when they leave. To be honest, there wasn't a great deal of training."

I laugh louder than necessary and glance again at the magazine. What is she reading? A red *V* is visible. *Vanity Fair? Vogue?*

"But people appreciate that," I tell her. "You're doing a great job here."

"Well, thanks."

A moment passes in silence. I would love to bring her back to the house, late night, when Dad's asleep, and . . .

"What are you doing later?" I ask her.

"Me? Oh, I'm going over to my boyfriend's house for Thanksgiving dinner," she says.

"Great! Enjoy that!" I say. Totally casual. I'm a mellow cat. Just being friendly. No big deal. But look at the time. I better get going. Holiday schedule. "Happy Thanksgiving," I say and head for the door.

"Bye." She waggles her fingers in a casual wave. "Happy Thanksgiving to you."

STAN BENNETT,
high school teacher

Let me tell you about passion. You don't know what true passion is. You've probably read about it but I lived it, man, day in and day out. Ask my ex-wife. She'll tell you. . . . When we played at home, in Rich Stadium, I was in the parking lot by ten a.m. sharp. Guaranteed. As a season-ticket holder, I felt it was my duty to tailgate. I stood behind the bumper of my Monte Carlo, cranking Rush and Van Halen tapes while my buddies cooked hot dogs and burgers on a hibachi, and my little brother sat in the front seat reading the sports page against the steering wheel. The Monte Carlo had just topped 150,000 miles and still drove great.

I'm gonna say this and I don't give a shit who doubts me. The Buffalo Bills were the best professional football team of the early nineties. Every Sunday they tore through their opponents, slaughtered them, on their way to four straight Super Bowls. I attended every home game, every home game. I was out there in the end zone, growling, "Deee-fense" and "Bruuuuuce" and "Let's Go Buff-a-lo!" I recognized a zone blitz package from three hundred feet away. I shouted warnings to Coach Levy. I shouted at the nearsighted referees when a bad penalty was called against us. I shouted at hot pretzel vendors. I couldn't contain myself.

When we scored, I stood patriotically with my comrades and sang "Buffalo's Talking Proud" and "The Bills make me want to shout, kick my heels up and shout!" I danced in the aisle, pumping my fists and my knees in the air. I laughed. I cried.

Where's the tape in this thing? . . . Ah, digital. Nice.

Let's be honest now. Some of my comrades hated me. Over the years a few punches had been thrown at me. Unjustifiably, I thought. . . . Once, a fifty-year-old man with a hearing aid, I mean the guy could have been my grandfather . . . This old guy was thrown out by security after he'd become a little too riled by my singing. When he grabbed my throat with two hands, my little brother tossed a beer in his face. That didn't calm him down.

Now, those were the good days. When the Bills were losing, which, granted, was a rare occurrence back then, but it happened. If I knew we were going to lose, I sat miserably in the end zone. Grumbling, pissed off, my arms folded on my chest, I knew my whole week was ruined. My asscheeks were frostbitten. The snow was packed tight under those metal benches. I had whooping cough. My life was shot. Nobody loved me. Life had no meaning. My wife was fucking the mailman. And Monday morning was a curse, a pox on the house of me.

I wasn't sure I was gonna tell you this, but I think I can trust you. Anybody ever tell you you have an honest face? If they did, they're a liar. You look like a convict. What are you gonna do with all these stories? Beat off to them? Are you a pervert? . . . Look, I have a secret that I've never told anyone before, but I'm gonna tell you. You ready for this? . . . I helped the Buffalo Bills during those miraculous years. Some may call it superstition, but nobody believed Galileo when he first piped up, either.

On Sundays I had certain rituals, set patterns—I followed them religiously—that directly contributed to the four straight

Super Bowl runs. It's true, it's true. Ask Doug from Schroeder's Bakery. I wore the same blue T-shirt to every game. Under layers of cotton, Gore-Tex and wool, I wore my lucky blue boxer shorts with the red Bills helmets. Without fail, I offered a single high five to each of my buddies after a field goal; three high fives were distributed to each man after a touchdown. I always ate a hot dog with mustard during the second quarter. And when my own supply of smuggled beer ran out, I bought big cups of Labatt's on the upper deck from the Alpha Sigma Whatever sorority girls, who were fulfilling their charter-required act of weekly community service. Yes, I did. I did. . . . I admired their philanthropy. It brought a tear to my eye. Young girls. Winter caps pulled down over that long shining hair. Are you kidding me? Those girls were making the world a better place. . . . Now, during the third quarter I bought a hot pretzel. Always. And the fourth quarter was Nacho Time.

The Bills' record with me in attendance? Lifetime? You ready for this? . . . Fifty-two wins, six losses. How's that for a winning percentage? We're talking over .800. But we tanked all four Super Bowls. Some say we were overmatched in size and skill, and sure, there's something to be said for that, but on bad days, on dark days, like in February, I still think we fell short because I was not there, in the flesh, with my hot pretzel and special underwear.

celebration

Rodney straps himself into the passenger seat of my rental car. He turns down the volume on the car's stereo. "What," he says, "is that?"

"That's Stan the Bills Fan," I tell him. "You remember when I made that oral history of Buffalo."

He shakes his head. "Can't say that I do."

Stan was a lucky find. I met him outside a B-Kwik Market on West Klein Road. He seemed representative of a type of man you see all over Buffalo. An overweight guy in his forties with a lopsided goatee, Stan wore a Bills winter jacket and stonewashed jeans tucked into his Timberlands. He was drinking a twenty-ounce Mountain Dew and climbing into his minivan. Even though he was a perfect stranger, I asked him straight off to talk about the Bills, a logical opener, and he regaled me with tales about rooting for a team that always broke his heart. I had formed an early shallow impression of him, based on his appearance, that was soon belied by his intelligence and self-deprecatory humor. During our interview he talked about many things, including his wife and kids, but he was most animated when recalling the glory years of his favorite team.

I commiserated with him. For two decades I worshipped at the altar of the Buffalo Bills. It was in my blood. When six-year-old Buffalo boys were thrown together by their mommies, they threw rocks at trees, kicked things and talked Bills and Sabres. We were tiny zealots. We knew the names, the numbers, the vital statistics. I remained faithful through adolescence and into my early twenties. My holy trinity consisted of Jim Kelly, Thurman Thomas and Andre Reed. A well-executed screen play was more beautiful to me than any ballet. The no-huddle offense was fiendish and unstoppable. For about seven years the Bills were gorgeous to watch. When Jim Kelly hit Andre Reed on a slant for a clutch first down, or when Steve Tasker extended his body and flew through the air to block a punt, I felt grateful to have witnessed such perfection. The Bills gave us something to talk about on Monday mornings at work. We ballooned with pride after victories. At last, our noble city warranted national attention for something other than natural disasters. The Bills gave us hope. But they lost four big games with class and dignity, and, in the end, that taught us even more.

"My oral history of Buffalo," I say, attempting to jog my father's memory. "That was my big project for a while. My life's work. Remember? I was an urban ethnographer."

He stares out his window. "I believe you."

We have 6:30 reservations at the Greenfield Club. Tonight I'm the designated driver. Dad's had a few stiff drinks already and anticipates having a few more. I don't blame him for putting on a pre-dinner buzz. Mom's absence must be even harder for him to take on holidays.

Kate and Allison hold hands and whisper at the table. Their shoulders seem to have magnets in them; they lean into each other. They are always touching. When you're in love like they are, nothing penetrates that armor—not a world-wide oil crisis, not the degradation of the environment, not even the death of your mother. But that doesn't mean that other people want to see it all the time. The closest thing I have to a romantic relationship is a loose arrangement with Michelle, a young woman who lives above me in Brooklyn. We sleep with each other when we're both depressed and lonely.

"Do you want to get the fondue?" Kate says, meaning: *I want the fondue*.

"Do you think that's too heavy for an appetizer?" Allison says, meaning: *I don't*.

"James is taking Lactaid pills these days," my father says. He sips his Tanqueray on the rocks with an olive. "He says it helps his bowels."

"I don't think they need to know that, Dad," I tell him.

Allison looks at Kate. "You tried Lactaid and it didn't work for you, right?"

"Yes. And you did, too, I think."

"Well, I'm not lactose intolerant, baby girl."

"Neither am I, it turns out."

They laugh and bask in each other's admiration.

"James is," my father says. "He gets pretty uncomfortable if he doesn't take his fart pills."

"We covered that, Dad," I tell him.

When the waiter appears, I order a Heineken. My sister scrunches up her face, as if to say: *Aren't you on the wagon?* I smile back at her, as if to say: *Everybody knows that beer doesn't count when you're riding the wagon.* This doesn't convince her. Her frown says, *You told us you were dry.* I hold my smile until I feel the strain in my cheeks. *I'm not* bone *dry.*

She stares at me for a moment longer before turning to my father. "So: how has Mom been lately?"

"Good," he says enthusiastically. "Great. She's been communicative and smiling for most of the week. She doesn't fight the aides as much. Got her hair done on Friday and seemed happy."

He's not consciously lying, but I think he's incapable of seeing what's before his eyes. Drawing instructors tell their students to draw what they see, and not what they remember an object looks like; the mind will attempt to create a vision out of its vault of memory. The mind lies. Rodney sees only what he needs to see. He ignores anything that's unpleasant.

"Mom's dying of Alzheimer's," I say.

"The stylist, Mrs. Andrews, comes in on Fridays," he says, ignoring me. "She works so well with the residents. Puts them right at ease."

Is this pathology or genius? He doesn't dwell on problems. He wasn't raised to complain about things he can't control. I drain my beer in three minutes.

Barnes & Noble Booksellers #2937
12193 Fair Lakes Promenade Drive
Fairfax, VA 22033
703-278-0300

STR:2937 REG:004 TRN:8151 CSHR:Victoria H

$3.99 TP Asst		
9780594459460	T1	
(1 @ 3.99)		3.99
$3.99 TP Asst		
9780594459460	T1	
(1 @ 3.99)		3.99
$3.99 TP Asst		
9780594459460	T1	
(1 @ 3.99)		3.99
$3.99 TP Asst		
9780594459460	T1	
(1 @ 3.99)		3.99
$3.99 TP Asst		
9780594459460	T1	
(1 @ 3.99)		3.99

Subtotal	19.95
Sales Tax T1 (6.000%)	1.20
TOTAL	**21.15**
CASH	**21.15**

A MEMBER WOULD HAVE SAVED   2.00

Thanks for shopping at
Barnes & Noble

101.34B   08/09/2014 11:03PM

CUSTOMER COPY

for purchases made by check less than 7 days prior to the date of return, (ii) when a gift receipt is presented within 60 days of purchase, (iii) for textbooks, or (iv) for products purchased at Barnes & Noble College bookstores that are listed for sale in the Barnes & Noble Booksellers inventory management system.

Opened music CDs/DVDs/audio books may not be returned, and can be exchanged only for the same title and only if defective. NOOKs purchased from other retailers or sellers are returnable only to the retailer or seller from which they are purchased, pursuant to such retailer's or seller's return policy. Magazines, newspapers, eBooks, digital downloads, and used books are not returnable or exchangeable. Defective NOOKs may be exchanged at the store in accordance with the applicable warranty.

Returns or exchanges will not be permitted (i) after 14 days or without receipt or (ii) for product not carried by Barnes & Noble or Barnes & Noble.com.

Policy on receipt may appear in two sections.

Return Policy

With a sales receipt or Barnes & Noble.com packing slip, a full refund in the original form of payment will be issued from any Barnes & Noble Booksellers store for returns of undamaged NOOKs, new and unread books, and unopened and undamaged music CDs, DVDs, and audio books made within 14 days of purchase from a Barnes & Noble Booksellers store or Barnes & Noble.com with the below exceptions:

A store credit for the purchase price will be issued (i) for purchases made by check less than 7 days prior to the date of return, (ii) when a gift receipt is presented within 60 days of purchase, (iii) for textbooks, or (iv) for products purchased at Barnes & Noble College bookstores that are listed for sale in the Barnes & Noble Booksellers inventory management system.

Opened music CDs/DVDs/audio books may not be returned, and can be exchanged only for the same title and only if defective. NOOKs purchased from other retailers or sellers are returnable only to the retailer or seller from which they are purchased, pursuant to such retailer's or seller's return policy. Magazines, newspapers, eBooks, digital downloads, and used books are not returnable or exchangeable. Defective NOOKs may be exchanged at the store in

In his less tight-lipped moments, Rodney has told me a few interesting stories about his childhood. His folks owned a lunch counter in Cassadaga, New York. They opened the doors at five a.m. for the deer and duck hunters. They sold hot and cold sandwiches, burgers, fried chicken and biscuits, spaghetti and meatballs, mashed potatoes, baked beans, ice cream sodas and floats, glossy magazines, cigarettes and hard candies. Rodney's father also sold hunting and fishing and marriage licenses. Grandpa Fitzroy was the Village Treasurer, Stockton Town Clerk, manager of the cemetery and a tool redeemer.

Rodney and his younger brother were put to work as soon as they could be productive. If they wanted to connect with their folks, if they wanted to get to know them, they did it in the lunch counter. But if Rodney was in the lunch counter, there was always work for him to do. The doors of the family business closed for only one hour, from four o'clock to five o'clock, so that the whole family could race upstairs and eat supper at their own table. Then they were all back at work. Some nights Rodney helped his mother in the kitchen while his younger brother, David, refilled coffee cups and water glasses. The place stayed open until midnight, and sometimes later if there was a prom or a mixer at the school. Rodney bussed all the tables. Sometimes his classmates would come in and give him a hard time.

The waiter moves around the table taking drink orders. After a moment of rumination, Kate says, "I'll have a Cabernet, I think."

Allison touches Kate's hand and says, "Are you sure that's a good idea, babe?"

"One glass couldn't hurt," Kate says.

They share some private smile over this.

"*One* glass." Allison looks up at the waiter. "I'll have a gin martini, extra dry. Thank you."

Billy Meadows is now standing over our table, looking down at us from his sovereign height of six feet six inches. When we were both kids, Billy and I were exiled to the same summer camp in Maine. He's the one who taught me how to blow smoke rings. After graduating from Vassar, he floated around Los Angeles for five years trying to make it as a soap opera actor. Now he's back in Buffalo and working as an investment banker, a position his old man lined up for him. Billy drives a new Acura, lives in a waterfront condo and belongs to a club frequented by seventy-year-olds. When you get something for nothing, though, it's amazing what you end up paying for it. He has always resented his powerful and successful father, a heart surgeon at Millard Fillmore Hospital. "Happy Thanksgiving, everybody," Billy says merrily, holding a lowball glass of bourbon. "It's always good to see *you*, my friend," he says, clapping his paw on my shoulder. "Gracing us with your illustrious presence. How's New York treating you?"

"Good," I say. "No complaints."

"Making a million dollars out there?"

"No."

"Half a million?"

"Not even close."

Billy laughs. "What are you waiting for, amigo?"

Go fuck yourself.

Rodney smiles up at Billy Meadows. "William," he says pleasantly. "How are you this evening?"

"Evening, Rod. Great as always. Wait a minute! Is that Kate?" He peers across the table at my sister. "I don't believe it."

"Hello, Billy," she says. "How's it going?"

"I hear you're living out in California. How do you like it?"

"Oregon," she says, and glances at Allison. "I love it."

"Terrific." He takes another sip and punches me companionably on the shoulder. "Give me a call, man. Let's hang out. It's been too long. Meantime, let me give you a solid tip. Keep your ear to the ground. The market's moving into an inverted yield curve soon."

I have no idea what he's talking about. "Sounds good," I say.

"And you know what that means," he says with a slight nod.

"Remind me."

He stage-whispers: "Buy bonds." Smiling, he points a finger-gun at Rodney. "Anyway, you folks have a great meal."

After he leaves, I say, "Well, that was pleasant."

"Yes," Kate says. "Always nice to see Billy Meadows."

"I can't trust a grown man named Billy," Allison says. "You know what I mean? Billy, Bobby, Andy. It just sounds creepy."

I smile at her. "And he's a little obsessed with money, right?"

Rodney studies the menu. "There are worse things to spend your time on, James."

A hit! A very palpable hit.

Rodney, Kate and Allison order the "authentic turkey dinner." I had enough authentic turkey in the dementia ward, so I order a steak. Conversation buzzes around me like a cloud of shiny green flies. Every now and then one lands on my nose, and I look up from my plate to find everyone looking at me.

"Sorry, what?" I say, cheek bulging with chewed bread.

The conversation resumes without me.

Thanksgiving dinner at the Greenfield Club: my mother would not approve. She would see the sadness in it.

"Earlier today Kate and I were talking about your job," Rodney says to me.

"Dad says that you're really advancing in the greeting card field," Kate says. "What's the glass ceiling on a job like that?"

THANK YOU, BIG SISTER, FOR YOUR WONDERFUL WORDS OF SUPPORT.

"I need another drink," I say, scanning the room for our waiter. "Where'd he go?"

"Rodney says you got a promotion to the humor division?" Allison adds kindly. "That must feel good."

Staring, they all wait for more information. I'm not feeling chatty, folks. I don't want to sit here and play nice while Mom lies awake in her hospital bed with a cold shit in her diaper.

"Give us your funniest one," Kate says.

Is she just being cordial? Am I imagining the ridicule I detect? They smile at me, waiting. I see the faces they've prepared to meet mine. I've hidden so much of myself from them, a habit I've found hard to break. Even now, when I have nothing to conceal and could actually tell a story that they might enjoy, I fiddle with my cloth napkin, eyes lowered. Where can I find the beauty in this situation? I dredge up a smile for them.

"You were always so funny," she says. "Didn't you want to be a stand-up comedian when we were kids?"

It was a short career. When I was nine years old, I discovered the book *Truly Tasteless Jokes*. I imagined a popular kid telling joke after joke as his friends laughed and clapped for more. When I actually tried to perform in the cafeteria, though, my classmates looked horrified. They barely knew my name. "Gross. That's not funny," they said. "You're a weirdo," they said. These were children who did not yet appreciate the poetry of naughty American nouns. Making friends, I learned, required more effort than just blurting jokes. Usually I sat alone during lunch period, tuna sandwich in hand, my head bursting with *cunt* and *dogshit*.

"Enough about me," I say to Kate. "How's the physical therapy business? People still getting injured?"

"Every hour," she says.

Allison says, "Speaking of that, I think I tore my rotator cuff in the gym today."

"Babe! You didn't tell me that."

"I'm exaggerating," Allison says with a shy smile. She

turns to Rodney. "I was trying to do some dead lifts. Bad idea."

"Allison is really strong," Kate tells us with a look of great seriousness on her face. "She's stronger than most men actually."

"Where's our fucking waiter?" I say.

I drink three beers with dinner before switching to whiskey. After dinner and digestifs, Kate and I stand in the parking lot, shivering. I've asked her out here because I want one uninterrupted goddamn minute with my sister to talk about this goddamn situation.

"Doesn't it make you want to just smash something?" I say.

She scrunches her face. "What do you mean?"

I just stare at her. "Mom."

"What about her?"

This is maddening, too. I fight to keep my voice steady. "You're joking, right?"

"James. What are you saying?" She hugs herself to stay warm. "They're waiting for us."

"Are you blind? She's in hell. That is hell. You really are your father's daughter, aren't you? You don't think that place is horrible? You don't think Mom shitting her diapers—"

"Oh, God. Stop. You're drunk again." Kate stares over my shoulder, watching for Allison and Dad. "What do you want from me?"

"I want you to be as pissed off as I am," I say, trying not

to slur my words. "I want you to have a serious talk with me. I want you to help me."

Still looking over my shoulder, Kate's face brightens and she waves, holds her index finger up, *one more minute*, before turning her attention back to me. "James, I love you and I would do anything for you. Anything. You know that."

"Help me to save her," I say.

"I don't understand what you're saying. What do you mean, *save* her? You're going to do what trained medical professionals can't do? Come on. This is silly."

"Remember this conversation," I say. "I'm going to do this."

"Good luck," Kate says, walking away. "Let me know how that works out."

My father decides that he'd better drive, but I tell him that I'm fine. After a self-administered field sobriety test, in which I locate my nose with my fingertip and stand on one foot for a full eight seconds, Rodney capitulates. He's not sober enough to argue with me.

buffalo lockjaw

After dropping Rodney off, I pilot the Ford through a weave of falling snow. Going nowhere. Scanning the deserted streets for the partiers and thugs and college girls I once knew. In Buffalo I'm always looking for ghosts. I glide past low-lit bars and diners, strip malls and liquor stores, Dairy Queens boarded up for winter, bookstores, factories, churches and record shops. Where are all the people I hung out with a decade ago? I'm peering through the windshield trying to raise the dead.

Gently pumping the brake pedal, I slide to a stop at a red light on Grant Street. A duct-taped Torino shudders past in the opposite lane, ignoring the traffic signal. The driver plays a syncopated horn solo all the way through the intersection. His winking taillights disappear in the soupy whiteness behind me. Now that guy's drunk. If I ever get as bad as him, I'll stop drinking and driving forever.

Three bundled pedestrians venture into the road, inches from the grille of my car. Stiff-necked and scowling, teeth gritted, they split the twin bars of the headlights, one right after another. They trudge past with identical Buffalo lockjaw faces. The light turns green well before they complete their pilgrimage. I watch them intently, blowing warm air into my cupped bare hands. What's keeping me from running them down? It would be no problem at all. Ease my boot off the brake pedal and stomp the gas. Simple as that.

Too late it occurs to me that I might have been useful in this situation. They're trudging through blinding drifts of snow, their heads down. The temperature has now dropped into the teens. Snow clumps down around them. Rolling down my window, I shout, "Do you need a lift?" I have nowhere to be. "I'll take you wherever." They do not turn around. I probably wouldn't accept a ride from me, either.

Now I'm listening to a Canadian rock station and banging my palms against the steering wheel. Whipping past power lines and smokestacks. Maybe I'll get a coffee, forget the whole idea of sleep tonight and just give rides to pedestrians all across town. The Peace Shuttle. I'll charge a nickel or a dime for fare, no more than that.

Craving coffee, I hit the drive-thru at Tim Hortons, a chain coffee-and-doughnut shop named for a dead hockey player. Tim Hortons is Buffalo's equivalent to Dunkin' Donuts. You know you're getting close to Canada when local businesses are named after gritty NHL defensemen. Horton played for the Toronto Maple Leafs and for the Buffalo Sabres, but now he's known primarily for having the best coffee in town. There are probably a hundred locations in the United States and Canada, and nobody seems to care about the missing apostrophe in "Tim Hortons Coffee & Baked Goods." Then again, nobody mentions that "Leafs" is not a proper word. But each sport has its own syntax, and most of them are strangely beautiful.

Sipping coffee, I drive through the streets of my past, past the soup kitchens and homeless shelters, past the advertised Ponzi schemes and pyramid offers, EARN A MILLION—CALL THIS NUMBER, past the ubiquitous billboards of two smug-looking personal injury lawyers. The DJ promises even more "killer cuts" after the commercial break. I hope he's telling the truth. The Judas Priest selection was perfect. "Living After Midnight." A prostitute waves from a doorway on Niagara Street, leans her knit-capped head out. I think it's a she, anyway. None of my business. I keep driving. The Peace Shuttle doesn't stop for hookers, thieves or drug addicts.

At the intersection of Niagara and Porter, I hear the flatulent rumble of a muscle car pulling alongside my rental. I stare out my steamed window at Regis Cartwright and his driver, Granger. They're in a mint 1971 Chevelle Malibu Super Sport. A beautiful car. A two-door hardtop. Metallic blue paint with white racing stripes down the hood. You don't see many cars like this one on Buffalo's salty, ice-slick roads. Most people would put it in a garage somewhere and drive it only in the summertime. Regis's assistant, Granger, is a thick-necked ex–rugby flanker with a protruding brow and enormous hands. A loyal, slow-witted classmate from high school, he acts as a sort of manservant for Regis. He never leaves his master's side.

At first, neither of them acknowledges my presence. Sprawled comfortably in the passenger seat, Regis flicks a cigarette ash and yawns. He shattered his leg in a fall from a broken ladder on a Niagara Falls casino construction site, and in 2003 he won a multimillion-dollar settlement. His thinning black hair is pulled back into a ponytail. His dark eyes are luminous, penetrating and cruel. His trimmed black beard is threaded with gray hairs. Beside him, Granger wears a fur-lined denim jacket. He grips the steering wheel like a circus strongman trying to bend a steel rod. He turns his frowning face toward me. "Fuck you," he says over the deafening roar of his revving engine.

I can't help thinking it's all a joke, but the two of them look totally serious. They are dedicated to the art of intimidation. Regis has a brown belt in Tae Kwon Do, I've heard, and Granger can bench-press four hundred pounds.

"Roll down your window," Regis shouts at me. He moves his thick leather glove in a clockwise motion. "Roll it down, James."

The traffic signal is green. I'm tempted to stomp on the accelerator, but there's no traffic behind us and this could be worth a laugh or two, so I do as he says.

"Hiya, Regis," I say. "What's new?"

He doesn't waste any time. "I heard you were back in town. Don't get any ideas while you're here."

Is there some kind of slacker grapevine or gazette that I don't know about? This town is becoming more and more like one of those old Western sets. Bank. Schoolhouse. Saloon. How does everyone know when I'm in Buffalo?

"Stay away from Corinne," he shouts over the bass rumble of our two idling engines. "She doesn't want to see you."

What is he talking about? Is he high? I probably shouldn't provoke him, but I can't resist. "Pardon me?" I say, cupping a hand to my left ear. "Didn't hear you, Regis. Could you speak up?"

"Stay. Away. From. Corinne. Patterson," he says, adding her last name, as if that will make things more clear to me.

I've known Regis since elementary school. I remember him holding a KISS lunchbox and bawling like an infant when Dave Snedden hit him in the face with a dodgeball. Regis lived in an apartment complex with his mom on Hertel Avenue. He wore Toughskins jeans every day to school and he ate bologna sandwiches on Wonder bread for lunch. A few times we played tackle football in Shoshone Park on Sunday afternoons. I don't fully understand what has happened to him since then, but I wish he wouldn't include me in whatever it is he's working through.

Granger's history I know even less about. This might be simplistic of me, because the guy must have hidden depths not visible to the naked eye, but I consider Granger a dangerous moron. Unlike Regis, Granger seems to be a guy lacking any type of subtlety, a garden-variety meathead. He punches you first and asks questions afterward. Type of guy who drives across the border for the "Canadian Ballet," pays for a lap dance, gets thrown out for squeezing a tit. There must be more to him, but I won't take the time to find out.

"Hi, Granger!" I wave to him. *"Que pása?"*

"You hear what he just said, pussy?" Granger wants to know.

Stifling the grin threatening to burst forth on my face, I nod my head soberly. "Loud and clear, friend."

"I'm watching you. Remember that," Regis says and points to his right eye. "I didn't get that Lasik surgery done for nothing."

Granger leans across and spits on the door of my rental car. He grins. Regis slaps him across the back of the head.

"Dude," he says. "You almost got that on me." Then they pull ahead and disappear down a side street.

How is a man to behave when he finds himself in a cartoon?

Still, it's exciting to be back in Buffalo again, where the absurd still thrives.

excavation

I drive all night, block after block, until I'm quite certain my father has pushed himself up from his armchair and stumbled off to bed. It's past two o'clock when I park the car on the street outside the house and trudge up the pristine white driveway. My footsteps will be erased in an hour. I let myself in through the garage, past the tool bench and retired bicycles and the blue plastic recycling bin and stacked newspapers and a number of shovels.

After pouring myself a lowball glass of vodka, I start yanking open drawers. Three dented metal filing cabinets stand against the far wall in her office. I'm not looking for anything in particular. Not looking for a green light. Evidence. A permission note from Mother. I would just like to know her better.

She saved a lot of stuff, kept files on the many things that interested her. Dozens of her manila folders are crammed full of clipped newspaper and magazine articles, word-processed manuscripts, photocopied essays from medical journals, notes on napkins and scraps of paper, ticket stubs, photographs, old brochures. Notes are scribbled on the fronts of most of the folders in her tiny, crimped penmanship. *Research Consent Forms—Stories of Homeless Women.*

She did most of her research and clinical work before she owned a computer.

I start with cabinet one, file one. Sitting with my back to the wall, I read until my eyes blur.

The quality of care Americans receive in hospitals and other settings is directly related to the services provided by registered nurses.

Nursing <u>is</u> a reflection of social reality.
Nursing preceded medicine.
1650–1850 — a dark period in nursing.

I'm digging through one of the fattest folders now, pulling out yellowed clippings and faded photocopies. She saved birth notices and obituaries of friends. She saved all the drafts of her handwritten letters, including this one:

May 26

Dear Pat,

I have decided to resign from the School of Nursing as of the end of June. You know that I respect you and the wonderful team you have assembled to guide and teach the ever-increasing number of students who want to become Family Nurse Practitioners. However, I am not handling the pressures here very well, and think that it is time for me to vacate the premises.

Thanks for the opportunity to work with you, your

*great staff, and the outstanding group of students we
have in the Program.*

> *Fond regards,*
> *Ellen*

The description of my parents' wedding ceremony from
the *Buffalo Evening News*, a squib written by a Caitlin Mul-
len, staff reporter, painstakingly details all the women's
clothes and manages to ignore all the men in attendance:

Ellen Fitzroy (née Lundgren) married Rodney Fitzroy
at Saint Anthony of Padua Catholic Church yesterday.
Escorted to the altar by her father, the bride wore an
A-line linen gown with peau d'ange lace detailing the
hi-rise bodice, and scalloped elbow-length sleeves and
skirt. A detachable shoulder train was edged in matching lace and a crown of seed pearls held her three-tiered
silk illusion veil. She carried a crescent-shaped bou-
quet of glamelias and stephanotis with ivy.

Her sister Rita, the matron of honor, was attired in a
seafoam green A-line linen gown with empire bodice
and elbow-length sleeves. Dyed-to-match Venice lace
edged the hemline and sleeves. The other bridesmaids
wore similar gowns in blue mist. All wore matching
bows in their hair and carried crescent-shaped bou-
quets of dyed-to-match carnations with ivy.

The bride's mother attended the wedding in a pink
crepe dress with a coat of pink lace and wore a corsage
of Happiness roses. The bridegroom's mother selected

a pink lace sheath with matching jacket and flowers of pink glamelias.

A reception was held at the Holiday Inn following the ceremony. Mr. And Mrs. Fitzroy will honeymoon this week in Hawaii.

It would take years to go through these files with any degree of thoroughness. Much of her life is documented here. There are extensive files on euthanasia and physician-assisted suicide. I'm too tired to read anymore. Before heading upstairs, I pluck three or four books from her office shelves.

I left *Assisted Suicide for Dummies* in the backseat of the rental car.

With all the pillows bunched behind my back, I try to read in bed, angling the annotated pages under the dim lamp. Let's see: what did I end up with here? I've got *Streetlives* and *Communicating with Mental Patients* and *What You Can Do to Help the Homeless* and *How We Die*. Great. Wash it all down with two aspirin and a glass of strychnine and call it a night. These books do not engage me, but I hope to find a deeper connection to Ellen Fitzroy, some unknown footpath constructed of her own asterisks and underlines. Maybe this selective reading can lead me to the question I still haven't figured out how to ask.

bonding

Morning. Rodney stands before his open refrigerator, staring. It's packed with condiments, sauces, miscellaneous mustards. The main shelves are empty, save for a quart of milk, an unopened deck of processed orange cheese slices, a foil-wrapped brick of something, and three cans of Coke.

"She made delicious omelets," he says with his back to me. He scratches his bald head, shuts the fridge and pulls open the rattling silverware drawer. Every room of this house must remind him of her. He's as lost as I am. What is he looking for right now? Does he want a snack? I sit on a wooden stool at the Formica island, watching him.

"On Sundays before Mass we ate omelets," he says with his back to me. "She was always experimenting with new ingredients. Of course I would've been happy with, you know, American cheese, maybe a few mushrooms, but she liked to put in tomatoes or spinach or feta cheese. One time she even used salsa." He shakes his head in sheer admiration of his wife's culinary daring. "American cheese would have been just fine, but Ellen's an original."

I understand how Rodney can hold on to these trivial things. Sometimes, when I'm hungry, I long for cinnamon toast. She specialized in comfort foods. Meat loaf. Mashed potatoes. Chili. Kate and I loved some foods simply because

Mom had made them. When she was a little kid, Kate bragged to the neighbor kids about *our* peanut butter and jelly sandwiches. Mom's secret? She kept the bread in the freezer, so the peanut butter didn't tear the bread. Some nights after dinner, when we demanded dessert, Mom cored an apple by pressing a spoked wheel down on top of it. Eight slices of apple bloomed outward, a flower of fruit, and the core stood alone, intact on the cutting board. We thought it was a magic trick.

I watch my father flex his fingers. He stretches his hand, all five fingers extended, and inspects the knuckles.

"When she stopped cooking, we were in a real jam," he says. "I can't even boil water." Rodney grins. "So we went out to dinner a lot, until that became too difficult."

He repeats himself often, I notice, tells the same stories. For a few years now he's been telling me that he can't boil water. Abruptly I experience the snap of a brand-new thought: What if my father has a degenerative brain disease, too? It's possible. Who's to say that dementia hits only one person per marriage? Everybody expects Mom to die first. Yet my father could die before her. So could I.

"What year were you and Mom married?" I ask him, testing the waters.

"Nineteen sixty-eight," he says. "Why?"

"Just curious. And what year were you born?"

His eyes narrow behind the lenses of his glasses. "Nineteen forty."

Nodding, I continue my inquest. "Who's the current president of the United States?"

Placing his arthritic hands on the counter, my father

leans close and peers into my eyes. "Are you taking drugs again, James?"

"I'm just curious."

"I think you're acting pretty strange."

My cell phone vibrates in my pocket, saving me. I excuse myself and adjourn to the next room.

welcome home

My lifelong buddies in Buffalo greet me effusively whenever I'm back in town. "Hey, fucknob, I heard you came home for Thanksgiving. Gunther said he saw you on Elmwood."

"Who's Gunther?"

"Whatever," Brickteeth says. "You remember Gunther. Anyway, I'm having a few people over tonight. Why don't you come by?"

Silence.

"Why don't you come by tonight, Jimmy?"

I can hear him thunking the strings of his electric guitar, and the scene chez Brickteeth materializes in my mind. A few stoned people wander around in their underwear, slowly becoming lucid and considering breakfast. Two untrained Rottweilers jump on the torn-up couches with muddy paws. His dirty blond hair hanging down over his face, Brickteeth repeats the same simple blues riff over and over again. Faded jeans torn at the knee. One bare foot resting on the dusty 50-watt amp. Cell phone pressed between upraised shoulder and cheek. A partisan of all things illicit, Brickteeth carries himself with a ragged dignity that inspires allegiance in his crew.

"Not tonight," I tell him. "I promised my old man I'd be around. Now that he's alone in the house, I kind of worry about him."

"Yeah, I hear you, let me give you my address. I live on Herkimer now. Almost right behind your old place on Lafayette. Side door. Upper rear apartment. I don't have a bell. Name's not up yet on the mailbox, gotta do that soon, but just head up the stairs, man. You'll hear us."

"I'll try to make it."

"You better show up. Costello's in town. He's back from Miami."

"Is he?"

"Yeah. He's been back for a couple of months now. He keeps asking about you. So come over tonight. We wanna see you, man."

"I don't know. What time should I come by?"

"Come by whenever you want. I'm cooking on the grill. Burgers, Italian sausages, chicken breasts. I'll *feed* you. Takes a fucking blizzard to keep me off the grill."

"Should I bring something?"

"Dude," he says. "Why are you being so formal all of a sudden? We're your family. Just come over. Lot of people looking forward to seeing you, including me. Don't bring anything. Just bring a twelve-pack of something. See you tonight."

FLOYD THE FIGURE MODEL,
landscaper & figure model

Listen, I know what you want. The perfect party. I've been all over the world looking for it, but it only exists here—right here in my head. Mountains of uncut blow. Unprotected sex on the first date. Old hipsters playing sax on the street. Back in '67, I lived in a studio on Elmwood, and you couldn't keep the party out. The streets were electric. Walls were permeable. You caught a contact buzz in the post office. I mean, even when I locked the door of my apartment, this guy Roger always turned up in my bedroom wanting to talk religion. I'm not kidding. He'd climb in through a window if he had to. Roger would sit on the edge of my bed, rapping about God.

. . . Once I actually walked down to the Psych Center to commit myself. True story. I did. I packed a lunch and some clean socks. But they wouldn't take me. Fucking cowards. I pounded on the admissions desk. They said they'd call the cops if I didn't leave. So I went to Pano's instead and ordered a chicken souvlaki with extra tzatziki sauce.

After that, I stopped in at the Royal Pheasant. "Give me a White Russian," I said. "Because I'm gonna kill myself tonight and I've never had a White Russian before." The bartender was like, "Good for you. A man with a plan." She made my drink in the shaker and poured it into a highball glass. Right to the rim. It looked all frothy and delicious. Then she filled a lowball glass to the rim. Then she pushed both glasses toward me. I said hold on, sister, I didn't order two drinks. "That's the dividend," she said. "I always make too much." And she winked at me.

The dividend. What a bartender! That night I decided not to kill myself. With women like her in the world, why pull the plug?

TALL JEFF,
graduate student

You should've seen the freaks they hired for the figure drawing classes at Upton Hall. We had some real characters. There was this one guy—what was his name? Floyd the Figure Model. He was in his late fifties. Built like a former ironworker. Barrel-chested. Always sucked in his gut. He was a total exhibitionist. He loved being naked, loved having his wang hanging out. Most figure models would throw on a robe during breaks. Not Floyd. He'd stroll down to the drinking fountain in the hallway, then he'd swing by the vending machines, asscheeks jiggling. You can ask hundreds of people if they know his name and they'll just start laughing.

Middle of winter he'd be copping a smoke out front of Upton Hall. Totally buck naked, standing outdoors, no big deal. Students and professors walking by, all bundled up in heavy coats and boots, and there was Floyd the Figure Model, getting a last drag off his Winston. The school finally fired Floyd when a drawing instructor caught Floyd wrapping rubber bands around his dick during breaks. Floyd was trying to gorge it with blood to make it look fatter. The instructor, an adjunct named Courtney Something, walked into the room looking for a stool, and there was Floyd with like a rainbow of rubber bands on his pecker. Floyd claimed he was doing it for the students.

. . . Exhibitionism is very popular in Buffalo. It's a result of cabin fever, I think. We're a people who hibernate. From late October until April, we spend a lot of time indoors. So when the temperature goes above forty degrees there's this overwhelming urge to go wild! Look at the birth figures for Buffalo: more children are born in January than any other time of the year. They're all being conceived in April and May.

When it's nice out I sit on the front porch, reading, and before summer ends maybe a hundred men and women flash me. It doesn't even surprise me. I wave and comment on their kibbles and bits. When April hits, people go bananas! Getting naked is just one of the preferred activities.

pompeii

Empty beer bottles and cans are scattered on the kitchen counter. Plastic vodka gallons and ash-filled plastic cups litter the floor. A sink full of dirty dishes. A bucket of slushy ice stands on one of the electric burners of the stove. It's an apartment I've been in a thousand times before. There are old newspapers strewn on the floor, under combat boots and basketball sneakers. If the ashtray isn't within arm's reach, you simply ash on the worn-out carpet, or in the numerous soup-scabbed plates and bowls within reach. Or, if you're polite, you tap ash on the thighs of your own jeans and rub it in. The CDs that have fallen out of favor have become coasters for drinks. Enormous hairy armchairs squat in the corners of the room like unhealthy gorillas at the zoo. There's a prickly green-and-ochre plaid sofa, a garbage-picked futon and two mismatched bar stools—one tall, one short. Stains on everything that can be stained. Seeds and stems ground into dust by boot heels. A poster of the Himalayan mountains on one wall. Poster of Hendrix (ripped), near the kitchen entrance, flapping in the weak breath of the overhead fan. Always hot, stuffy—wet-towel humid. Poor lighting. No ventilation.

Somebody is sprawled on the futon, one arm flung over his face to protect his eyes from the naked lightbulb overhead. His T-shirt reads SQUISH THE FISH. A fallen stick of incense has burned a tear-shaped groove into the coffee table.

"Is Brickteeth here?" I say, leaning over him. "Hey, man. Is Brickteeth here?"

Groaning, he rolls away from me. "They're out back," the dying man whispers. "Kill the light, bro."

Carrying a twelve-pack, I head down the stairs and into the snowy backyard. Eight or nine people are hanging out tonight. They're mostly Kenmorons, old friends who live in Kenmore. They're all holding drinks: red plastic cups or green bottles of Canadian beer. A Pixies song blasts from a speaker propped in the kitchen window. It's about thirty degrees Fahrenheit outside.

Brickteeth stands by the grill, black-crusted tongs in his bare hand. A reddish purple ink stamp from last night's club still adorns his broad flat hand like a bruise. There are burn holes in his untucked flannel shirt. His red thermal underwear is visible through the rips in his jeans. "Yes," he says, his breath visible in the air. His greasy blond hair curls out from under a black knit cap. "How you been, brother? Come here." He gathers me into a bear hug.

Abruptly Costello appears beside me, grinning. He's a stumpy, broad-shouldered man about five feet eight inches tall. Two hundred thirty pounds of hard-packed muscle. He's missing a front tooth, one of the important ones on top. Holding an icy bottle of beer in his bare left hand, he slaps me hard on the shoulder with his right fist. "Jimmy," he says. "Fuck. Yes. Right on."

"Good to see you too, Costello."

Most of the people out here tonight are dressed in quilted parkas and bulky winter coats with fur hoods, or at least multiple layers—hoodies and scarves and knit caps and gloves—but Costello is wearing a black Miami Heat muscle shirt and baggy black jeans. His thick muscled arms are bare, ruddy and stippled like chicken flesh.

"Dogs are done," Brickteeth calls out. "Grab a bun, Jim."

Things have not changed much here, but there are a few noticeable differences. McQuilken has cut his long red Axl Rose hair off. Now he's got some kind of crew cut. His fiancée and longtime sidekick, Kelly the Funnel, fled town eight months ago and ended up in Atlanta or Charlotte, and McQuilken still wears the sad grin of a heartbroken and sedated man. Mattress Lips plays his favorite game on the picnic table. Eyes shut, he's tic-tacking a knife blade in rapid succession between the spread fingers of his left hand. He will stab himself before he's through. He never misses. I'm not sure he fully understands the object of this game, as most players conceive of it, but maybe I am missing something.

Beautiful erratic Samantha, always shorter and more freckled than I remember her to be, steps forward and hugs me. Her forehead presses into my lower chest. "Hey, stranger," she says. "Christopher said you might stop by." Samantha's the only one who uses Brickteeth's first name. "He says you're doing awesome in the City."

"Well, I'm doing okay."

"Cool," Sam says. "How's your mom?"

"The same."

A floodlight bathes us in unforgiving light, stretches our

shadows behind us. Deep in the yard half a tree is visible, dead stripped bark. A half-built motorcycle gleams against the dark wall of the garage.

"Sausages!" Brickteeth calls out. "Hey, I got hot sausages just sitting here. Yo, Five Boroughs. Mustard and ketchup's on the table. Dig in."

A young woman with dark, abundant hair is seated alone at the picnic table. Dark eyebrows. A slender, intelligent face. My attention shifts carnivorously. Her pale face is illuminated by a candle flickering beneath her chin. Finally she looks up at me. She's gorgeous. Ecstatic blue eyes. She should be advertising purses or shoes in a women's magazine. I imagine she works in a bar or a coffee shop on Chippewa Street, making minimum plus tips.

Costello sees where I'm looking and shepherds me over to her. "You never met my fiancée, Kim." He gives me a possessive squeeze. "I grew up with this wild man. We're like brothers, me and this guy."

I say, "Pleased to meet you."

"Hi." She lights a cigarette by dipping her face into the candle's flame, holding her black mane back with one pale, elegant hand. This is textbook Buffalo: ugly guys like Costello walking around with lovely women like this.

I head back to the grill, where Samantha says, "I know you probably don't want to talk about it, but I miss your mom. She was really really nice to me."

"I miss her, too."

What more can I say? I agree with her.

After standing around and eating, we settle in and drink. The women drink as much as the men around here.

Because it's late autumn. Because it's a Friday in Buffalo. Because the disappointment would be too great without it. The candle on the table blows out and Brickteeth relights it. Somebody burps.

Mattress Lips packs a bowl. A look of great calm comes over his face as he arranges his materials. There is something ecclesiastical in his devotion to this act, the thumb gently pressing a disc of black hash onto a bed of weed. He has shellacked black hair, sunken vampire eyes, and a gaunt face bordered by bristling sideburns and silver hoop earrings. He dresses only in black: black trench coat, black jeans, black boots, as if to inspire some new assessment of his persona, but it's too late for all that. His bulging pouting lips earned him his moniker years ago, when we were all still in high school, and those same bulbous lips have inspired a number of men to punch him in the mouth. Brickteeth named him in ninth grade, so you might as well put Mattress Lips on his death certificate. This is the danger of having lifelong friends. Each remains forever locked in his role, his most vulnerable pose, like the victims of Pompeii.

Mattress Lips returned the favor. "At least I don't have giant teeth like bricks in my mouth," he said, and fifteen years later, this is how they remain, bound to each other by spontaneous insults.

For a few years I was Bartender Jim, but I worked so many different jobs that the name didn't make sense anymore.

One winter I rode around in a guy's van delivering books to schools and offices. I humped heavy boxes up icy sidewalks, sweating an awful boozy stink into my thermal underwear. The pay was thirty bucks a day under the table. One morning I staggered into the boys' bathroom and violently puked: a nauseous Gulliver down on his knees, hugging the tiny bowl. The stall had no door. Two schoolkids came in and started giggling and pointing at me. When I turned and glared at them, they got scared and hurried out. My boss, Peter the Book Guy, never fired me, I suspect, because he couldn't find anyone else to do the job. But he knew I was a drunk. Some mornings I showed up; other mornings I didn't. It was pitiful. I couldn't even ride around Buffalo in a customized van and deliver books. And yet I maintained this secret exalted opinion of myself: *If people only knew what I'm capable of . . . Nobody knows how talented I am. . . .* Et cetera. I lived every day in fantasy. Riding in the van one morning, when I was feeling particularly low and bitter, I turned to Peter and said, "You know, I could never imagine being the Book Guy." Peter had his big hairy arm draped over the steering wheel. He didn't even look over at me. After a brief silence, he said: "Well, shit, Jim. I could never imagine being the Book Guy's *assistant.*"

That brought me back to reality. Somehow I had convinced myself that whatever I was doing at the time wasn't my real life. I was enduring it only for the sake of the glorious future that I was certain awaited me. If I didn't rid myself of this tendency, I understood that eventually I would go mad.

Brickteeth pulls Samantha closer. She rests her head on his shoulder. Sitting around the picnic table, the guys all tell stories on each other, shivering in the cold, performing for the pretty girls, one-upping each other and laughing at once deeply shameful memories, now shared history—cars smashed into trees and fences, drunken nudity, emotional pain. The women are clearly not impressed by this lore. Bored, they make eye contact and communicate wordlessly. *Here they go again.* I agree with them. But when I attempt to change the topic, my friends think I'm being superior, I guess, highfalutin, a Big City guy, which I've never been and never claimed to be, and they knock me down even further, calling me Captain Hallmark, asking me if they still give Pulitzer Prizes for greeting cards.

"All right, this was fun and all," Brickteeth says, "but I can't feel my fingers anymore." He turns off the grill. "I'm going inside."

We all come to our senses at once. What the hell are we doing out here? It's not summer. We follow him in.

"I've got blisters on me fingers!" McQuilken shouts, doing Ringo Starr at the end of "Helter Skelter." Now alone in the backyard, he's pissing on a tree.

I wait for him by the back door. "Let me ask you something," I say. "I've been meaning to talk to somebody about this." I wait for him to approach before continuing. I don't want to blurt out my question. McQuilken reads a lot of true-crime books. He might have some insight into this. When he's close enough to hear me, I say in a quiet voice, "What do you think of mercy killings? I mean, you know, in general."

A cigarette dangles from his lower lip. He strikes a match, cups his hand around the flame. Inhales. "You live in Brooklyn, right?" he says, ignoring my question. Steam issues from his nostrils and mouth. "Is it any cheaper than Manhattan, where they charge nine bucks for a fucking Grolsch on

New Year's Eve? I hear Brooklyn's just like a bigger version of Buffalo."

Two can play that game. "I guess the real question I'm asking is: Can a murder ever be considered moral?"

He nods and says, "Because this town is dead, bro. I gotta get out of here one of these days. My uncle lives in Toronto." McQuilken frowns and drags on his cigarette. "What are rents like in Brooklyn? Affordable?"

"Mercy killing is misunderstood," I say. "You see stories on the news sometimes, but they never show what the family members were going through. It's just like a two-second shock piece, and then the weather."

More than once Ellen pressed the accelerator when she meant to press the brake pedal. Sometimes the car lurched forward when she thought she was in reverse. Eventually she might have killed somebody, a child crossing the street on the way to school, and she would have ended up a fifteen-second spectacle on the six o'clock news, a blinking unrepentant woman unsure of what she'd even done wrong, despised by those viewers who watch the evening news only to judge and condemn others. *Throw her in jail!* they'd say over their TV trays. *She must have been drunk!* And now she lives on a locked ward. Her bed has rails. The mattress is narrow, thin and plastic-coated.

"Hold up," McQuilken says. "Why are you even talking about this?"

"No reason. It's kind of a hot political issue right now."

"But why do you care?"

"Because if somebody is in so much pain, physical or

mental pain, *anguish*, isn't it more merciful to help them die than to make them live?"

He holds my gaze for an uncomfortable moment. His eyes are bloodshot. He hasn't shaved in days. "I think I'd want to evaluate that on a case-by-case basis," he says. "It's nothing I ever thought about before."

I look away, conscious of his prolonged staring. "Yeah," I say. "I hear you."

"You gotta be more specific, Jimmy. Are we talking like shotgun blasts or what? Lethal injection?"

"Ha," I say, shivering. It's snot-stiffening cold out here. Why did I think I could talk to this guy about anything? "Purely an academic question. Anyway . . ."

"Let me get this straight. Start at the beginning. Who do you want to kill?"

This is not going well. "The rents in Brooklyn are a little cheaper than Manhattan," I tell him, "but it's catching up."

I should start hanging out at botanical gardens and art galleries and cultural events. This town is full of intelligent and fascinating people. If I weren't drinking beer in some-body's backyard right now, I would certainly meet an array of sophisticates, maybe even my future bride. Not that I am in any hurry to get married, that "pleasant prison dream," as Gregory Corso calls it, but a thoughtful companion would be a welcome boon.

"Dude," McQuilken says. "What are you saying? Say what you're saying."

"Fine. Do you know anyone who would be willing to dis-cuss this topic with me? I'm being dead serious now. Do you know anyone who would be willing to work out some kind of a deal?"

"You mean, like a hit man? You're asking me if I happen to know a hit man?" He flicks his cigarette into the snow. "Are you nuts? Seriously. Are you a stupid fucking asshole? Answer me."

"No. I don't believe that I'm a stupid fucking asshole. But what kind of stupid fucking asshole has the type of clarity that he would recognize—"

"You wanna go to prison?"

"—I mean, isn't that the nature of the stupid fucking asshole, that he doesn't realize what he is, if he ever does, until it's much too—"

"And you think I'm just hanging around with professional killers? You think I'll just say, Sure, let me put you in touch with my boy Knuckles or Muscles or whatever?"

"This has been a good talk, McQuilken." I glance at my wrist, where a watch would be if I wore one. "But look at the time. I better get going."

"You're an idiot," he says.

"Right," I say, shivering. "Got it. Okay, I'm getting out of here. It's late. I'm beat."

He grabs my arm, stops me. "Wait. I'm still confused. You're planning on killing your mother? Or your father? Which one?"

"Forget it. I'm not going to kill anyone."

"Hey, man. You brought it up. But if you do end up killing your parents, you might have to kill me, too. I know too much now. I might squeal. To the fuzz."

There's nothing more to say. McQuilken and I shake hands. "Good to see you again, bro," he says.

"I was only kidding."

"Whatever," he says. "Try not to waste anyone on your way home tonight, Bundy."

"Thanks for your support."

"No problem."

McQuilken climbs the stairs to Brickteeth's apartment. I should go home now, make an attempt at sleeping. Stay out of trouble.

reunion

Two o'clock in the morning. I'm camped on a stool at Mc-Glennon's. There's no good reason for me to be here. One beer and then I'll head home, get some rest. I attempt to wave the bartender over. Moth to a flame. He finishes reading a page of his book before coming over. "Pint of Labatt's," I tell him.

"Jackson!" A young woman emerges from the gloom and takes the stool beside me. "When did you get back in town?"

It doesn't seem appropriate to inform her that we've never met before, not to mention that my name is not Jackson. "A few days ago," I say tentatively.

Climbing onto the stool beside me, she gives me a big smile. Fiery red hair. Bright green eyes. A pretty, narrow-shouldered girl, she makes herself comfortable immediately, without coquetry or self-reproach, and there's no question that she belongs here. Slender forearms resting on the bar, she surveys the bottles on the shelves. When she swings her attention back to me, her nose ring glitters silver in the bar's dim light. She tells me how "stoked" she is to see me again. Soon we're old drinking buddies, talking about the weather, music, Iraq, drugs, genetic engineering, Buffalo, all kinds of fascinating topics. She downs shots and cocktails. Now she's telling me about her artwork. She isn't painting pastries anymore, she says. She's doing cheeseburgers now. Dripping with red juice. It's a radical change in philosophy and process.

"*Viva la revolucion*," I say, hoisting my pint glass.

It's a slow night in McGlennon's. The bartender flips another page of his thick paperback. He wears black-framed glasses with rectangular lenses, the kind worn by architects and graduate students. His shaved white skull gleams in the murky greenish light. A thick, ropy muscle flexes in his neck. I can't see the cover of his book from where I'm sitting. Five bucks says it's some critical-theory text. *The Hegemony of Hermeneutics* or some such nonsense. Whenever we have the temerity to request service, he makes a big production of tucking in his tasseled bookmark before carefully placing his paperback beside the register. I have grown to hate him in the last four minutes. He should be taken out back and beaten. Why am I so angry all of a sudden? When he finally arrives at our end, I say to him, "Glad you could stop by. The lady will have another shot of Jägermeister and a vodka tonic. I'll take a Crown Royal and a pint of Labatt's."

Now he hates me. So we're even.

Nobody shoots pool on the warped table in the back room tonight. Even the electronic dartboard stands unplugged by the men's room. Christmas lights blink off-on in the bar's plate-glass window. Outside, Elmwood Avenue is quiet and dark.

"So what are you doing with yourself these days?" she asks me. "Do you have a job?" A question heard more frequently in Buffalo than in New York City. She downs the last gulp in her highball glass. A lemon rind is capsized on the slush of the ice cubes.

"I write greeting cards," I tell her.

She finds this hilarious. "*You?* That's awesome, Jackson. Congratulations." She lifts her empty glass and smiles. She's in the mood to toast everything. It's almost four a.m.

I reach out and touch a coiled strand of red hair. "You have nice hair," I say.

Her third-floor apartment is tiny and cramped. She lives alone, except for the cats. She got sick of having room-mates, she says. Paintings are stacked against the living room walls. Wooden stretcher boards lie across the hard-wood floor. While she uses the bathroom, I examine a small canvas hanging over the fake fireplace.

"Nice cheeseburger," I call out. "Ground chuck."

"Thanks. There's beer in the fridge," she says from the other room. "Hey, have you seen Costello and them since you're back?"

She knows I'm friends with Costello? Maybe she and I have met before. My memory is strangely selective. Why can I remember my second-grade teacher's name but not this? It doesn't make sense. I blame my blackouts, which have stolen thousands of hours from my life. I'm fine when I stick with beer. It's the booze that kills me.

"I saw him tonight actually," I say. "Over at Brickteeth's. I just came from there."

"Those guys are crazy." The toilet flushes. Water splashes

in the sink. "I always thought you were the most normal one in the bunch." A door shuts with a click. "And the cutest."

She dims the halogen torch, blurring the edges of everything in the room.

I'm tempted to say, "I'm sorry. Where do I know you from?" But even in my drunken state, I recognize that an identity question at this particular moment might be considered insulting. I try a different angle. "Why do you keep calling me Jackson?"

"For real? You don't remember?" She smiles at me. "Action Jackson? That night in Tonawanda."

"Oh. Yeah." Nothing. No memory of that at all. I've lost entire weeks of my life. Tonawanda? I hope it was fun. "Yeah," I say again, unable to think of anything else to say. "Wild night, right?"

She slides her arm around my waist. I turn toward her, fully prepared to admit my confusion. *I am not who you think I am.* She kisses me hard on the mouth, and tugs my hand. I follow. That settles that. Her little bedroom smells sweet and clean, like expensive soap or scented candles. Vanilla. Tangerines. She lifts my T-shirt over my head and unbuckles my jeans. "I can't believe we're doing this," she says into my ear. "You know what I mean?"

"It's really good to see you again," I say.

invitation

The next morning I wake up early, slide out of her bed. My brain hurts. Can't find one of my socks. My mouth tastes like death. I don't think I ever learned this woman's name. Jana? Jenna? Does that sound right? She raises herself on one elbow and watches me fumble with my clothes at the foot of her bed. Sunlight slants in from an east-facing window, and I notice, for the first time, that each wall in her room has been painted a different color: blood orange, lemon yellow, avocado, lavender. An enigmatic smile flashes on her face but she says nothing. Silence. I should make her breakfast and tell jokes and do all the strategic things that will make her fall in love with me. But I feel like a porcupine, its quills sharp and protective. I have nothing to offer her.

"Well, I guess I better get going."

"Uh . . . okay."

"I've got a lot of stuff to do today."

"I understand," she says, not moving. "See you around, I guess."

Parked outside Tim Hortons, I lower my forehead to the steering wheel. "Idiot," I say. Now I want to go back, hat in hand, and make a speech about my complicated feelings, to explain that I've got problems, that too many thoughts of euthanasia have darkened my mood. Or if that's too intense, I might say, "Do you like pancakes? I bought blueberries." But I left like a scared child. What's done is done. And if I'd actually stayed there, I'm sure I'd be desperate to escape right now.

I'll bring Mom a gift in jail. Yes, that's good thinking. Charity. Tolerance. . . . It's impossible to know what she might like—she usually prefers the shiny wrapping paper to whatever's inside—but I can drive out to the Walden Galleria mall and look. Maybe I'll get her a stuffed animal, a teddy bear, something like that, something she can squeeze and pet for hours. All the literature suggests that tactile pleasures are most important to dementia patients. This seems like a noble plan, the right thing to do, but I sit unmoving in the driver's seat, my hands gripping the wheel. Staring out the windshield, I listen to the oral history CD and retreat into memory.

When I was eighteen, I finally moved out of my parents' house. Soon afterward I walked into my first bar using a fake ID. I ordered a beer and drank it. I ordered another. What freedom! This is what I had been looking for all those years when I was staring out the bus window on the way to school. I had become a grown man drinking beer in a bar. I belonged somewhere, and soon I found others who shared my enthusiasm for this way of life. Other than a few mystery bruises and some crippling morning nausea, there were no serious consequences during those first few years of drinking.

Driving out to the mall, I scan the streets looking for the people I once knew, as if a decade hasn't passed since then. In my imagination, Dan Spinelli still tends the bar in the Essex Street Pub and drunkenly explains to somebody why Todd Rundgren is a genius. The Haitian lead singer of Jolson's Lip begs for cheese on the corner of Elmwood and Allen. "Oh, please, give me big pieces of cheese." Sublime-smiled Lynn Robbins, wearing her floppy hat and thrift store corduroys, lights a cigarette off the gas burner of her stove. Mike Friedlander paints LUCY I LOVE YOU in thirty-foot letters on a brick wall, after she leaves him for a bassist in somebody else's band. Bald Victor the Goth pedals a stripped ten-speed bike the wrong way down Pearl Street. Ani DiFranco packs up her life and moves to New York City, breaking the hearts of a growing army of acolytes.

In the early nineties, Buffalo was an immense outdoor theater. There was always free entertainment. Rampant nudity. Dramatic drunkenness. Pathology disguised as performance art. I walked up and down the streets, buzzed and grinning. The Great Thinkers were not dead or incarcerated only in dusty library stacks: they were alive and performing on the streets of Buffalo. Elmwood, Allen, Grant, Chippewa, Franklin. The major boulevards of the world. Who was Friedrich Nietzsche next to one-armed Carlos "Soul Patch" Quintana expounding on promiscuity as he chewed a steak taco from La Nova? What could Eugène Ionesco teach me about the absurd after I'd listened to Sean McManus pontificate for an hour at the Essex Street Pub?

But I always felt more like a witness than a participant. More interested in reading a novel than going to a house party, I found myself on the fringes of everything. I prized solitude above anything else. I felt no pressure to succeed at anything. There was no hurry to get anywhere. Nobody I knew had accomplished anything of note. After leaving my part-time shift at the Village Green bookstore, I'd stop in at Merlins or Faherty's to drink pints of draft beer before heading to the Lenox Hotel on North Street, where I worked the overnight auditor's shift. I read a paperback at the front desk all night, while johns and prostitutes paid thirty-nine dollars for the sour-smelling rooms on the second and third floors. Broken people who just wanted to smoke some crack in peace. They kept the hotel's utility bills paid. Occasionally, though, late at night, an entire family would come in smelling of smoke after an East Side arson fire ignited by the owner to collect insurance. Sitting with my feet up on the counter, I watched them straggle in, defeated—father, uncle, two or three children, a sleepy-eyed child looking at me over the mother's shoulder—and despite my orders to place them on the third and fourth floors, I gave these families the clean suites on the sixth and seventh floors, which were intended for out-of-town actors and musicians and other luminaries.

A flash of blue and yellow catches my eye in the side mirror. I look back and see that two kids are hanging on my bumper. Leaning back on their heels, they're bumper skiing through the ice and snow. Sliding along at twenty miles per hour, they're laughing hysterically. One of them is wearing a blue Buffalo Sabres cap with a yellow ball of yarn on top.

The other one is bareheaded. "Faster, Grandpa!" he shouts. This is brilliant fun for these boys until the moment I drive over a patch of dry road. Then it's a broken ankle or a face full of Ford trunk. Unable to deal with this possibility, I pull over to the side of the road. At the same moment they both let go, sliding on their heels until they both fall back on their butts in the middle of the street. Now I'm parked on the corner, watching them run off. They slap high fives and don't look back at me.

I formulated my plan to compile an oral history of Buffalo at the Lenox Hotel's front desk. The nights were long for a third-shift worker. You sat there at three a.m. just hoping not to get robbed. It was a successful shift if nobody walked in off the street and messed with you. Because anybody could look in that window and see an easy mark sitting there. Just a boy and his cash register. In the small hours, to keep myself entertained, I came up with all kinds of future projects: teaching abroad, forming a cult, learning harmonica. Ultimately, the oral history was the right choice for me. I could hide behind the recorder and ask people questions. It gave me confidence. Turned out that Buffalonians loved talking about Buffalo, especially during happy hour, which lasted from five o'clock to midnight. Many of them felt an immense tenderness for this town. They were proud and protective of Buffalo. They dipped their pizza crusts in puddles of blue cheese and argued about where to find the best chicken wings in the city. They participated in bowling leagues and dart leagues. They celebrated happy hour most nights and ate fish fry on Fridays. They had distinctive vowel-strangled accents, and the nasal sounds of certain words ("*car*" and "*bar*") rivaled Long Island's more jarring and annoying tonal variations. Their last names were Szwejbka and O'Shaughnessy and Torrentino. They distrusted book learning. Money talked and bullshit walked. They had provincial worldviews, and they definitely considered you show-offish if you used words like "provincial."

If someday I'm demented and exiled to a wheelchair, which of these long-term memories will persist? Will I choose to remember the good or bad moments from my life? Will I be able to tell the difference?

My cell phone vibrates in my pocket. Perfect timing. I need an escape from the morbid spiral of my thoughts. I examine the unfamiliar number—716 area code—then plug a finger in my left ear and answer on the third ring. "Hello?"

"Hey, asshole."

"Hi!" I say brightly. "Who is this?"

"You know who it is."

"Actually I don't. That's why I asked."

"It's Regis Cartwright," he says.

"Oh, hey. What's up?"

"Stay away from Corinne," he says. "That's over for you."

"What?"

"Find some other chick to pork."

"Nice, Regis," I say. "Did you just use 'pork' as a verb?"

I hear a rustling on the other end of the line.

"I'm gonna come over there and kick your ass," says a higher-pitched voice.

"You realize we're not in fifth grade anymore, right? . . . Regis?"

"This ain't Regis," the voice says.

"Is this a joke? You just said you were Regis."

"It's not gonna be a joke when I kick your ribs through your spine!"

"Right, okay. Where did you get my number, by the way?"

"Don't worry about it, pussy."

"Okay, then. Where are you calling from?"

"Where am I?" he echoes. "Where are you, bitch?"

"Metaphysically speaking? Well, I guess I'm trying to find myself."

These guys don't have much range in their repertoire of insults. If this conversation continues any longer, I'll probably be called *motherfucker* or *faggot* or *cocksucker*.

"Look across the street, douchebag," he says.

Or *douchebag*, that old chestnut.

Startled, I look across the street. Regis nods at me from the patio of a Greek diner. The creased brim of a baseball cap is pulled down low on his forehead. A heated propane lamp bathes him in orange light. He's seated across the table from an elephant in a fur-lined denim jacket—an elephant with a tiny cell phone clamped to his ear. Granger extends his thick middle finger and mouths, "Fuck you," apparently forgetting that I can hear him.

"Hi, Granger," I say into the phone. "Did you watch a lot of cartoons when you were a child?"

"Fuck you," he says audibly this time.

Regis pulls the cell phone away from his articulate personal assistant. "James," he says, "do us both a favor. Stay away from Corinne."

"This is getting way too creepy," I say. "Are you guys following me?"

"I'm not gonna tell you again. You stepped over the line the other night, but I'm going to overlook it. This time."

"Here's the thing. I don't know what you're talking about. Honestly."

"Stay off Niagara Street altogether," he says. "Don't go past Richmond, or we'll hurt you."

"Regis. Come on. You're a smart guy. You've been around. Do you have any idea how ridiculous you sound?"

"No joke, loser. We will kill you."

Loser. Great. Of course.

But that word has less juice than any of them. I've never thought of *loser* as a slur. I've always been more interested in books and songs about people who don't triumph in the end. They don't get the suitcase full of drugs or the blowjob or whatever they're after. All my favorite movies—*La Strada, Double Indemnity, Withnail & I*—focus on losers. At the end of the race, the people I care most about don't stand on the raised platform while their country's anthem plays. I'm fascinated by the athlete who trains diligently for years, making incredible sacrifices of his time and energy, only to pull a hamstring at mile nineteen and limp off the course yelping like a dog. What has he learned from this experience? I like the artists who toil for decades only to arrive at a dead end and then change course in middle age and find a new path to enlightenment. When I interviewed people for the oral history, I always asked about their losses. They perked up. Turns out they had learned a lot more from losing than from winning.

"James," Regis says.

"Remember when Dave Snedden hit you in the face with

a dodgeball? How old were we then? How do you think that affected you?"

"I'm done talking to you."

"Talk to you later." I hang up on him. And by hanging up I mean that I press END very forcefully on my cell phone. Hopefully he hears and sees the masculinity in the *click*. I sit there for a moment, facing him, my hands on the wheel. A more bluff and hearty man might get out and head across the street. But I'm far too shaky for this machismo bullshit. I start the car's engine and drive away before Granger can leap the short patio fence and challenge me to a brawl in the street.

JOEY DONOFRIO,
barber

Look around. We're in serious trouble here. City streets are more
dangerous than ever. The kids these days'll shoot you without
even thinking about it. There's no shared humanity, no sense that
we're all in this together, we're all connected. . . . Probably
hundreds of reasons for why a city goes down the tubes, but I'll
tell ya what I think. You wanna hear what I think? I think we're too
segregated. Not just black and white. I'm talking about the class
divide. I grew up poor. I know the difference. When we were kids
we knew there were places you just didn't go, places you weren't
welcome. Cops would follow you in their cruisers—"What is he
doing here?" You know what I mean? "Greasy wop. Dago." So I can
just imagine what the black kids today feel if they make a wrong
turn. . . . Only way to end that stupidity is to pack everybody right
on top of each other. Your neighbors are Jews, blacks, Chinese,
and Puerto Ricans—what are you gonna do, ignore them for forty
years? Look the other way? You're going to say, "Good morning.
How are you today?" Cities like Chicago, Cleveland and even
Columbus have something called metro government. A safeguard.
Prevents suburban sprawl. The core of strength is the city. In
Buffalo, though, the city is shrinking and the suburbs are thriving.
You don't push all the poor people to the east side of town. That
doesn't help your economy and it doesn't help your schools and
it doesn't help nothing. There's a ripple effect. Now, if our

politicians had implemented a metro government fifty years ago, when they should have, there would be no suburbs called West Seneca and Cheektowaga. They would be part of Buffalo proper. See what I'm saying? So imagine your nose is Buffalo, right? If you drew a big circle around it and all its suburbs, including your ears and your chin, you'd have a medium-sized city, maybe a million people. More. A million five. But the city of Buffalo never defined its borders like that. So let me reiterate: I blame the politicians for this. If they had established a metro government, Buffalo would now expand all the way to the Grand Island Bridge to North Tonawanda and Clarence, right past your shoulders through Lancaster, East Aurora, and Hamburg. And the city of Buffalo would be a medium-sized American city, a metroplex with a radius of, what, thirty miles by thirty miles roughly? Now this is a reversible problem. This can be fixed. We can fix this. But these jack-me-off politicians would be signing away their own power. You see? That's why they never vote for metro government. They would lose their seats. Right now they are like little dukes and duchesses of their own zip codes. It all comes down to power and greed.

AL POLONIS,
eavesdropper

You're talking about a lack of foresight, Joe, if I understand you correctly. And that's just one element of a larger picture here. I'm not even going to . . . Toronto built an international airport back when— What year did they build that, Joe? Was that 1960? Everybody travels through Toronto now. Who travels through Buffalo? . . . What are you working on here, a school project? . . . Just curious, eh? You ever hear what that did to the cat? . . . I'm just having fun with you. We're having fun here. But let's be serious now. You want to know what killed Buffalo? I'll tell ya. The Saint Lawrence Seaway. Nothing hurt this city more than that. You gotta understand: Let me break this down for you. Hold that thing closer. Closer. . . . Okay. Buffalo is a port city. Before the Saint Lawrence Seaway, all the ships docked in Buffalo and unloaded their cargo. Flour. Grain. You following me? Then they want to make a water route between the Great Lakes and the Atlantic Ocean that bypasses Buffalo. Joe, correct me if I'm lying. And what do our beloved city leaders say? Do they protest this insanity? I mean, anyone could see this was gonna destroy our shipping industry. The mayor says, "Let's do it. Where do I sign?" Freaking idiots. That killed Buffalo. The Saint Lawrence Seaway. Losing Bethlehem Steel was child's play compared to making our ports obsolete. And when Toronto starts building a major airport, do you think that woke them up? Hell no. They were asleep at the wheel. And we're paying the price for it today.

a gift

Today she's wearing baggy gray sweatpants and an oversized rainbow T-shirt that belongs to someone else. Where are all her sweaters? She's in a lineup of wheelchairs near the door: a motorcycle gang whose members all ran out of gas at the same time.

"Oh, we were just about to take her upstairs to the piano recital," says one of the aides, a late-forties brunette with a thick braid of hair tucked into the collar of her scrubs. "Do you want to stay with her?"

"I'll stay with her," I say. "Sure."

My mother looks up at me, blinks. She's wearing her spare glasses today—the good ones must be missing again. The fingers of both her hands are interlocked, as if she's playing a silent game of "Here's the church, here's the steeple." Around her neck she wears a crumb-crusted harness, a padded horseshoe, so she can lean her head back and snooze, just another weary traveler on a cross-country flight.

"Hey, I'm sticking with you, kid," I tell her.

She smiles, recognizing one of her favorite old phrases. Or she smiles in response to my tone of voice. Or she smiles because . . .

This morning I bought her a green stuffed frog at the

K-B Toys in the Galleria mall. I have it hidden behind my back right now. It has very soft material with polyester filling and, according to the label, PVC pellets in the hands or paws or whatever a frog has at the end of his arms. I imagined her squeezing the pellet paws and petting the toy for hours. The PVC pellets, whatever they are, convinced me that the green frog was the pick of the litter.

I lean down and whisper in her ear, "I'm busting you out of this joint. Let's go to the Nature Room."

"Yuh," she manages, breathing uneasily. She's playing with a strap on the wheelchair, trying to sound out words. "Puh-puh-puh."

I rarely pursue these fragments of speech because it only frustrates her to search for a lost word or a clipped thread of a sentence. Many times—before we knew what was happening to her—I pushed her to finish her sentences, not realizing that I was being cruel, asking her to do something beyond her capabilities.

"So we're almost . . . ," she'd begin.

Half a minute would pass. She'd look at me and nod.

"So we're almost *what*, Mom?"

"Do you think we should . . . ," she'd say, smoothing the unwrinkled cloth of her slacks.

"Leave? Sure, we could do anything you want," I'd say, "or we could sit here for a while."

"I think that would be . . . ," she'd reply maddeningly.

In the Nature Room, I hold out the stuffed frog to her. "Look what I brought today. This is for you."

Her eyes light up. She takes the stuffed animal into her arms, presses it to her chest.

"Doesn't that feel good? It's pretty soft."

"You're . . . wonderful."

"I am? Thank you."

Too bad Rodney isn't here. He longs for these flashes of clarity. I bend down and hug her. She holds the frog in one arm, and pats the back of my head with her free hand.

The stuffed frog wears a green bow tie. She's playing with it now, pulling at it.

"That's a bow tie you're playing with. Can you see what this thing is? He's a frog. Look at him. He's funny."

She looks at me.

"Look at this frog, Mom."

She smiles at me.

"See the frog?"

She nods, still staring at me. "Wonderful," she says and tugs on the frog's bow tie, trying to pull it off his neck.

Now she's distracted by a purple lint ball on her rainbow shirt. She stops playing with the frog and devotes all her attention to this new fascination.

There are moments, sudden flashes of lucidity, when she escapes the captivity of her dementia. Becoming her younger self again, she speaks fluently and answers questions with insight, humor and grace. Eyes alert, she smiles and nods her head, apparently comprehending everything. Ignoring the wheelchair and the food on her face, you imagine that this is the same Ellen who, fifteen years ago, rolled up her pant legs and waded out into the cold water of Lake Erie on her birthday. Laughing, she turned and called out to us, "Come on in. The water's fine." That Ellen remains trapped inside her. But because I have a functional memory, minus a few lapses, that same Ellen remains preserved within me. If I try, I can feel the slick rocks beneath my bare feet, the icy water on my ankles, as I follow her out into the lake. I can reach her if I go out far enough.

Wheelchair-bound Ellen clamps her eyelids shut. Her lips quiver. She sneezes. It's a big wet explosive one. She looks horrified by the noise she's made. It scares her. I try to imagine how frightening a sneeze would be if I didn't know what it was.

She begins to cry.

"Oh, hey, that's okay," I say. "That's just a sneeze, honey. That's normal. God bless you. In fact, I bet there's another one coming. They usually come in twos."

She glares at me. Furious all of a sudden. She throws the stuffed frog on the floor. "Stupid," she says and turns her attention to the strap attached to her chair. She folds it up into loops, then unfolds it. Folds it into loops, unfolds it. Her nostrils quiver. Here comes the second sneeze. She's ready for it this time, even tries to block it, but it will not be prevented:

"Ebb-chaa!"

I touch her shoulder. "Gesundheit, Mom."

She folds the strap into a loop, unfolds it. "Stoopy," she says. "Stoo . . . stupid."

In some ways this has been her first childhood. Ellen was the oldest of five kids. She had two younger brothers and two younger sisters. In her parents' absence, these little kids begged her for haircuts and clean clothes. They demanded that she read to them in bed at night. Sometimes she skipped doing her own homework, knowing that her teachers would reprimand her the following morning. In the late 1950s, Ellen's mother and father had discovered a religion that they believed would change the world: the Baha'i Faith, a unique choice for a self-employed carpenter and a secretary in a dairy-equipment company. Smitten, they attended meetings every night. They went off on spiritual retreats. And they left their oldest daughter, a ten-year-old girl, in charge of the ramshackle house on Victoria Avenue. She became a caregiver, a mother, before she hit adolescence.

"What's that strap you're playing with?" I say.

"I . . . don't . . ." She shakes her head angrily. "Don't!"

"Well, it gives you something to do with your hands. Right? That's a good thing. Probably more fun than quilting a blanket that nobody wants."

"Blan-ket," she says.

I've read that it's helpful to talk to dementia patients just as you might talk to anyone else. Doesn't matter whether they understand you or not. It's supposedly good for their self-esteem to be treated as adults and equals.

She laughs and smiles at me, swinging through arcs of emotion. She reaches her hand out and tries to caress my cheek but is really just poking me in the face.

Ignore it.

"That's my beard," I say. "I wear a beard now."

"I . . . know . . . that." She continues to touch my face. For a split second I wonder, guiltily, where her hands have been. When was the last time anybody washed her hands? Ignore it!

"Do you know where you are?" I ask.

She pokes at my lips with her sticky kindergarten hands. "Yes." She begins worrying the strap, turning it over and over. "I don't . . . know."

If she knows where she is, it must be a devastating blow. This is her worst nightmare come true. My mother's greatest fear was not spiders or snakes or rats. She was afraid of ending up in an adult care nursing home, sitting in a wheelchair unable to speak. She told us this. It became a family joke. "If I ever get like that," she said, "do me in." She meant it. She supported assisted suicide in cases of terminal illness. She supported the patient's right to choose. In fact, she published articles in *JAMA* arguing for judicial leniency in well-known right-to-die cases in New York and Michigan.

"It's not the best place in the world, that's for sure," I say to her. "But you're safe and warm here. We should be grateful for that. You're eating well, and . . ."

She's not listening anymore.

"He was my principal," an aide shouts at a resident. "Yeah, your son! Mr. Roszak. Mis-ter Ros-zak!" she shouts in the old woman's face. "I couldn't believe it when I saw the photo in your memory box. I said, 'Hey, what's old Mr. Roszak doing in there?'"

"He was your *what*?" the confused old woman says.

"My principal!" She points at her own chest. "Your son!" Now she points at the old woman's chest. Satisfied that everything is now perfectly clear, the aide lowers her voice and speaks at a decibel level one would expect of a person standing on an airport runway. "Mr. Roszak knew all our names, and there were over a thousand of us. We loved him for that. We'd say, 'How are ya, Mr. Roszak?' And you know what he used to tell us? 'Best day of my life so far.' I've never forgotten that. 'Best day of my life so far.'"

A sign on the wall warns: IF YOU SEE SOMETHING, SAY SOMETHING. I glance around the Nature Room, on the lookout for evildoers. Eighty-nine-year-old Mr. Jacobson over there, with his pendulous testicles emerging grotesquely from his open bathrobe, appears to be capable of all kinds of mischief, except that he's asleep.

Perry Como sings, "Zing Zing Zoom Zoom."

A squat, bearded man enters D-Unit. He's wearing a gray knit cap and a leather trench coat. His chapped cheeks are flushed pink from the cold outside.

"Oh, oh, oh, I'm so happy to see you," says a woman in yellow cotton pajamas. She pushes herself up from the stained couch in the Common Room. "I'm so happy to see you."

"I'm happy to see *you*," he says, gathering her into his short, thick arms.

"Oh, things aren't working out here, George," she says into his chest. "And I'm ready to leave."

"I'm not George, Mother."

"Oh, oh—I know."

"George is out in Boston, remember?"

"Yes," she says softly, "he said he was going out there for a while."

"I'm Terry," he introduces himself.

At the Elms, you hear this type of exchange a dozen times a day. Maybe someday this will all seem incredibly primitive, like bloodletting or leeching. In the future, people will have heard of Alzheimer's, but it will sound to them like polio does to me: a disease people contracted before we knew anything important about medicine and the human body.

"This is my son," says the pajama-clad woman to nobody in particular.

I will find the beauty in this situation even if it kills me.

Ellen turns her head toward me. She smiles. In good conscience I can't let my mom sit here with so much goop in her teeth. She's so unaware, helpless. So I excuse myself and wash my hands in a nearby bathroom sink, cherry-scented soap, then I snap off a foot-long strand of green dental floss and position myself behind her chair. Leaning like a dentist over her right shoulder, I say, "Can you open your mouth, Mom? Go ahead. It's okay. Open your mouth."

She's not having it.

I peel back her upper lip to reveal yellow, gritted, food-clotted teeth—*they shoot horses, don't they?*—and try to get the floss into her mouth. Uncertain, she pooches her lips, now trying to help. "Okay, good," I say *sotto voce*, dentist-style. "Now open." Her tongue pokes out. "Better. Try to open. Can you say, 'Ahhh'?" The floss is taut, a green tightrope between my clenched fists. "Let me just . . . Come on. You'll be happy when I—" Just as I'm about to give up, her mouth opens wide. "Great. Good work, Mom." I work the floss between her lower teeth, plink-plink-plink, fast, before she changes her mind, and tiny wet clumps of food tumble out behind her teeth. She closes her mouth. She chews.

"That's a little snack for you," I say.

Tomorrow maybe I'll try the upper teeth. It's a necessary violation. The attack will soon be forgotten, but the results will be enjoyed for the rest of the day.

The other residents in the Nature Room are napping, narrating unintelligible tales, or staring at the Humphrey Bogart film on the Turner Classics channel. Ellen hasn't even glanced at the TV since we came in here. Instead, she is keeping an eye on the nurses' station. Marianne is there, so is Fran, and three aides. Ellen watches them intently. She holds the stuffed frog in her lap. I realize that she has more nursing experience in a clinical setting than any of them.

From this distance we can't hear what the staff members are saying. Marianne raises her arms and motions wildly, acting out some routine. The other women shake their heads, as if to say, "Marianne, you're so crazy." Marianne turns away from them, feigning disgust, and then glances back over her shoulder at them. Gales of laughter carry to where the two of us sit. I'm inclined to say that Mom's watching them *longingly*, but I can't know for certain. She might be incapable of longing or even remembering that she spent so many years around nurses' stations herself. Maybe they're annoying her. Or maybe she's thirsty and wants something to drink.

Does my presence have any tangible effect on her? Impossible to tell. Nevertheless, I sit beside her and pretend to be a grown-up. What can I bring to this situation? How can I help? Minutes pass in silence. Ten minutes, twenty minutes. My mind wanders. My ass hurts. I shift in the seat.

Amazing: Rodney comes here and does this every day? God bless him.

When Mom falls asleep holding my hand, there's nothing to do but daydream. One day, I imagine, I will create the great work that will finally vindicate me, and everybody will recognize my worth and intelligence, especially all those pinch-faced lunch ladies and barking crossing guards and after-school thugs with cigarettes lodged behind their ears. They will finally understand that Quiet James's moody silences were not the symptoms of mild retardation, but rather the gestation of a superior intellect gathering data. They will open the newspaper and read my name. "Guess I was wrong about that one," they'll admit. "Turns out that mute kid was a freaking genius." However, eighteen years have passed and still—still!—I have not made the shattering impact that I daydreamed about as a ten-year-old schoolboy. My foot is asleep. I rotate the ankle. Mom senses my movement and grips my hand even tighter.

If I were to kill her, I would probably choose this time of day, the hour between two and three, when she's usually taking her nap. She's awake now only because I am here with her. Visitors, because of their scarcity, trump scheduling. Normally, she naps for an hour or two after lunch. Nobody enters her room during that time. I could tiptoe into the room without waking her, smother her with a pillow and be in my car cruising down Delaware before the staff knew anything.

At three o'clock the next shift starts. A staff nurse, Tricia Vacanti, enters the Nature Room and heads toward Ellen's chair. Her slender face has an impish, doll-like quality. She's the only member of the staff who has expressed any interest in Ellen's past medical career. Tricia says that someday she wants to read Ellen's adult health nursing textbook all the way through. Nobody I know has read the whole thing, including me. It's over a thousand pages long. For eight or nine years it was an assigned text in American nursing programs.

"You guys want something to drink in here?" Tricia asks. "Juice? Ginger ale?"

I squeeze Ellen's hand. "You want something to drink, Mom?"

She lets go of my hand. She finds the strap and folds it, unfolds it. The stuffed frog sits on the table beside her, forgotten.

"I guess we'll have a ginger ale, Tricia."

She returns a minute later holding a green can with a bent white straw sticking out of it. "Is this your baby, Ellen?" she says loudly. "He looks just like you!"

Ellen smiles up at Tricia. The two women make eye contact. "Do you have any brothers or sisters?" Tricia asks me.

"One sister," I say. "She was here this morning."

I learned this from the guest book when I signed in.

"It's not root beer, though," Tricia says, looking down at my mother. "I know how Ellen likes her root beer."

Does she? Since when?

Holding the straw to my mother's lips, I ask Tricia if she had a good Thanksgiving. Nodding, she talks about her son, Donny. "He's fifteen," she says. "His dad gave him a full Pearl drum kit. At night Donny keeps everybody awake, but at least he's finally gotten interested in something constructive. He wants to start an Aerosmith cover band."

I smile hugely at Tricia, thanking her again for the ginger ale. I want the staff to associate my mother with smiling, friendly people. "Do you live in Buffalo?"

"Nah, we live out in the sticks, past Darien Lake."

"That's quite a commute, isn't it?"

"Oh, twenty miles, give or take." She straightens the pillows on the urine-scented couch. Ignore it. "You know, your dad is so sweet," she says. "He brings us a big box of doughnuts every Saturday."

I hold the straw to Ellen's lips.

"The aides start hanging around the station, waiting for him to arrive," Tricia continues. "And I make sure I'm working at the desk." She laughs. "Every Saturday morning he brings doughnuts. Every Saturday."

"He's a good guy."

"You can say that again." She nods vigorously. "Visits your mom every day. Same time. Sits there with her. Clips her fingernails."

Rodney is our family's ambassador here. Doughnuts? That's genius.

Al-Qaeda doesn't stand a chance against good Americans like us. The evildoers hate our freedom to start Aerosmith cover bands and bring doughnuts to nursing homes. LOVE IT OR LEAVE IT. UNITED WE STAND.

"It hasn't been easy on him," I say.

"Well, you don't see that dedication around here much," Tricia says. "Sometimes I see him brushing her hair. Heartbreaking." Tricia bends over and picks up a discarded tissue. "You just hate to see somebody suffer like that. I would help him in any way that I could. You can let him know that, too. That's just the kind of person I am." She reaches over and adjusts Mom's neck pillow. "If you need anything, just give me a shout."

"That means a lot to me, Tricia. Thank you."

When the staff nurse walks away, I find Ellen staring at me with a look of pride and wonder. Well, I imagine her expression reveals pride and wonder. Her eyes are bright, merry and focused. She likes seeing me in the world, communicating, engaged with others. Or maybe she likes watching a nurse do her job well.

Like most of the employees here, Tricia is more mechanic than saint. To Tricia and her coworkers, my mother is not entirely human—not a daughter, not a mother, not a wife. Her past wiped out, she is just another sack of flesh, dehumanized. She has become a freak. Staff members put food in Ellen's mouth, strip clothes off her body, dress her and lay her in bed—she's an oversized doll, an animate toy—but she does not belong to their species any longer. I understand this. It's a human impulse to think: *I will never be like that.*

My cell phone vibrates in my pocket. The call is coming from a 646 number that I don't recognize. Against my better judgment, I answer it.

"Hello?"

"James. It's Derek from Laffs," he says, his voice echoing. "Listen, sorry to bother you, but I need your help."

"Where are you?"

"I'm in a stall in the men's room. So we've got a mock-up here that needs a better punch line. This is the gag. Hot blonde in a bikini. Huge rack. Nipples out to here. Cover caption: 'They told me it's your birthday.'"

"Okay. Hold on." I think about it for a minute. "'Time to get excited,'" I say to him.

"I'll give it a try," he says. "Thanks."

Time to get excited. Happy Arbor Day.

There is something freakish about all human beings.

I once looked into the tired eyes of Sandy Allen, the world's tallest living woman. She was in the Guinness Museum in Toronto, a live exhibit, a human oddity sitting in an enormous chair with carved wooden arms. All day she sat there, I realize now, because it was too difficult for her to stand upright. She must have needed the money. Why else would she sit through that kind of scrutiny? But then again, where else could a woman that size have worked?

"Make her stand, Mum," a kid said in a loud voice. I turned to scowl at him, trying to indicate with a forbidding expression that he was being an asshole. There were about twenty of us crowded around Sandy Allen. We were all assholes.

The boy's mother tried to shush him, but he was adamant.

"Make that giant stand."

Finally, Sandy Allen, seven feet seven inches tall, pushed herself up with great effort, her huge hands gripping the arms of the chair, knuckles the size of golf balls, and managed to stand. Towering above everyone in the room, she leaned on a cane for support. She weighed almost four hundred pounds.

"Ha ha ha," the boy said happily, and turned to another exhibit.

Briefly, I met Sandy Allen's eyes and tried to impart silently that I was not like him, that all of us were not like this rude little boy, but I knew it wasn't true. I had been gawking at her along with everybody else. I had paid for my admission ticket expressly to see her, and on some level was probably thinking: *I'm glad I'm not her*. Ultimately, that's what all the Guinness World Records were for me: a chance to flip through the book's pages and think: This sad bastard was struck by lightning seven times. This kook has finger-nails 261 inches long. I'm glad that's not me. They are not like me.

But they are me. Every one of them. And so is my mother.

The word *"Achtung!"* rings out at the end of the corridor. Oh no. Mr. Myers is awake.

The smell of urine is strong now. Ellen squirms and tugs at the elastic waistband of her sweatpants. Evidently she did not need any ginger ale. She attempts to remove her pants, hooking her thumbs into the waistband, mumbling to herself.

"Do you need to be changed, sweetie?"

I have taken to calling her sweetie and honey and dear, as the aides and nurses do. It's an affectation that doesn't seem natural to me. I find it odd to hear other people's words emerging from my mouth.

Embarrassed, my mother nods. With that slight move-ment her glasses catch the overhead light, and for a moment I can't see her eyes.

"That's okay," I say, swinging her chair around. "That's fine. No problem."

Perry Como sings, "Papa loves mambo."

I wheel Mom down to her room, D-116. It amazes me that the body can produce so much waste, even as meals are reduced in portion and frequency, and her liquids are limited to a few sips at various times of the day.

She jams her left hand into her loose pants. I watch with growing horror and revulsion as she rummages around in there. Soon her wet-fingered hand emerges, a trophy, an exhibit, and she wriggles the glistening fingers. She lifts them to her nostrils, and sniffs. Now she has urine on her nose.

Oh, Mom.

"I'm going to get someone to help you," I tell her.

"Where?" she says.

"They'll come here. You just stay put. They'll help you out."

Three deep creases have appeared in her forehead. She begins to cry again.

"Here. Look at this." I hand her a Thanksgiving card from her sister Donna. "Isn't that nice?"

"Lovely," she says, force of habit, even as tangles and plaques strangle her brain.

please

Two aides enter the room a few minutes later, wheeling the cumbersome Hoyer Lift. "We'll take care of her," one of them says to me. "We have to put her in bed first."

"Okay." Then, for the first time, I say: "Can I watch?"

"Uhhhh, okay." One aide glances at the other. This must be an unprecedented question. "But when we undress her, you have to leave. You can't watch that."

"No, no, just the lift. I want to see how this thing works."

"You can watch, I guess," says the first aide. She shuts the door. "One warning: she doesn't like it very much. She gets scared sometimes."

"I don't blame her," says the other aide. "I didn't like it either. I thought I was gonna fall out."

"We all get lifted during our orientations," explains the first one, "so we can know what it's like."

They attach the netting underneath her body to the hooks on the lift. So the loops she was playing with earlier become a part of this operation. I can't believe I didn't figure that out before now.

"Okay, Ellen, we're gonna lift you up now."

My mother presses the green frog to her chest. She holds

it like it's a baby, with one hand beneath its butt. Legs dangling, the frog rests tranquilly on her chest.

She watches me. Abruptly the sling goes taut—she's still watching me as the pouch closes around her body, embracing her—and the Hoyer Lift's strong arm swings the bulging cargo of Ellen Fitzroy through the air. Cartoon images of stork and baby flit through my head. Ellen's chuckling and shaking her head, marveling at the strangeness of the world. Her body is lowered into bed. The aides unhook the straps and pull the sling out from under her.

"Wow. She usually screams when we do that."

"Yeah, you should visit every day."

"I'll be right outside the door," I say. "See you in one minute, Mom. Thanks for letting me watch," I tell them, and I leave the room.

Outside her room I lean my head back against the wall, trying not to envision what the aides are doing to my mother—trying not to imagine the faces they make when they change her soiled diaper, trying not to imagine Ellen's shame.

Afterward, she lies awake in her bed, worrying the frayed seam of the thin blanket on her chest. "Please," she whispers. Her head is turned toward me. Her legs are twisted to one side.

When the snow stops falling in her mind and she can see clearly, it must enrage and demoralize Ellen to find herself here. Nursing homes, convalescent homes, terminal wards.

Minutes slow as frozen syrup. Silent suffering. The crushing loss of dignity. She wrote all about this. She treated people in this condition. She stood by their beds, spoke kindly to them. And now she's here.

"Please," she repeats. She wheezes with each inhalation of breath.

Body temperature, pulse, respiration, blood pressure.

Her blue eyes have a ferocious intensity, a burning quality, communicating what language cannot. What is she trying to tell me? Does she want me to end her suffering?

"I want to help you," I say. "Are you in pain?" Reaching over the metal rails, I lay my palm flat on the side of her face. I feel the warmth of her face, the blood rushing just beneath the skin.

I sit beside her trying to imagine what she thinks and feels. If it's true that she experiences no physical pain, and that mentally she is no more cognizant of her condition than a baby is—the baby doesn't recognize the helplessness of her life because she has nothing to compare it to—then this is my problem and not hers. But if she is suffering with the knowledge of loss, if she recognizes the absence of dignity, which I suspect is the case, then her shame and despair must consume her. And she has nothing but time, the regulated ticking of minutes on a clock, to remind her of that.

How can Dad and Katie stay so calm about this? Don't they see what's happening? Do they smell urine and bleach and chemical violets when they enter the D-Unit? Do they recognize this impostor in Mom's wheelchair?

I know I can't smash or destroy anything because that's not a proper response to the flaming despair I feel—*Why don't you talk about your feelings, James?*—but I haven't got the language, the words—old Quiet James in the back of the classroom doodling anarchy symbols on his notebook—I have no language to express the rage that a human life has all come to this, to nothing. After all the struggle and sacrifice, after all the unspoken opinions and missed opportunities. I wonder why anyone in their right mind chooses a life of humility, or modesty, unless they truly believe, on the basis of no evidence, that something awaits them on the other side.

Ellen is flat on her back staring at the ceiling. She lives now only in the memories of those who knew her. For years she lived in our house, making dinner every night, asking us about our school subjects, dabbing our cuts with iodine, a woman with grace and intelligence, and I wanted only to escape her and to meet up with my know-nothing friends. I considered her and Rodney enemies to my development as a partier. My folks were fools, I thought. Dinosaurs. They did not have my best interests in mind, and yet I implicitly trusted every adolescent gasoline huffer and pill popper in Buffalo. Mom fed me fresh vegetables at night and I resented her. But if one of the Critter brothers pulled a hit of blotter acid from his grimy pocket and offered it to me, saying, "Watch out, it's Purple Unicorn," I put it on my tongue without asking a single question.

I spent my free time interviewing fools, never thinking to seek answers in my own home.

"I'm here," I say, leaning over the guardrails. "Are you awake? Mom?"

Still holding my hand, she wades into sleep. Her eyes move quickly behind the lids, as if she's following schools of swimming fish. After a moment, she pulls away from me, leaving me standing alone on the shore.

ALAN FARMER,
former district councilman

Every so often the Psych Center attempts to re-acclimate some
of the patients back into society. But most of them, when given
outpatient privileges, don't wander past the confines of
Elmwood Avenue. You see them hanging out on street corners,
shopping at Wilson Farms and settling onto a bar stool somewhere to kill an afternoon. They really do want to fit in and they
try hard to become one of the crowd. Unfortunately, their
obvious quirks and the drug-induced frizziness of their hair
gives them away. Quite often Jerry, the bartender at No Names,
will let them sit there because they aren't bothering anyone.
Sometimes, though, I've seen him ask one of them to leave. It
always hurts him to do this. Jerry is a kind man. Jerry is a soulful
man. And I can imagine how important it must be for insane
people to feel like they're enjoying some moments of normalcy.
When Jerry does ask one of these unfortunates to leave, the
person usually understands. You might expect them to put up a
fight, to scream or bark like a dog, but most of them are pretty
docile people. It's as if . . . as if they know they don't fit in and are
only hoping to play along with everybody else for a while. Jerry
the bartender is quite often the one who has to bring reality
back into the game. And I feel implicated because I'm sitting
there quietly with my shot and beer, watching everything. I am a
witness to the savage dance of the world.

windows

When I was twelve years old, I hated day camp even more than I hated school. Apparently some children looked forward to it all year. To me, it always felt like a punishment, like more school. At eight o'clock in the morning, the yellow bus pulled up in front of our house. My sister and I climbed aboard and shared a seat. I hoped the ride would never end. Barely awake, I would stare out the window, daydreaming. Looking at all the houses and people, all those mystery lives, I prayed that the bus driver would lose his way and we'd never arrive at our destination.

Kate loved camp. She made a lot of friends there. But what I enjoyed most was that bus ride, the fantasy, the waiting for something to happen. Twenty minutes of peace, twenty minutes of imagination, just watching the world and thinking about anything I wanted, before finding myself in a cramped, rotting wood cabin with the other boys in my age group, our activities overseen by our teenaged counselor with his acne-ravaged face, the schedule precise every day and planned down to the minute. Every day we had to swim laps in an over-chlorinated pool while a tanned old bald man with a zinc strip on his nose shouted "stroke stroke stroke breathe" through a bullhorn. I churned through the pissy water in the shallow end, knowing that my neighborhood friends—Costello and McQuilken—would wake up at noon and ride their skateboards to a half-pipe. They were living the good life, smoking cigarettes and drinking chocolate milk and eating Funyuns and Doritos, howling with laughter after the drudgery of the school year. I imagined them meeting cute girls and loitering outside Wilson Farms, asking old people to buy them beer. At the end of a normal day at camp, I had a vicious sunburn and way too much sand in the crack of my ass.

Now, when I come to Buffalo, I drive around for hours, staring out the window, the kid who doesn't want the ride to end. Zeppelin bursts through the front speakers. I turn it down, then off, a twist of the dial. It's evening again. Neon bar signs illuminate otherwise pitch-black blocks, a glowing smear of green and red on snow. I slow down, then accelerate, using the correct pedals without thinking.

I park outside McGlennon's. I'll pump some quarters into the jukebox, camp out on a stool and maybe, with luck, bump into the red-haired painter again. Jana. Jenna. On Elmwood Avenue there is a bar on every block, each filled with young people in no hurry to go home and face their empty beds.

McGlennon's is jammed with people tonight. "What's up?" yells a different bartender from the other night. This one has blond dreadlocks and chalk-white skin. "What can I get ya?"

"Pint of Blue," I shout over the din. George Clinton's big voice booms out of speakers above my head: *"Flashlight."* Drums and bass pound my back companionably. I scan the crowd. A blur of diffident eyes, wet teeth, upraised glasses.

She's not here. I could drive by her place instead. She might let me in. No. That would be creepy.

"Flashlight!"

I'm perched on a wobbly stool surrounded by buzzed, raucous teenagers. Beside me, a girl yells to her friend, "Because he *told* me!"

"What did he say?"

"He told me about *her.*"

Outside, twenty or thirty people are smoking cigarettes, talking on cell phones. It's a Saturday night in Buffalo.

There's a soccer match on the TV suspended above the bar. The yellow team has the green team backpedaling. Both squads are playing reckless footie.

While I'm nursing my second pint of draft beer, Jana/Jenna enters with two girlfriends. Before I can wiggle my way through the crowd to reach her, she falls into a conversation with a smirking boy in baggy jeans. He can't be much older than eighteen.

A player on the green team just scored. He blasted a rising shot into the upper left corner of the net. *Top shelf where Mama hides the cookies!* Clutching his head to keep his brains from exploding, the goal scorer sprints across the pitch in a zigzag pattern. His teammates chase after him as if he's stolen their wallets. The fans are going bananas. Exhausted, the hero drops to his knees, his arms raised. That must feel amazing.

Three o'clock ticks by. Nobody notices. I drink a few more pints on a stool at the bar, waiting. She's still engaged with the kid by the dartboard. Is he her little brother or something? Is she babysitting?

Sting is singing about taking giant steps on the moon.

At last, when she breaks away from her companion, I approach her.

Leaning over the jukebox, she chooses the third of her four songs. Her curly red hair shrouds her face. "Hey," she says absently, her sea-green eyes still fixed on the smudged jukebox glass.

"How's it going?" I say.

"Fine." Jana/Jenna selects her final song.

"Look. I'm sorry about the other morning," I say. "How I left. I've been thinking about it. I was going to call. . . ."

"Don't worry about it. It's cool."

I shake my head. "No, it's not. I know that."

She says nothing.

"I like you, and . . . but right now . . ." *I can only think about language, memory and death.* "It's kind of a strange time for me."

"It's cool, I said." She stares evenly at me. "You don't need to explain."

"This is awkward," I say, shaking my head. "I'm awkward."

She smiles at me. "Yeah," she says. "You're kind of a freak."

For some reason I'm inclined to take this as a compliment. "Thank you."

Jana/Jenna peers across the bar. "After I hear my songs I'm taking off," she says. "I have to pull an all-nighter in my studio. There's a group show in December and I promised I'd have something new by then."

I say, "Can I come with you?"

She looks into my eyes before responding. "Where?"

"To your studio."

"If you want to." She shrugs. "Sure. But I'm going to be painting the whole time."

"Come get me at the bar before you leave."

Maybe it will help take my mind off my task.

"HANDSOME" TOM DRUCKER,
bartender

I don't know any Buffalo stories. . . . Oh, wait. Yes, I do. Yeah,
okay, this is a good one. My dad told me this one. Grover
Cleveland—Yeah, I'll be with you in a second!—Sorry about that.
Grover Cleveland, our thirty-fourth president, worked as a hang-
man in Buffalo for years before he went to the White House.—Two
more? The same? You got it, sweetheart!—And so he's the only
paid killer to become the president, far as I know. Dude,
Cleveland offed something like thirty or forty men. And hanging
is a pretty gruesome death. They say he dreamed about the
killings in the White House, woke up sweating at night. Dead
men stood around his bed and talked to him. He admitted this
to a close friend of his. The corpses were like, "Why, Grover?"
Cleveland couldn't fall back asleep when this happened. His wife
slept in another room when it got too bad. She thought he was
going cuckoo for Cocoa Puffs. He also had major physical
problems, on account of the stress from having murdered so
many men. He was a big fat sombitch with a bad ticker. . . . What
a guy! One of Buffalo's finest exports. And a Democrat.

rough hands

Three cracked attic windows covered in insulating plastic. A paint-freckled boom box on a stack of oversized art books. The soothing stench of turpentine and linseed oil. Cigarette butts floating in the week-old water at the bottom of a coffee can. On a rusty chain affixed to the ceiling a naked 100-watt bulb dangles above Jana's head. Her shadow attacks me every time she moves her body.

Slumped in an armchair in the corner, I watch her prepare her palette: warm colors on the left, cool colors on the right. Her red hair is pulled up in a loose bun. She has changed into old sneakers, gray sweatpants and a ribbed white halter top—splatter-friendly clothes. She twists the handle of her paint squeezer like a can opener, dribbling wet paint on the clear glass palette. The Dead Kennedys' *Fresh Fruit for Rotting Vegetables* plays on low volume on the boom box in the corner.

In her studio, she says, she often listens to lecture tapes borrowed from the public library downtown. We share an appreciation for that place. Listening rather than reading, she teaches herself about Hinduism, ecopolitics, the Weimar Republic, string theory. When she doesn't want to become too meditative and just wants to attack, she listens to early-eighties punk music—Black Flag and Minor Threat and Dag Nasty. She lunges at the canvas, slashing at it with her big fat brushes that could paint a house, or she dabs and swipes with long skinny brushes, trying to conjure beauty. I admire the physicality of what she does every night. Who needs aerobics classes when you're a painter? She works up a good sweat doing this.

"We have the capacity to remember a billion faces," she says, her back to me. "But what we really remember are only caricatures—a drooping eye or a bent nose. And when I hate other people's behavior, I think what I'm really seeing is a caricature of myself, my own behavior, personified in them."

"Do you have any cookies?" I say.

"Maybe I recognize a neediness, some kind of helpless yearning, that I've tried to kill in myself. And it pisses me off when I see it in them."

"I could really go for chocolate chip. Warm. Fresh from the oven."

She ignores me, keeps painting.

An Easton Black Magic aluminum baseball bat leans against the wall. I heft it in my hands. "Nice," I say, inspecting the barrel. Thirty ounces. Thirty-three inches. "You play?"

"It's my brother's."

"Does he live in Buffalo?"

"He's in prison," she says. "In Wende."

"For what?"

"Drugs."

I lean the bat against the wall. "Rockefeller?"

"You got it. Fifteen years for five ounces of coke."

"Damn, that's criminal," I say. "What's it like out there?"

"Wende? What do you think it's like? It's a prison. Barbed wire and armed guards. Just like in the movies. The first time I went, maybe five years ago, one of the guards said he had to strip-search me, but Marcus told me to just ignore him. They fired that asshole. Usually I try to go during the week, like on a Wednesday, because the weekends are way too busy. All these buses from New York City show up. It's loud and crowded. On a Sunday it's impossible."

"How long has he been in for? Marcus."

"Six years now." She looks out the attic windows. "When it's nice you can sit on an outside deck. At a picnic table. In the summer you can even grill out there. They give you charcoal and lighter fluid."

"Sounds nice."

"It's not nice," she says. "I think they're doing something to Marcus. He won't admit it. He'd never tell me. But I can see it in his eyes. They're doing something to him in there."

A good ethnographer knows when to ask questions and when to keep his mouth shut. I say nothing. Jana keeps working and before long she tells me other stories.

Every year she shows her work at the Elmwood Art Festival, where hundreds of people herd by, licking ice cream cones and drinking bottled beer from paper bags, ignoring her. For those two days she sits on a lawn chair, smiling, her sunglasses on the crown of her head, prepared to answer questions, prepared to haggle about the already underpriced work, but nobody ever stops to ask what inspired her to paint a certain image, or how she got started with conté crayons and a cheap newsprint pad, back when she was eighteen, on the roof of a friend's apartment building in east Los Angeles. On Sunday night, in the gloaming of Elmwood in July, she packs up her shit, loads everything into the back of her pickup and returns to this run-down house on Niagara Street.

It's a HUD house. The landlord quit collecting rent two months earlier. He moved to Georgia and left no forwarding address. In the mail every month she receives an eviction notice stamped with the signature of Jack Kemp, the former quarterback of the Buffalo Bills. These days he's the Something of Housing and Urban Development. "Resident must vacate the building within thirty days." And every month she recycles the form letter with her junk mail and *ARTnews*.

She's so alive in this studio. I romanticize her solitary life in my imagination. On these long and empty winter nights, when gusts of wind rattle the windows, carrying the bad news from Lake Erie and beyond, visions open before her and offer their numerous gifts. And when she can ignore her fears and silence the voices of insecurity and hatred long enough to experience them, Jana/Jenna is the most beautiful of children, smiling, splashing paint, alive, alive, alive.

Briefly ignoring her canvas, she turns her attention to me. She rubs the fingertips of her right hand on a soiled rag. "You said your ma is pretty sick, didn't you? Do you have anybody who helps you with her?"

I imagine Rodney sitting alone tonight in a house already

sold, waiting for the packers and movers and estate sale vultures to descend. On Monday morning they will tell him what his past is worth. Nights he sits ossified in his armchair, alone in his museum of memories. A lowball glass of Scotch rests reliably beside him. His TV belches the evening news.

"My dad," I say, "but it's hard to tell what he's feeling. I thought it was just a generational thing, but my sister acts just like him."

"Well, it must be tough for all of you." Jana pulls back her hair, gathering all the loose ones, and makes a tighter knot at the back of her head. Her forehead shines under the naked bulb.

I want to say *chignon*. I don't know if that's the correct term or not. Unbidden, it surfaces. *Chignon, chignon*, a word that carries with it a memory of Emma Naessén, an exchange student from Uppsala. Pale blonde hair coiled at the back of her head, a brown chopstick sticking through it. Dark eyebrows. Slight overbite. Nineteen years old. Adorable. Emma told me that Sweden had the highest suicide rate in the world. I said sure, because they're all killing themselves in the long winter, all that unrelenting darkness. And she said no, no, what's fascinating is that they're killing themselves during summer *in anticipation of* the darkness. She spoke with a pitch-perfect American accent, and her best friend, Marie, had an impeccable British accent. They grew up on the same street. When I asked how it was possible that they sounded so unlike each other, Emma said, "In my house we watched American television, and in her house they watched BBC."

"So, is your mom still . . . ?" Jenna says. I imagine she's trying to find a diplomatic expression for *recognizably human.* "Is she able to . . . ?"

I don't want to talk about it. I say, "How's this painting coming along?"

Smiling, she dabs her brush in a puddle of orange paint and turns back to her work. "It's getting there. Slowly."

I wonder how many young women like her are living in derelict buildings in this city. Each day is a temporary reprieve for them. Soon the wrecking ball will crumble this house and all its ghosts. How many people have lived and died here? How many woke up one morning and were unable to recognize themselves?

"Undertones," Jana says softly.

Startled, I open my eyes and look up at her. "What?"

Bending over me, she peers into my face. "Purples and blues. Greens. Beautiful in your skin. Under your eyes and in your cheeks, just below the curve where the light strikes." She touches my face with her rough finger. "Right there."

A square wooden box of knives and paint-stiffened rags rests at her feet. How much time has passed? Five minutes? An hour?

"You fell asleep," she says, "just like a little baby."

"Shut up," I say, smiling.

"Your skin is so thin, Jackson. It's like paper. And it's so pale, almost translucent."

"The Swedish and Irish conspire within me," I tell her. High summer is always torture for me. I slather on the sunblock. I come alive in autumn and thrive in deep winter. "I am a wonder of whiteness."

She motions to the canvas. "Look what I started."

Flesh-colored grapes? A benign tumor? "Oh, hold on. Is that supposed to be me?"

Wiping her fingertips on a crusty rag, she nods and inspects her work. "It will be. That's just your head."

What time is it? I wonder, looking around for a nonexistent clock. Must be close to five a.m. From this angle the windows appear black behind the plastic. Buffalo in winter. Snow sifts down outside like grated cheese. I close my eyes and open them.

"Hey, listen, I was wondering something," she says. "Would you model for me sometime? I'd really appreciate it. I couldn't pay you anything, but—"

"Naked?" I say.

"Well, yeah." She laughs. "But if you're too lame you can keep your underwear on. It costs fifteen bucks an hour to get a model in here, and males are always harder to find than females."

"I'll have to think about it."

"You'd be doing me a big favor."

"I'll think about it."

While she paints, I try to snap out of my funk. I'm young and healthy, I tell myself. I have memory and language. The quickest way to stop being selfish is to do something selfless. I'm scared to stand naked before her. That's why I should do it.

"What the hell," I say. "Let's do this."

Two empty tea mugs rest on the floor of her studio. A

Fugazi CD spins in the boom box. Hunched over, Jana uses her palette knife on the canvas, scraping at something. I can't see what she's doing.

She says, "You can get changed in the other room."

In her frigid hallway with its splintered wooden floor, I strip off all my clothes. Why did I think this would make me feel better about myself? My penis recoils in the bitter cold, and I remember Floyd's old trick. "By any chance, do you have any rubber bands?" I call out.

"What?"

"Nothing."

She pops her gum. "Ready whenever you are," she says.

Stripping off her pink bathrobe, I step up onto the small wooden platform in the center of her studio. My whole body is blushing. This is Art, I tell myself. Painters need figure models. I'm providing a valuable service. Yes, I'm naked, but there's nothing sexual or erotic about this. Standing nude in front of her, I am not aroused in the slightest. I feel cold, misshapen and dangly. "This is a big change from cheeseburgers," I say.

"Okay, turn to your left a little." Jenna waves her brush. "Just a little more. Okay. Good. Great. Try to stay like that. Okay?"

"Like this?" My legs feel like they're shaking. "Am I good?"

"Yeah. Perfect." She swirls her brush in a dollop of yellow ochre paint, not looking up at me. "Don't move."

She doesn't talk much while painting. It's rather disconcerting. She stares at me, then looks at her canvas, dabbing and slashing. At times I can tell exactly where she's looking.

Occasionally our eyes meet, but it feels like an unwelcome collision and I'm compelled to look away. I could be any man passing her on the street, making eye contact and disappearing forever. My naked body is only a pattern of shapes and lines to her. An object. Actually I can't begin to imagine how I look through her eyes.

"Just relax," she says. "Think of something calm."

I watch her work. "Couldn't you buy one of those little ceramic space heaters?" I say, shivering. "I mean I know you're attached to the whole impoverishment of the artist trip, but this is ridiculous."

"You're doing fine," she says. "I really appreciate this. You're a good guy, Jackson. Thank you." She works directly on the canvas. "Just loose and quick," she says, more to herself than to me. "No sketches or photos here. I'm just . . . trying . . . I'm just trying to capture the essence here. Just working on color and value. . . . Nobody will even know it's you."

There's something naïve, almost childish, about this pursuit. Why do some people insist on capturing a fleeting moment, locking it up in a frame, imprisoning it? I understand Jana's desire, but the odds are against her. I know she lives for that moment of grace, when a well-executed brushstroke can get her higher than any drug. That one shimmering second is worth a thousand hours of suicidal struggle. Most likely she won't ever make an impact on the world, but she probably doesn't give a shit about that. She paints because it gives her life meaning.

Even the greats wasted their lives. Marcel Proust lost twenty-five years trying to capture the first twenty-five years of his life. He locked himself in a cork-lined room and chased that elusive time, his youth. He caught it, a tiger's tail, but then lost the present in his pursuit of the past. He was fifty by the time he documented his life up to the age of twenty-five. Is it childish of me to ask where I can find the beauty in a moment, even if I'm sitting beside a dying woman in a nursing home? Certainly others would wonder: Where can I find the money in this situation? Where can I locate a profit? They may be better suited to this world. Attics and basements all across the country are filled with men and women like Jana, seeking that elusive buzz. Nobody will know their names. The question is, Why do they keep doing it? Beauty may not be the answer at all. I remember a line of Rilke that Mara Coursey liked to quote: "Beauty is nothing but the beginning of terror."

Twenty minutes after beginning this project, she says, "Okay, great. Take a break."

I fall into the armchair, lean my head back and shut my eyes. I'm wearing her thick soft bathrobe again. Naked underneath. I feel so comfortable in her studio.

"It's nice up here," I say.

"Yep," Jenna agrees and ashes her cigarette in a coffee can. "A little cold maybe."

Watching her work, I dig into my bag of favorite questions. "Tell me a lie you've told so often you believe it yourself."

She laughs. "Am I being interviewed now?" She loosens her hair and lets it hang over her shoulders. "No, that's a good question but I don't lie. I never lie."

"Okay. I don't believe you, but okay. Just tell me a story."

"About what?"

"I don't know. Anything."

She drags on her cigarette and exhales twin blasts of smoke through her nostrils. "In Albany once I saw a woman—this was probably ten years ago. I saw a young woman, maybe ten years old, give mouth-to-stoma resuscitation to an old man. You know what that is? He had throat cancer. She cupped her hand over his nose and mouth and breathed into his neck hole. This happened in a store in the mall. Like a Bed Bath and Beyond?" She flicks her thumb against the cigarette's filter. "The old guy lived. And she bought herself a big pillow."

It has been my experience that when I say "Tell me a story" to the right people, I am never disappointed.

My cell phone vibrates in my rumpled jeans. I dig it out just before it clicks over to voice mail. "Hello," I say.

"Looking good over there, gayrod. Pink's really your color. It matches your little pussy."

"What?" I sit up and look out the window.

Across the street, Regis Cartwright and Granger wave to me from a third-floor window. Regis is holding binoculars. Granger holds the tiny phone to his ear.

"We have some really nice photos of you." Granger laughs. "They'll look great on the Internet."

Between them there's a camera on a tripod. Granger reaches over and holds it up so I can see the tremendous zoom lens.

Granger hands the phone to his master. "I thought I told you to stay away from Corinne," Regis says. "I guess you didn't understand me."

My God. It makes perfect sense to me now. *This* is Corinne. Amazing. So where did I get Jana or Jenna from?

I remember her now, I think. She had much lighter hair when I last knew her. She must be wearing tinted contacts because I don't remember her eyes being this green. And all this time I thought Regis and Granger were maniacs, and I suppose they still are, but this explains a lot. I misjudged them. They are romantics. Still, I can't resist taunting them.

"Is that what you said, Regis?" I smack my forehead with my palm. "Shit. I thought you said, 'Visit Corinne. She's lonely. She would appreciate the company of a man.'"

Corinne looks up suddenly. "Who are you talking to?" she says.

This whole scene is too much for me. I pass the phone off to Corinne. "Your boyfriend is on the line." I strip off the pink bathrobe, gather up my clothes and carry them into the hallway.

"Shut up for a minute, Regis. James, wait!" she says, following after me with the phone pressed to her cheek. "What happened? No, I'm not talking to you, Regis." She hands the phone back to me. "I don't want to talk to him."

"Why not?" I say. "Isn't he your man?"

"Regis Cartwright? Hell no. We dated for what, three weeks? And I dumped him years ago. It's over. It's been over. But he won't leave me alone."

"Well, he thinks—"

"It doesn't matter what he thinks," she says, holding out my cell phone. "Here." She pushes it into my hand. "I don't want this."

I feel idiotic now. "Anyway, I'm gonna go," I say. "I'm tired."

"Don't," she says. "Stay."

"I'll call you tomorrow." I hug her. "Thanks for letting me come over."

And I'm out the door and down the stairs before she can say anything else.

act casual

Sunday morning. The house is empty again. Kate and Allison have left no traces of their presence. Rodney's coat and keys are missing. Where is everybody? Where do they go during the day? I feel bad for being so scarce lately, but why am I not included in the plans?

I sit on the couch reading an Iris Murdoch novel. *The Sea, the Sea*. Murdoch's the greatest writer in the world when you're in the mood. I'm not in the mood. Bored, I head over to the computer and check my four e-mail accounts. Eleven messages: two from coworkers asking when I'll be back in the office, one from a friend inviting me to a show at Southpaw tonight, a group e-mail sent out by Michelle in the apartment above mine in Brooklyn ("Cynthia's turning 30 this weekend!"), and seven slices of spam. A Miami man opened fire on a busload of schoolchildren, wounding six. In other news, my fantasy football team is tied for third place. I need a big game out of Peyton Manning this weekend.

I run outside and retrieve *Assisted Suicide for Dummies* from the car. Once I get it inside, though, I realize that actually it's not that helpful. The authors assume that the person who wishes to die will be a willing participant in the act. My mom is way past that point now. So how does one prepare for a mercy killing when the patient is incapable of assisting you? What's the first step in the procedure? Clueless, I Google "assassin," but that doesn't give me what I'm looking for. Then I Google "hired hit." That's not right either. I Google "euthanasia." I Google "mercy killing." My heart rate soars. I'm sweating. Can they trace this to my father's house? If I do kill my mom, will this be considered evidence?

Digoxin is a drug derived from the foxglove plant. Inject ten milligrams into somebody's arm, and five minutes later her heart will stop beating, according to an Australian euthanasia Web site. There are lengthy definitions of "assisted suicide" and "voluntary euthanasia," expansive essays about the legal precedents in these cases. I don't want to make a mistake here. And I don't want to spend my life in prison.

Great subject for a line of greeting cards. ON THIS DAY YOU DID THE DEED, A LOYAL SON WHO MADE HIS MOMMY BLEED. NOW YOU'RE IN THE CLINK, WITH NOTHING TO DO BUT SIT AND THINK. HAPPY ANNIVERSARY.

I return to the couch and begin reading the same paragraph I read two minutes earlier. It makes as little sense this time as it did the last. I click on the TV, watch ten minutes of a *Three's Company* rerun, in which Larry and Jack are drinking beer at the Regal Beagle. Larry explains to Jack that he's lined up a couple of hot chicks for them, except there's a catch: he's told the women that he's an airline pilot. Jack can't believe his ears. Larry nods and tells him there's more: he's told them that Jack is a surgeon. Indignant, Jack stands and heads toward the door, prepared to leave the Regal Beagle, exercising his moral superiority over lecherous Larry, but at that moment, as luck would have it, the women enter the bar. Larry wasn't kidding. These chicks are gorgeous. Jack reaches out his hand and says, "I am Dr. Tripper. And this is my associate . . ."

I glance at the Regulator wall clock. Stopped dead at 2:17. My father must have forgotten to wind it this morning. I remember when he built it from a kit, downstairs on his basement workbench, and then proudly hung it on the living room wall. It kept time for us for years. I know where the key is. I could wind it for him. This would be a small gesture of kindness, one I'm sure he'll appreciate.

My phone rings. "Yo, Hallmark Kid, come on over," says Brickteeth. "We're having a little get-together. The two girls from the gas station are on their way. You don't want to miss this."

Brickteeth isn't really into hellos and good-byes. He doesn't traffic in small talk.

"Can't," I say. "I'm gonna hang out with my family today. This time I mean it."

"We're playing spades. We need a fourth."

Nothing has changed in this town. Nothing. Don't they have any ambition beyond hanging out, playing games and getting fucked up? We're almost thirty years old.

"You're playing spades with the two girls from the gas station?"

"Them?" He laughs. "Nah, they don't play cards. That's not why the two girls from the gas station come over."

During the temperate months he's a housepainter, but in

winter he plows driveways. Mattress Lips, McQuilken and other employees hop out and shovel, doing the detail work. Brickteeth is the boss, the brains.

"So who's playing then? You and Mattress Lips and Costello?"

"Naaaah. Costello's too sick, man. That's why we need a fourth."

"Costello's sick? What's the matter with him?"

"He's got pneumonia or something. Who knows. Guy's flat on his back in bed."

"Does he have a fever?"

"What do I look like? Dr. Strangelove?"

I laugh. "No, I just thought—"

"Who am I supposed to be? Nurse Wretched?"

"Okay, okay." I walk into the kitchen and turn on the light. "I get the point."

Ratched.

"So come on over," Brickteeth says. "We start throwing down at noon."

"Can't do it, man. Sorry. Not today."

Brickteeth hangs up.

Peering into the fridge, I notice that Rodney went shopping recently. I admire his extensive collection of condiments: whole-grain Dijon mustard, habanero hot sauces from Jamaica and Peru, a half-eaten loaf of nine-grain bread. Everything is an adjunct, a supporting player. There is nothing edible on its own, except maybe for the Spanish capers.

"Pneumonia," I say aloud.

I grab my coat and hurry out to my car. I drive toward Summer Street, where Costello lives now. Elmwood Avenue is clogged with cars. The traffic signals are staggered so that you can get through only two lights at a time before you have to stop again.

Costello has a one-bedroom in a house on the corner of Summer and Elmwood, across the street from the crack hotel. His apartment is on the second floor. I park in the Wilson Farms lot and head across the street on foot.

"This parking lot is reserved for customers of Wilson Farms," yells a rent-a-cop. He leans out the door and waves at me. "You will be towed."

"I'm coming right back," I call out. "Give me five minutes."

Standing on Costello's porch, I ring the bell three times. Nobody comes to the door. I try the handle—it's open. I let myself in and head up the dirty, carpeted stairs. His apartment door is ajar. Maybe the patient left it unlocked for that gorgeous, dark-haired fiancée of his. Lucky bastard. Maybe she's bringing hot soup and vitamins. The love of a good woman. That's what I need. She stands beside me, whispering, "Don't listen to them. They don't understand you," or, "You've taught me so much about life."

Costello's dark bedroom is cluttered with booby traps and potentially fatal obstacles, including a weight bench and dumbbells, a tangle of strewn clothes, razor-edged ice skates, hockey sticks, empty beer cans and bottles. In his disarrayed bed Costello snores louder than anyone I've ever heard. The windows are rattling. At my own peril I plunge into the stale, warm air of the bedroom, mincing across the room, and begin shaking the sleeping giant's shoulder. "Costello," I say, "Costello! Get up."

"Wha'?" His sheets are twisted, sweaty. He buries his head under the pillow. "No. Fuck that."

"Come on," I encourage him. "Get up. The sooner you get up, the sooner you can get back to bed."

"I . . . *What?*"

"Rise and shine."

Costello sits up slowly and swings his legs over the side of the bed. He hasn't even opened his eyes yet. His skin exudes more heat than a fireplace. "I'm up, I'm up."

"Attaboy," I say. "Now get dressed."

"Jimmy," he murmurs. "What the fuck. What is this?"

"Okay, let's see here. Put this on," I say, snagging a maroon and yellow USC sweatshirt off the floor. I've never dressed a man before, other than myself. I don't know how parents of small children do it every morning.

He moans. "Oh. Oh. Gonna puke."

"Don't!" I tell him. There's no trash can in the room, as far as I can see. "Don't puke."

He stands unsteadily and rests his hand against the dresser.

"Do you have a nice pair of dress pants?" I ask, glancing around. Clothes are flung over the bed and end table. Drawers hang open. A few crumpled dollar bills lay scattered on the dresser, along with a pack of Camels and a green Bic lighter.

"Dress pants?" says Costello. He sits down on the bed again.

"No, no, no," I say, hurrying over to him. "No sitting.

Don't get discouraged. Throw on sweatpants, jeans. It doesn't matter."

In the car I try to keep Costello awake with some chatter. "The two girls from the gas station are going over to Brickteeth's, huh?" For some reason I adore this phrase: *the two girls from the gas station*. It is now lodged in my brain like a fly trapped in amber. "What's their story?"

"Fuck them," he says in a barely audible voice. "Those girls are crazy."

Costello doesn't want to talk about the two girls from the gas station.

"But what do they do?" I say. "The two girls from the gas station."

"The tall one stole my bong. The Toker Two. That bong has a lot of history, man. There's a lot of tradition that goes along with it."

"The best bong in Buffalo," I say.

"No doubt. And, you know, with great power, with great . . . power comes great responsibility. Those sluts don't get that."

We drive past a new purple neon sign on Kenmore Avenue: THE MAGIC TOUCH. *For relaxation and more.* It was not there the last time I came home. That was a tailor's shop.

"What's that place?" I ask him.

His eyes are shut. "What place?" His seat is fully reclined.

"Back there."

With some difficulty Costello turns his head. He glances behind us, peering over the tops of his sunglasses. "The rub-n-tug joint? Jesus, you hard up or something, Jimmy? Used to be you were always getting laid."

"No, I wasn't."

"What happened to you out in New York City?"

"Nothing. What do you mean? I'm just curious."

His eyes close again. "They're all over the place now. You know your city's shitting the bed when you see that. OTB. Checks cashed. Dollar stores. Rub your dick for you." Costello barks out a bitter laugh. "Only thing left after that is get the Senecas to run a casino downtown. Go stand on the unemployment line. Bring a sandwich."

He's sufficiently engaged now. Driving, I explain the plan to him. This is what Costello needs to do. Walk in, smile at the receptionist. Pretend to sign the guest book. Pick up the pen and fake it. Then walk onto the unit as if he belonged there and find my mother's room. Nod, say hello to people. Act casual. I give him the number: 116.

Costello leans his head against the passenger's-side window. He's sleeping.

"Costello!" I say.

"Casual, act casual," he murmurs. He really is a sick bastard. That's what you get for drinking beer outdoors in the middle of winter. "Now, pay attention." I continue to give detailed instructions, repeating myself three, four times to make sure I'm being understood.

"I'll wait in the car." I pull into the nursing home's parking lot. "I don't want them to see me with you." The mastermind at work. "Take your time. And don't forget: act casual."

I sit in the car and try not to consider what I'm doing here. I keep my hands on the steering wheel. A bald man parks a yacht-sized Ford LTD beside me. He nods at me and walks across the parking lot.

Forty minutes later, Costello staggers zombie-like to the car and knocks on the driver's-side window.

I roll it down. "What?"

"Let me in."

"Go around to the passenger side."

"Oh." He groans. "Yeah."

He stumbles around the rear of the car. He yanks open the door, falls into his seat. "Damn," he sighs. With great effort he pulls the door shut. "I'm beat."

I pull out of the parking lot and into the street. "How'd it go?" I ask him.

"So frigging beat," Costello says, leaning back against the headrest.

"Did you do it?"

"Yeah."

"So?" I watch the road. "What happened?"

Costello coughs wetly into his fist. "Uuuughh," he says. "I need to go home, Jimmy."

"We're on our way," I say consolingly. "Tell me what happened."

"I did what you said." He sneezes twice, drags his paw across his wet nose. "I, like, held her hand and leaned over.

Breathed on her. Coughed in her face and shit." He scratches his unshaved cheek. "She was *pissed*."

"Really?" I say, interested. "How could you tell?"

Costello coughs again. "What do you mean?"

"How could you tell she was angry? Was it her eyes? Her eyes were angry?"

"No, dude. She was like, 'Get outta my room, you son of a bitch.'"

I glance at him. "She said that out loud? She said 'son of a bitch'?"

"Yeah. She started yelling for security. And if she had legs I know she would've tried to kick me."

"What do you mean—legs?"

"Your ma's an amputee, right?"

My hands tighten on the steering wheel. "Hell no, she's not an amputee. What room were you in?"

"One-sixteen, like you told me."

"On the D-Unit?"

Costello closes his eyes. "There's different units?" he says softly.

GLORY ZYDEL,
small business owner

Oh, I almost forgot about the White Lady. She walked up and down Elmwood every day. She was even more interesting than the Walking Man. Her body was covered head to toe in white. White scarves. A white surgical mask. White plastic shopping bags over her feet and hands. We're talking everything immaculately white. I don't know how she kept everything so clean. I wanted to ask her what detergent she used. On her back she toted a big white bag full of plastic shopping bags. She was pathologically scared of germs, some people speculated. That seemed plausible to me. My friend's sister worked in the Psych Center, before she was fired for stealing drugs, and she said that everything in the White Lady's apartment was covered in tinfoil—furniture, walls, cabinets, floor, everything. Somebody else told me that the White Lady was "allergic to color," or believed that she was, which amounted to the same thing. I wasn't so sure about that, but I didn't really have a theory of my own. The White Lady said only one thing to me in the thirty years I lived on Elmwood: "Get out of my way, Stick."

the announcement

I interviewed Glory Zydel three separate times that year. She told me some pretty good stories. We sat on the sagging front porch of Buttercup, her fourteen-hundred-square-foot emporium of oddities. Pink paint flaked off the iron railings and the windows flashed with Christmas lights. With her explosive hair and her trademark silk kimonos, Glory Zydel was a cherished character on her block. She smoked extra-long cigarettes and spoke in French to the baffled mail-man. As a merchant, though, she was hopeless. One day I watched a guy sort through all the mismatched bowling shoes and voodoo masks and lug nuts and Dean Martin albums, and he said, "Hey, Glory, how much for these handcuffs?" and she came over to negotiate, her flip-flops slapping against the stripped hardwood floor. "Ohhhh, those are the real deal, man. They're nickel-plated. I could let you have them for . . . two hundred?" And he said, "Two hundred? Fuck *off*. I'll give you fifteen." Glory refused to consider his offer. Eventually he bought a ceramic skull ashtray for three bucks.

After dropping off Costello, I return home to find Rodney seated in his armchair, reading the newspaper. "Afternoon," he says. "You're alive. That's good. Father Brian sends his regards."

The Buffalo Bills game isn't televised today—they didn't sell out the stadium—so Rodney and I sit in the living room, listening to the game on 97 Rock. For visual stimulation, we have a Pittsburgh-Jacksonville game muted on the TV. The Sunday *Buffalo News* is stacked on the couch beside me.

At halftime, Kate calls from her cell phone, says that she and Allison are stopping at Mike's Giant Subs, and do we want anything? I say, "Hold on a sec," and consult Rodney. He wants half of a ham and cheese, no onions. I order a whole "Buffalo-style" chicken finger sub with extra hot sauce and blue cheese.

"You got it," she says and hangs up.

Kate eats at Mike's Subs whenever she comes back here. It's one of her long-standing traditions.

I look up at the TV. A Steelers safety just ran an interception the length of the field for a touchdown. Then he threw the ball in the air and leaped backward into the end zone stands, where he was caught by a throng of fat men dressed in gold-and-black clothing.

"Noam Chomsky says that being a fan of professional football is training in irrational jingoism," I tell my father.

"Yeah?" He's reading the Local News section. He has the newspaper spread open in front of his face. "Hm. That's different," he says, reading.

"But you have to wonder: Is it just the rationalization of the geek who never played sports and can't understand the appeal, the kid never chosen for the team, or does Chomsky maybe have a point? I mean, look at all that screaming and yelling and waving flags and banners and team colors."

Rodney doesn't even glance at the TV. "I hadn't thought of it that way," he says, folding back the page.

Just to test him, to see if he's actually listening, I say: "That's why I made an appointment to have myself castrated. I found a nice clinic in Queens that specializes in procedures of this sort. They said they could fit me in next month. It's a simple snip-snip and your balls are in the trash."

"That's good," Rodney murmurs.

Kate bursts through the back door carrying bags of subs. "Food!" she calls out.

Rodney lurches up from his chair, like a dog hearing a bell.

"Is it as good as you remember?" Kate asks, watching me eat. Allison stands next to her, easing her pinkie finger into a back pocket of Kate's jeans.

They ate already in Mike's—plastic trays, large sodas, shredded iceberg lettuce and pale tomatoes, extra napkins.

"It's all right," I say, biting into my soggy sub, "but I think you associate Mike's with fond memories from high school, and maybe you transfer those feelings onto the food."

"Yeah, maybe that's true," she allows.

"I, on the other hand, have no fond memories from high school, so it's just food."

"You were telling me some of those high school stories while we were in line, weren't you?" says Allison, smiling.

"But weren't you telling me some high school stories, too?"

They both laugh. They're like head injury victims.

"Tell me about your sub, Dad," I say.

"Good," Rodney grunts. "Ham and cheese."

"Well, I like Mike's," Kate says, shrugging. "I don't care if nobody else likes it."

"I like it," says Allison. "It was really good. Thanks for bringing me there, baby girl."

After we clean up the mess from lunch, Kate clicks off the radio during a promising Bills drive. Before I can protest, she asks Rodney and me to sit down. "We've been waiting for the right moment to tell you guys."

"We're pregnant!" Allison says.

Kate looks at her. "Al," she says. "I wanted to do it."

"I'm sorry," Allison says. She jumps up and stands beside my sister. "I'm just so excited about this."

"Congratulations!" Rodney says, clapping his hands. "That's wonderful."

"Good news," I say. "By the way, who's carrying it?"

Kate raises her hand. "Moi."

Allison stands behind her with a proud look on her face. She rubs Kate's shoulders.

"And who," I continue, searching for the proper term, "donated the seed?"

"In vitro fertilization," Kate says. "We chose an anonymous donor. A law student at Stanford."

"He's tall," Allison says. "About six three. German-Italian heritage. That's all we really know about him."

Rodney appraises Kate's midsection. "You're barely show-ing."

"Oh, it's early yet."

"How far along are you now?" Rodney says.

"A little over two months."

"No sickness or—"

"No, nothing. But it's only been nine weeks. Most people won't even announce that they're pregnant until they're four or five months, in case something goes wrong."

"But we just can't resist," Allison says.

Rodney stands and hugs them both. "I'm so happy for you," he says. Then his voice changes tone: "Kate, I would love to set up a 529 plan or a custodial account for the baby, and I've thought about how to make it work, if you or James ever . . . but all my money is tied up right now, and . . ."

"Dad, we're okay," she says. "Thank you. We just want you to come out and visit your grandchild after I give birth."

"I can do that!" he says with gusto.

We all watch the end of the Steelers-Jaguars game. Afterward, Allison starts pulling on her winter boots by the back door. "You want a latté, baby girl?" she asks Kate.

"You know how I like it," Kate calls out.

Allison smiles and zips her coat, resisting the rejoinder that would surely issue forth if they were alone. But Rodney is here and so am I, a couple of tenderhearted bachelors. Thankfully she restrains herself.

"You guys want anything?" Allison offers.

We don't.

"Back in a flash," she says and heads out the door.

I can't blame her. I would do the same if I found myself cooped up with someone else's family. Want me to run out and pick up groceries, a cord of wood, malt liquor? Watch me barrel down the street with utter confidence, just to get away for a moment.

Kate says, "How are the Bills doing this season, James?" but I'm still strangely distracted by that "baby girl" comment. It strikes a discordant note in my ear every time I hear it. I have never thought of my sister this way. Maybe this is the role she has assumed in the relationship—maybe she likes it, maybe she endures it—but certainly no one else in the world could call her this without a fight. Like Mom, she's always been active in women's rights issues, rallies, protests, etc.

For years my mother had a framed poster hanging on her office wall: GOD IS A GIRL, it read. When my sister acquired it five years ago, she had a local artist cross out the word GIRL and stencil WOMAN beneath it. The effect is pleasing. It teaches you a couple of lessons at once: two bayonet jabs at the patriarchy for the price of one. Take that, men! Now, my sister is some woman's "baby girl," and apparently loving it.

While Kate and Allison and Rodney watch *60 Minutes*, I continue excavating the filing cabinets. I don't know what I'm looking for specifically. Now I'm inspecting files Euthanasia through Malnutrition, seeking answers to questions nobody has asked.

"Find anything interesting?" Rodney says a few minutes later. He stands in the doorway.

"Yes." I have the Euthanasia folder open on my knees, my back against her office wall. "Mom thought terminal patients should be allowed to die. I think she would want us to mercy-kill her."

Rodney walks back into the living room. I can imagine the silent look he'll exchange with Kate: *Your brother is a disturbed young man.* Undeterred, I begin reading an early draft of an essay Ellen wrote in 1986:

> Modern life-support systems have evolved to the point where "life" by some definition can sometimes be sustained almost indefinitely. Death has become a technical event; not a cessation of breath and heartbeat but the withdrawal of a machine, an event hedged by legalities and all too often lacking in dignity and humanity. Gonda and Ruark (1984) describe this modern way of dying as *graceless death*, characterized by feelings of desperation, abandonment, humiliation, rage, and dehumanization. They indicate that graceless death often is the result of poorly managed terminal care and carries profound consequences, both immediate and long term.

One morning in 1986, Ellen makes a cup of coffee and lets the dog out. Then she sits down at her desk and types these words. How can she know that fifteen years later, she will be dying a graceless death herself? And if she could know, would it change what she has just written?

trust

Nine o'clock, Monday morning. The cabinets have been emptied. Drawers pillaged and dumped. Two packers from Allied Movers are here. They stand on opposite sides of the room, like gladiators competing against each other. Stationed behind overturned dishwasher shipping crates, they wrap my mother's antique glass bottles in paper. They use rolls of tape and wrapping paper and foam packing peanuts. The tools of their trade.

Rodney's moving to a two-bedroom apartment on January first. Almost as soon as he listed the house, it was snatched up by a young couple from Cheektowaga. They couldn't believe what they were getting for the price. They checked the foundation, the roof, the basement. They hired inspectors. No problems with the electricity, the plumbing, the heating system. Everything, including the wall jacks and the screens in the faucets, was brand new. They must have wondered: What's the scam? How could he sell this house for a hundred and twenty-nine thousand dollars?

When I asked him the same question, he said, "I don't want to live here anymore. Case closed."

"But a hundred and twenty-nine thousand dollars?" I said. "That's it?"

"That's the world we live in," he said.

I flee the house, intending to stay away for a few hours. After twenty minutes at Tim Hortons, though, I'm restless and bored. I should call Corinne right now. That's what a compassionate person would do. He would call and say, "I had a good time the other night." He would say, "It was nice spending time with you." He would be unselfish, tall, midwestern, with good hair and a well-paying job. She would be glad to hear again from a gentleman like that. "I was thinking about you, too," she would say. "Do you want to come over? I'll brew coffee." But where am I to begin? Should I say, "Hey, Corinne. This is Jackson"? Or: "Action Jackson misses you"? No. I am a fraud. My life is a web of lies. And my head hurts. After reading the house copy of *USA Today*, I buy four large coffees—one for me, one for Rodney, two for the packers—and head back home.

Tracking dirty slush across the kitchen floor, I walk in wearing my father's winter coat and gloves and boots. Rodney quit trying to keep the floor clean weeks ago. Too many people have stomped through in the last few days: acquaintances and a few family members coming to call on him, craning their necks to inspect the cut-rate goods; estate sale planners; these two stone-faced packing guys; and many others.

"You guys want coffee?" I ask the packers.

"I'm good," says one of them. A wiry man with a straggly gray beard, he bundles up my family's accumulated shit with a mute Zenlike indifference. His faded flannel shirt is rolled up to his elbows. His forearms are grooved with lean, striated muscles. Expending no more energy than necessary, he cradles each item in the cracked palms of his hands. He has better things to do than banter with me about coffee.

The other packer blinks at me from behind his glasses. They are the kind of prescription lenses that transform diabolically into sunglasses outdoors, and sometime indoors, for no good reason. They seem to have a mind of their own. I can barely see his eyes behind them. "You got an extra one?" he asks, holding a pewter bulldog in his hand.

"Yeah. It's extra."

"Okay." He joins me in the kitchen.

I pour the steaming black coffee into a SEXY SENIOR CITIZEN mug. My mom bought it for Rodney almost ten years ago. She thought it was pretty funny. "There you go, man. Milk in the fridge if you need it."

"Thanks." With both hands he lifts the mug to his nose and lets the coffee steam up his sunglasses.

"Sugar?" I ask.

He shakes his head. He leaves his mug on the kitchen counter, but comes out periodically to sip from it.

"You can take that in there with you, if you want," I tell him.

I can see the dark outlines of his eyelids behind the shaded lenses. He's wearing a blue Buffalo Bills cap with a sweat-stained brim. He sips his coffee tentatively, as if it's poisoned. Maybe these guys have orders not to drink or eat in people's homes. Maybe he thinks I'm trying to trick him into doing something against the rules so I can tattle on him. What the fuck do I care if he drinks coffee in this room or that? He could pour coffee on the floor for all we care. This house is dead to us. We're only caretakers now for the next family.

My father passes behind me, a stealthy shadow. Now he's seated on the tiny bench by the front door, pulling on his boots.

"Where are you off to?" I ask him.

"Just bringing some more of her things to the U.B. School of Nursing."

There's a plastic bag at his feet. "What's in the bag?" I say.

"Old equipment," he says. "Stethoscope, a hemostat. Percussion hammer."

"Give me that."

He looks up at me, surprised. "What?"

I snatch the bag off the floor. "I'm keeping these."

He sighs, one boot still impaled on his fist. "Come on. Where're you gonna put 'em?"

"I kept her black bag. Remember?" She called it her *black bag*. "I'll put them in there, where they belong."

The tools of her trade.

"What else is in here?" I say, peering into the plastic bag.

"There's an otoscope," he says, looking over my shoulder, "and those little plastic cone-shaped thingies that you put on the end of it."

"This is Mom's," I say, shaking the bag. "She's not dead. This is hers. I don't want it dumped in a drawer somewhere over at U.B."

He sits down on the little bench, sighs, removes the boot and stands up again. "Whatever you say, Captain."

"Yeah, that's right. Don't throw out any more of her stuff."

He turns away from me. "It won't bring her back," he says. "Don't be such a goddamned fool. Nothing you do will bring her back, James. You understand that?"

"I don't care."

Yesterday he had watched me excavate her filing cabinets. I read or skimmed almost everything she saved—newspaper clippings, scraps of paper, old advertisements, half-written essays. I opened every drawer of her desk, touched by what I found. Extra buttons for shirts long since donated or destroyed. Blank cards for all occasions. String, ribbons, tacks and nails.

One day you leave the house and don't come home and all your left-behind stuff becomes a shrine. People sort through it. They think about you. But the reverence soon wears off and most of it ends up in the trash.

"Ten years from now," he says, "fifteen years from now, you're going to say, 'Why did I save all this?' Like all those books you're keeping. We have fifteen boxes of books. Some of these things are going to surprise you when you unpack them. Being sentimental is one thing, but being obsessive? That's another."

The bearded packer is watching me. "Worst job I ever had," he says to somebody, me, I guess, "was my father-in-law's place. Three-story house out in Clarence. Old farmhouse. He'd been living there some thirty-five years, give or take. Couldn't convince him that every little piece of junk in there wasn't a brick of solid gold. Guy was moving into a mobile home and wanted to take it all. Everything. Had to make some tough decisions along the way."

It's a wonderful speech. My coffee offer must have loosened him up.

"How long did it take you to do his place?" I ask him.

"Weeks," he says, gently placing a glass plate on the stack of wrapping paper. "It was a real backbreaker. He had a lot of stuff. And he fought us every step of the way."

"So where does this job rank on the scale?"

"I seen tougher," he says.

His coworker sips his coffee and watches the two of us. His eyes are completely hidden behind his dark lenses.

"Anyway, I bought you a coffee," I tell the bearded one. "It's out here on the counter if you want it."

He says nothing. His point has been made. There's no reason to revisit the subject.

My stomach makes a familiar, post-coffee, yowling noise. Grabbing a *New Yorker* off the kitchen counter, I excuse myself for a session in the bathroom.

good cop, bad cop

At one o'clock, the estate sale planners—Don and Judy Sanderson—pull into the driveway in a white Cadillac. Judy is driving. She slams the car into park, hops out the door and hustles up the driveway. Her face is a mask of makeup, but you can still see the beauty there, in her high cheek-bones and hazel eyes. She carries her shoulders high. Her leather briefcase looks almost as expensive as her shoes. Clearly she means business. Old Don eases himself out of the car, one heavy leg at a time, and toddles behind his wife, stopping briefly to inspect the snow-covered shrub-bery. A tall man in his late sixties, Don takes his sweet time arriving at the front porch. Sporting gold-rimmed glasses, he has fluffy white hair, a high flaking forehead and an Adam's apple the size of a child's fist. I imagine him as a former ath-lete, a high school basketball player maybe, dressed in those shiny shorty-shorts players used to wear in the dark ages before Michael Jordan came along. Don looks like he knows how to pick and roll. He can square up for the twelve-foot set shot. When Don finally coaxes his reluctant body up into the house, Rodney takes both of their coats, hangs them up in the front closet and says, "Have a look around."

They wander through the house, fingering items on the mantle, whispering to each other.

The packers ignore them and continue wrapping up glass ashtrays and candlesticks and framed photographs, shoving everything into huge boxes. There is no logic to this. It's all last minute rushing and madness. It's the type of job estate sale planners must love. A desperate man who wishes to flee his past life will rarely bother to haggle or negotiate.

After a brief tour, Judy and Don sit at the dining room table with Rodney. He offers them drinks. They refuse. He pours himself a generous Scotch.

Judy plays bad cop. Don is good cop.

"To be honest, we thought most of this stuff that you're keeping would be out of the house," says Judy, eyeing the packers in the next room. "We didn't know so much stuff would still be in here. That makes it difficult for us. Presentation is important at an estate sale. Organization, presentation and efficiency."

"We're gonna light this place up like a Christmas tree," Don says. "People will come from miles around to see your enchanting house. We'll even bring our own lamps if we have to."

"It's going to make it much harder on us," says Judy. "Because we don't know what you want us to sell and what you're taking with you. Usually by the time we get to a house everything that is left, everything that we see, is what's staying." She casts a wary glance at the packers. "Right now I don't know what they're taking and what they're leaving."

"You have some very enchanting treasures here, Rodney," Don says. "Lovely items."

Rodney grunts and sips his drink.

"I assume that they will be done today. We won't be able to make an estimate until they do. And after they move on, anything you don't want sold, I suppose, will have to be locked in an enclosed room." Judy sighs. "That's to protect you and us."

"This is the best street in Buffalo," Don says.

"I've already told the packers what I'm taking with me," Rodney says. "They have their instructions."

"And the rest? Certainly some items are too big to be packed." She looks up from her BlackBerry. "How can we make an accurate inventory if we don't know what's staying and what's going? I suppose we can put stickers on everything that you're taking to your new place."

Don rests his hand on his wife's forearm. "Are you sure you don't want to take some more time," he says to my father. "This is a big decision, Rodney. Nobody would blame you if—"

"I want it all sold," Rodney says, cutting through the bullshit. "Everything." He waves his hand. "Anything that's not nailed down. Got it? Now let's talk about price."

The Sandersons glance at each other. Judy shrugs.

"Our rate," says Don, "is very reasonable."

"Okay, let's get down to brass tacks." Judy leans forward in her chair. "We charge twenty-five percent on everything sold. That's the going rate."

"And what about what doesn't sell?" Rodney says.

"It'll be hauled away, if you want." Don smiles at him. "Lickety-split."

"Fine," Rodney says. "You brought a contract with you?"

"We did," Judy says.

Don pulls it out of his satchel. "It's a short document—just forty-two pages."

"Don!" Judy laughs. "It's only two pages, Rodney."

My father uncaps his pen, flips to the last page and signs his name.

"Don't you— Do you maybe want to read that first, Rod?" Don says.

"I trust you." Rodney gulps down the rest of his drink. "I've got a meeting in the city in half an hour. I'm closing on a new apartment."

"Congratulations," Don says.

hello

I drive to the public library downtown. For an entire year, after Mara and I broke up, I hid in the stacks, where no drug dealers or congenial drunks offered me deals that I couldn't refuse. Nights I sat in the stacks until closing, my back against the wall, perusing hardcovers that hadn't been checked out in years. I scribbled names on paper scraps—Rabelais, Goncharov, Rulfo, Kawabata—names that passed me on to other unknown names, who in short time became living men and women as real to me as my own parents. Through printed words alone, the dead raised themselves across centuries to look me in the eye. In the library I learned how little I actually knew. A thousand books needed to be read and understood yesterday. I plucked heavy volumes at random from the shelves, held them in my hands, hefted them and promised to return. It was too much. I put them back where they belonged. Overwhelmed but hopeful, I trudged out of the library each night at 5:59, followed by the same friendly security guard in his sagging blue uniform.

At the downtown library I always visit my mother's textbook. Today I read the chapter on dementia first, then I read about more obscure ailments and how to treat them. It comforts me to know that Ellen has found her place here, among her colleagues, even though much of her research is now out of date. When I was fourteen years old, our dining room table was piled high with her reference books and yellow legal pads and messy stacks of photocopies. I liked flipping through her hardcover books and learning new words: *Corpus callosum. Staphylococcal. Phalanges.* Late into the night Ellen worked on her book. Sometimes she fell asleep at the table. Published in 1988, it was considered a success. Orders came in from colleges and universities. A whole generation of nursing students learned from her bio-psycho-social approach to nursing. Not long ago, the publishers requested an updated version. They offered Ellen a nice chunk of change, but she was incapable of spelling her own name. Rodney wrote back and respectfully declined the offer.

The tall windows behind me are frosted, veined with Buffalo cold. Alone in a swirl of sentences, my coat folded over the chair back, I take notes on a scrap of photocopy paper. *Amyloid. Neurofibrillary.* I'm trying to follow this meandering trail of words. I've read these sentences before, yet they seem new every time. Three hours pass and I look up, exhausted, to find that the light has shifted in the room. And now there is an attractive girl sitting one table away, twirling her hair around her thumb. She's facing me in a seat that was formerly occupied by an old man in a ragged winter coat. I stare at her until she looks up, until she sees me. We make eye contact for a split second. No emotion at all on her face, totally neutral. Instantly I look away, because I'm only a fantasy addict, incapable of even saying a single word, a word that would necessarily force me to admit to myself that she and I will not be in bed, naked, a half hour from now. That treacherous first word would shatter a carefully constructed scenario. I want her to know me right now. I want us to have thirty years of understanding, joy and shared pain between us. Instead, that first word would require a long process of dating, dinners, late-night conversations, meeting her closest friends and her family, ignoring her eczema and her abuse of laxatives, being understanding about her fear of dogs and darkness. But because I don't want to be alone forever, I know that a relationship has to start somewhere, and that it's not the destination that matters so much as the journey, so I should embrace this exciting beginning to our new life together. I should say that word. It's so obvious, so simple. I'm a pussy for averting my eyes as soon as my future wife recognized me. I imagine her telling the story, ten years from now, to our good friends Klaus and LaShawna at our annual Christmas Eve party: "He wouldn't even look at me at first. He was so timid, but you know his mother was dying at that time." I decide to look back, emboldened again, staring at her, willing my bride to look up and smile at me, but she has already resumed reading.

SALLY RICHTER,
musician

We were a grrrl band called the Vasdefernz, but we temporarily had a male lead singer. That gave us an identity crisis. All of us were becoming more political and we wanted to get away from male domination altogether. We pulled it off until Vivian quit. Somehow we ended up with a guy named Tim Johnstone on vocals. Then our drummer, Andrea, got accepted into law school. That was it for us. The end of an era.

Our last gig was at the Pipe Dragon, a warehouse bar downtown. We set up these huge canvases and invited artists to come and paint on them while we played. Cool idea, right? And it was really cool at first. The artists were splashing paint everywhere—on the canvas, on us, on our guitars. It was pretty wild. Then things got out of control. One of the artists, a guy named Pez or something, brought along a crucified Jesus made out of papier-mâché and barbed wire.

So Jesus was on a cross of two-by-fours nailed together and leaning out over the audience, kind of like a mermaid or what-ever on the prow of a ship. The stage was rocking, paint splashing everywhere, everybody was wasted, tripping on shrooms, and during an encore the Jesus head fell off. The crown of barbed-wire thorns came down like daggers on some poor kid in the front row. The kid screamed and rushed the stage. He freaked. Eleven people followed his lead. The stage collapsed and three or four people ended up in the hospital. To this day, I still remember an old naked man rushing the stage and punching Tim Johnstone in the chest.

Check out my guitar. You can still see yellow paint on the neck.

Looking back, the papier-mâché Jesus was a bad idea. Buffalo is a hard-core Catholic city. People get nervous when Jesus's head falls off. They don't find it amusing.

inspiration

I watch Rodney pour himself a glass of filtered water. He stands at the kitchen window looking out at the snow-plowed street. He has endured so much. Yet he never speaks about it. Never expresses his feelings, his fears. I'm tempted to imagine he doesn't feel anything.

I pour myself a glass and stand beside him. "Hey, Grandpa," I say. "How's it going?"

"Ha," he says, brimming with pride. "Can you believe it?"

Rodney's a paper tiger. In theory he's a conservative, but when he's confronted with a real-life situation that affects him personally, he acts on the dictates of his heart, not his politics.

Kate feared coming out to Rodney. My mother knew, and she supported Kate, and my sister's sexual preferences made no difference to me, but we all turned anxiously to Rodney—poor, unobservant, old-fashioned Rodney. I held my breath. The tension mounted. The day had finally arrived. I had a front-row seat in the living room. After some hesitation, Kate simply announced that she preferred women to men. Rodney just sat there and silently assessed the information. He had been raised in a conservative family. In college he fell in love with a liberal Democrat, a feminist nursing student named Ellen Lundgren, and married her. And now this. A gay daughter. Kate was on the verge of tears. Her reign as Family Hero was coming to an end. I thought my heart would explode. Winning by default wasn't an appealing prospect, but I must admit I yearned for glory. Just once, oh, just once I wanted to triumph, after so many years of second-place finishes. Of course I wouldn't showboat too much when my time came on the dais. I mentally prepared a few tasteful words on the subject. "How can we really know anyone," I would ask rhetorically, "when most of us don't even know ourselves?"

Eventually Rodney pushed himself off the couch and walked over to where Kate sat. He stood over her for a minute, rubbing his hands together. The tension was unbelievable. I hadn't been this worked up since Scott Norwood trotted onto the field for the game-ending kick in the Bills' first Super Bowl. I feared that Rodney would berate her. Would I need to throw myself between them, protecting my sister from my father's wrath?

"You're my girl," he said. "Come here."

She jumped up and hugged him. No drama. No controversy. If Kate liked women, that was her business, he said. He supported her no matter what.

I sat on the floor, deflated. My feelings about this were complicated. I didn't want Kate to be disowned or to suffer any lasting repercussions, but for once in her life I wanted her to experience at least ten minutes of disapproval. Would that have been so bad? Just so that she could comprehend what my entire childhood was like. Kate and I grew up with different parents, and I wanted my father— stern, disciplinarian Rodney—to come down on her a little, to give her the business. But it didn't happen. Somehow she had turned homosexuality into an asset. You couldn't compete with that. You bowed down before it and acknowledged your opponent's superiority. The spin control in Kate's camp was incredible.

On that day I no longer considered myself her competitor. We weren't even in the same field. It came as a relief to accept this. I stopped chasing her. Instead, I chose to admire her graceful stride through life. I felt like a weekend jogger, a two-mile-a-day guy who sits on his couch, a bag of Cool Ranch Doritos in his lap, and watches a professional Kenyan marathoner sprint to the finish line on TV.

Rodney and I stand together in the kitchen. We drink our waters and stare out at the snowy street. I don't know how many times I've stood right here and viewed the world through this window. A thousand times? Ten thousand times?

"I'm really gonna miss this house," I say to him. "A lot of memories."

All the rooms are historical. Right now I think I'll miss the basement the most of all, with its homemade wooden bar, the dusty bottles of brandy and crème de menthe and vermouth, all of which I sampled repeatedly with an ecstatic wince, the ceiling scarred by upraised hockey sticks, and the phone numbers of middle school girls scrawled on the wall in pencil, and the shuddering washers and dryers, and the beige corduroy couch where I tongue-kissed my seventh-grade girlfriend, and the second refrigerator serving only as a temple for a tapped beer keg, a constant temptation for me and my friends.

Still staring out the window, my father nods. "You can say that again."

Inspired, I touch his forearm, but can't think of anything more to say. My hand sits like a doily on his arm, flat and useless. Why is it so difficult? I should hug him and say, *No matter what, Dad, I will always—*

"You finished with that glass?" he asks me.

Rodney opens the dishwasher and places his glass, upside down, on the top shelf.

"Yeah," I say and put my empty glass beside his.

The dining room table is a graveyard of stacked plates, bowls, glasses, mugs, porcelain ducks, vases, saucers and a small wooden plaque that reads DON'T CRITICIZE YOUR WIFE'S JUDGMENT, LOOK WHO SHE MARRIED.

Everything on the table is priced and ready to be picked over by strangers.

What version of my family's history will this mausoleum of a house decide to tell them?

Bronzed baby shoe bookends, a Regulator wall clock, a chrome twelve-bottle wine rack, a stitch-control sewing machine, a digital clock radio, a hair dryer, random Craftsman tools, two rakes, three shovels, one broom, a woven wastebasket, four iron candle holders and a foot locker (empty).

Now we're both reading hardcover books in the living room. There is one lamp left in the room, and the two of us are huddled under its glow: my father in his armchair and me at the end of the couch. He's reading a thick historical novel about Teddy Roosevelt's presidency, and I'm immersed in a biography of Florence Nightingale, a book chosen at random from Mom's shelves.

"Before you leave town," he says, "I'd like you to come out and see my new place. Of course it still needs to be painted, and it's not furnished yet. . . . Maybe you can help me put up a shelf in the kitchen."

For days now I've been dreading this excursion. "Okay," I say, getting up from my place (her place) on the couch. "Maybe tomorrow."

I return the Nightingale biography to its slot on the shelf. It's a great story. As a young woman she rejected a lord's marriage proposal, which was unheard-of at that time. She became a world traveler, reforming military hospitals abroad and in England. Throughout her life, she battled prejudice and became an activist for women's rights. Inspiring. A life well lived. Someday, maybe, I'll read the whole thing. But seven hundred pages of nursing is a little too much for me right now. I select a new book to browse, *Great American Eccentrics*, and return to the couch.

"It's not much to look at right now," he says, "but it's in a good building with underground parking. Two bedrooms, two baths. A great view of the city."

"Sounds nice."

"Well, it will be." He shuts the book on his index finger, saving his place. "It will be, I hope. You can compare its shape now to its future condition. After it's renovated." Looking down at his right hand, Rodney flexes his fingers, working out some tightness there. "Maybe take some photographs."

I haven't even opened *Great American Eccentrics*.

"Dad." I'm unable to prevent a childish whine from entering my voice. "Why do you have to sell the house?"

"What?" he says. "We've talked about this."

"No, we haven't."

He sighs. "I can't afford to live here and pay her bills, too. It's simple mathematics. I'll be flat broke by 2012."

Obviously this is a topic he doesn't want to talk about, and I should just drop it, talk about something else, but when I press him for more information, he says that Medicaid will not cover even half of her expenses. He's paying out of pocket for almost everything. Eventually he will have nothing left: her money and his money will be gone. He'll still receive Social Security, of course, but that's it.

"But what if Mom were to die? Then you wouldn't have to pay for her treatment."

He stares at me for a moment. He searches my face with his tired eyes. Has he thought the same thing, too?

"She's not going to die any time soon," he says. "I mean, she's only fifty-six. Physically, she's as healthy as you or me. It's just her brain that's out of whack."

"But don't you think she deserves a more graceful death?"

"I do," he says. "Hell yes. We both want the same thing for her, James. But that's not the hand we've been dealt here."

I lean forward, elbows on knees. "Is there anything we can do?"

He seems to consider this. "Well, we can try to make her as comfortable as possible."

"No. I mean, you know, about hastening the process. Is there anything we can do on that front?"

Again he stares at me for a moment. "We can have faith that this will happen exactly as it's supposed to happen." He opens his book and begins to read. "It's not our place to intercede in any other way."

I'm still confused. He has signed a number of legal documents—the do-not-resuscitate forms, the no-life-support contracts. Essentially he's saying that we're hoping she'll die soon. We *are* hoping that. That's no big secret. So my question is simple: If it is what we're hoping for, why not bring it about ourselves and end her suffering right now?

"Mom advocated for the patient's right to choose," I remind him. "She felt that a terminal patient had the right to decide not to live anymore. She wrote about it. You've read her writing. You know where Mom stood on this stuff."

"But she wouldn't be choosing here. *You'd* be choosing for her. It's murder."

"It's mercy."

"No!" My father removes his glasses, rubs the lenses with

his handkerchief. Two pink indentations ornament the bridge of his nose. "She wouldn't want us to do it. She would never put you in that position."

"She did, though. I am in that position."

He shakes his head, replaces his glasses. "Only if you imagine yourself to be."

I am responsible. He knows this as well as I do. I talked Mom out of killing herself. *You're fine*, I told her, and she believed me, or pretended to believe me, to keep the peace, and because of this capitulation she ended up exactly where she least wanted to go. She's in prison right now because I put her there. *Don't worry*, I said. *Don't worry*. This is my mess.

"Come to the Elms," I say, quoting the sign in front of the aluminum-sided building, *"a leafy, shaded environment for a more leisured lifestyle."*

"James," my father says in a soft voice. "What's your point?"

"There aren't any trees there." I look up at him again. "Why do you call a place the Elms if—"

"Give me a break. Read your book."

Now I'm standing, pacing. "We can't leave her to rot there."

My father shuts his eyes, then opens them slowly. "What do you suggest as an alternative?"

"Don't get angry. I just think—"

"I am not angry, James. Just back it up. What's your big plan for her? Because I will listen to any better solution. Believe me, I welcome some thoughtful input on this. Her brothers and sisters are nowhere to be found."

I stand before him with my arms crossed on my chest, but I don't want to appear judgmental or petulant, so I sit down on the couch again. I lean forward, prepared to brainstorm. "What about a home worker, a home aide? Whatever they're called."

"I looked into that, of course."

"And?"

"Ellen is well beyond that point now. It takes two people and a special machine to get her in and out of her chair."

"I'll move back to town," I say. "I'll quit my job. We can look after her together."

"I don't see how that helps her. She's basically bedridden. The house isn't wheelchair accessible." He takes in the entire room in a glance. "She doesn't know where she is, James. She can look around this house and see nothing that means anything to her. This house has no value for her."

"Does it have any value for you?"

He sighs and looks up at the ceiling. "How is keeping her at home preferable to a care facility where they have three shift turnovers, nurses, the proper equipment, regular meals? If you think she's gonna snap out of this, you're nuts."

"I don't think that."

"Maybe you think she'll just rub her eyes one fine morning and say, 'Holy cow, that was strange. I had the craziest dream.'"

"You don't need to mock me. I'm just trying to talk to you. Why can't we talk about this?"

"For three and a half years . . . Every day. You know what that's like? I gave her baths. I dressed her. I washed the sheets and blankets when she messed the bed. She messed the bed damn near every night. I fed her three or four times a day and—"

"I am not blaming you."

"You have to accept this. This is happening. What Ellen needs is the best care we can give her before she dies. I can't offer that to her at home. Can you?"

I imagine he has rehearsed this speech in his head. He has answered his silent critics many times before. He probably didn't expect his son to demand an explanation, and I'm not sure that is what I'm demanding. How and why did this happen? That's all I want to know. But I see his point: it's a pointless question.

"Can you offer her that?" he asks again.

"No."

"Then what more is there to talk about?"

A minute later he's reading about TR again, and I scurry out of the living room, embarrassed. There is nothing more to talk about.

the most popular
guy in town

I drive past my old college. A pretty girl sits in a bus stop
shelter on the street. I consider stopping, asking if she needs
a ride. The old smooth-talker leans across the seat, smiles
toothily. He lowers the passenger window. "The Peace
Shuttle is free and goes everywhere!" And she laughs, gathers her things and joins him in his overheated rental car.
"Thank you so much. It's really coming down now, huh?"
But this isn't a pornographic movie or a good dream. It's my
life. I don't even stop. The light is green. Green means go. I
keep driving.

A four-foot assassin in a bloodred snowsuit leaps out
from behind a Dumpster on Grant Street. He drills my passenger door with an iceball, jolting me out of a dangerous
reverie, a driving version of sleepwalking. His mittened
hands cover the astonished O of his mouth. Even he didn't
expect such a percussive result. Frozen in place, he waits to
see how I'll react.

It's hilarious, I think, exactly the type of thing I used to
do when I was ten years old, but there are rules of etiquette
to observe here. This kid will only be satisfied if I acknowledge what he's done and appear to be outraged, even though
I couldn't care less. So I slam on the brakes, fishtailing in
the snowy street, and shout, "You little prick! Come back

here! I'll kill you," my head hanging out the rolled-down window, watching the thrilled kid scamper like a jackrabbit through a gap in a chain-link fence. Of course he had his escape route mapped out beforehand. A solid performance.

July 18

Dear James,

Bonkers had his anal gland surgery last Thursday and is doing very well. He stayed overnight at the vet and when we picked him up, all the girls in the vet's office said what a great dog he was! They took him out and played with him—they thought he was the most affectionate, gentle dog.

I am sitting here at the dining room table working on the book—wishing I was doing something else. Things are very quiet in the neighborhood—no Tuckers, no Morellis, no kids at all at our end of the street. Sabine is here visiting the Puchanskis but I've only seen her once—in the supermarket.

I hope things are going OK for you at sleep-away camp. I was very happy when Dad told me "Uncle Al" said you were doing better. If you decide to do something, you can do it—and do it well. You're a lot like me, I think. I had a lot of fears too when I was your age, but if you can admit that it is a little scary for you, people will help. No one will help you if you act like you know it all already.

I want you to think about your life and your future while you're up there. Your report card came the day you left—it was not good—you passed, just barely. You didn't work very hard in middle school, and in the fall you will enter St. Joe's. They won't put up with someone who doesn't want to work there. It's a hard school. You have great potential (I think you don't believe that about yourself, but it is true). When you are being yourself, and not those alter egos you assume in certain situations—your real true self—you are a kind, caring and intelligent young man. Somehow you have to learn to feel good about who you are as a person. Not because you have the right clothes, the right haircut and sneakers, but because you are <u>you</u>—a young man with good looks and a <u>brain</u>.

I know you didn't want to go away this summer, but the truth is we needed a break from all the problems and conflicts of the past year. We're all exhausted. I bet you needed a break from us, too. We're all making the best of it. And you'll be home before you know it. While you're up there, though, I think you need to think about doing <u>two</u> things: (1) applying your brain to some things that don't interest you initially (your school subjects, for example) and (2) make an effort to be more outgoing and sociable. When you meet people, ask them questions about themselves. Where do you live? Where do you go to school? How do you like it? Do you have any pets? Any brothers or sisters? Do you like sports? What groups do you listen to? Ever go to a rock concert? What do you plan to do when you grow up? etc etc. People respond positively to someone who expresses interest in them. Let them talk about themselves—but listen, sincerely—and ask good follow-up questions. You'll have friends for life and be the most popular guy in town.

I hope you won't be annoyed with this letter and I hope you can read my writing. You can start a new chapter in your life right now—and you can have the greatest 4 years in high school anyone ever had. It's up to you—I can't do it for you—you have to do it yourself. Dad and I will help you when we can—but you have to turn yourself around. You can start by following my suggestions about getting to know people better and focusing on them rather than on yourself. I did that to get over feeling so insecure—it works.

You asked for a longer letter from me—hope you're not sorry you did!

I love you,
Mom

like life

Judy Sanderson enters twenty minutes after her crew has arrived.

"Here's the boss," calls out Don Sanderson.

Sculpted hair and gold shell earrings, Judy bursts through the door laughing. The rectangular lenses of her designer glasses fog up. The frames have a colorful starburst pattern. "I'm blind!" she says, removing her glasses and rubbing them on her blouse. She is almost twenty years younger than her elderly husband. Sometimes her brazen good health must enrage him.

"Chilly out there," Don says to her.

"I'm dressed like a polar bear," Judy announces to the room. One of her male assistants rushes forward and helps her off with her fur coat. He peels the dead animal off her and disappears. "Now, Rodney," she says, wasting no time, "we had to bring our own dinette set and some other furniture—lamps and so forth—because there's simply not enough to sell here. Or we won't come out even. You understand. We often sell some of our own stuff, too. Common practice. Now, come on, boys, let's get cracking," she says to her workers. She claps her hands twice. "Time is money."

"Two degrees outside, the radio said," Don observes.

"This is Buffalo," Judy says. "We live in Buffalo, Don."

She turns to me and smiles. "I don't know what people expect. You want warm, move to Florida."

Don looks hurt. "All I'm saying is it's cold."

"It's cold. Let's move on." She sits down on a living room chair and massages her ankles. She gazes at me meaningfully over her colorful glasses. "Your father seems to be holding up well—or is he?"

"Oh, yeah, he's doing fine. He's a trouper."

"Terrible, what happened to your mom. Rodney says she's in a nursing care—a nursing home?"

"Yes."

"So young."

"Yes."

"So, so young."

"Yup."

She leans forward and taps my knee, as if to say, *Enough about that.* "Now, *this* is nice," she says, patting the arms of the chair. "And that davenport. It's nice, isn't it? How old is that piece?"

"I have no idea."

"Rodney, how old is the davenport?" she calls out.

My father strolls into the room, forking up tuna fish from a plastic container. "Well, it must be—ah, fourteen years, at least."

"You've taken *great* care with it, great care. That's what I like to see."

"Judy, holy cow. Are you sitting down?" Don says from the next room.

"Lemme tell ya," she says privately to my father, "I work for Heslington Real Estate as well, and I've worked a half day already. I have this great house in East Aurora, Rodney, listed at six hundred thousand dollars? And to drum up interest I'm thinking of making a magazine where each room of the house gets its own page? Three floors, nineteen rooms in all. You have to do anything you can to sell a house like that."

"Right," Rodney says. He walks out of the room.

"Gotta be clever," I say to her.

"That's it," she says. "Exactly. Clever." She raises an admonitory finger. "But honest."

"Yes," I say solemnly.

"Honesty is the best policy," she reminds me.

"I've heard that, I think."

"It's one of those truths," she says.

"Do you know how much a studio apartment goes for in Manhattan?" I ask her.

"Amazing, isn't it? You can have nineteen rooms here or half a room there. Which would you choose?"

I think some houses should get funerals. Favorite bedrooms deserve obituaries. Certain kitchens have earned memorials. Instead, we just walk away from the wrecks like amnesiacs.

"Should I go to work in here?" one of Judy Sanderson's assistants asks, peeking out of my mother's office. She picks up a three-ring binder: a family scrapbook of sorts. "What's this?" Flips through it. "Neat."

Ellen's book of collages. For three decades she clipped up theater bulletins, photographs, maps, ticket stubs, graduation announcements and newspaper articles, taped them crisscross and jumbled on a piece of cardboard taken from

Rodney's dry-cleaned shirts. She dated each collage and placed it in the book. Thirty-one years of their marriage are represented in one three-ring binder. You can flip through it and imagine what their lives were like, year after year. All sorts of things are recorded—funerals, graduations, movies watched, trips taken—without privileging one event over another. They are anarchic: jumbled, confusing and surprising. Like life.

The book ends suddenly, marking the time when she stopped driving and forgot how to use her checkbook and lost her bearings in her own neighborhood.

But the collages still remain, offering more evidence of a time forgotten.

I can flip to the year of my birth. My folks bought their first washer and dryer that year. They moved into a new house. They saw *A Doll's House* at Studio Arena. I was born in Children's Hospital—weighed eight pounds, thirteen ounces. Length: twenty inches.

All this information she dutifully recorded, saved, kept safe for us to see one day.

"I'll take that," I say, stepping forward and plucking it out of her hands. "That's not for sale."

Judy is giving Don detailed instructions in the next room. They make quite a couple, these two. They live together, they work together. That's a lot of time in the presence of your spouse. They both assume that she will outlive him, which of course is not a certainty, but the odds are in Judy's favor, and this gives her an imperial power over him. Or maybe Don just likes a more subservient role. Takes the pressure off. "Don't look at me," he might say, sidestepping responsibility. "Talk to the boss."

My father carries something into the back of the house. In his arms he has winter coats, hats, gloves and scarves. He doesn't want them swept up in the fire sale, I guess.

Two of Judy's movers are carrying in a round table of a distinctly early-1970s vintage. The chairs are wicker, blond wood and ugly. It's a *Three's Company* dinette set.

"Christ," Rodney mutters.

Kate and Allison are flying out in an hour. They have a two-hour changeover in Chicago. Kate hugs me just inside the front door. "Come out to Portland and visit."

"I will. And congratulations again. I'm gonna be the world's greatest uncle. You watch."

"I'm serious. Come visit us." She leans down and picks up her shoulder bag. "You're welcome any time."

"Maybe I'll come in the spring."

"That would be great." She wags her finger in mock warning. "I'm holding you to that."

I smile at her. "I promise, baby girl."

She holds her bag by its strap. "What?"

"Nothing."

"What the hell does that mean?"

"Oh, I thought you liked that."

"Why would you think that?"

"Because Allison calls you 'baby girl.'"

"No, she doesn't."

"She doesn't call you baby girl?"

"I don't think so. . . . Does she?"

"Okay. Whatever."

My sister glares at me. "You're so annoying," she says.

Allison comes over and hugs me. "Great to see you again," she says. "I hope you will come out and see us."

"I'm gonna be the coolest uncle," I tell her. "The one who gives the kid the best stuff. You know, like a dirt bike and a carton of cigarettes."

"You better not!"

"All right. Let's say an iPod and a signed jersey from his favorite sports star. Whatever the kid wants. What do I care about the expense? I'm Uncle Awesome."

DEAREST NEPHEW, THE TEENAGE YEARS ARE LONG AND HARD BUT, YO, HERE'S FIFTY BUCKS AND A LAME-ASS CARD.

Kate tries not to smile. "And if it's a girl?"

"No prob." I snap my fingers. "A cell phone and a leotard. Merry Christmas, Little Brittany."

"A leotard?" Kate says.

"Brittany?" Allison says.

"Oh, and let's not forget the stocking stuffers: butterfly barrettes and a Hello Kitty coin purse. Shazam! Uncle Awesome is in the house. Let the party begin."

Kate and Allison turn away from me. "Uncle Awesome needs a psychiatrist," one of them says, leaving me to contemplate my latest card composition.

DEAREST NIECE, SURVIVE CHILDHOOD AS BEST YOU CAN— No, that's not quite right. ENDURE THESE YEARS AS BEST YOU CAN— Why so negative, jerk? Maybe Little Brittany loves being a kid. She can't get enough of it. So give her the sweet stuff. DEAREST NIECE, YOUR TWO MOMMIES

LOVE YOU AND SO DO I, AND NO MATTER WHAT THOSE OTHER KIDS SAY— True. I do need a psychiatrist.

They head out the side door. The trunk of Rodney's car thumps shut in the garage. I hear the automatic garage door lift with a shudder and climb up its track, hovering over the reversing Buick. Rodney eases out into the driveway, presses a button on the dash, and the garage door coughs and lowers again.

Standing at the front door, I watch the car crawl down the driveway onto the snowy street. All three of them wave from their windows. I raise my hand and press it to the steamed glass. My mother used to stand right here, behind the storm door, waving politely until all the cars and people disappeared.

slush

One winter she began paying for everything with twenty-dollar bills. Before she hit upon this dangerous system, she held up lines at the grocery store, couldn't comprehend what $11.25 meant, or $31.19. Fellow shoppers glared at her while she listened again to the complex sum, concentrating, hoping that this time it would make sense to her. Her once-intelligent face clenched in incomprehension, she looked plaintively at the cashier. "Thirty-one nineteen," repeated the cashier. Eventually Mom worked out the twenty-dollar-bill system: she handed over a twenty and hoped that that was enough. She knew, then, that if the cashier repeated the amount—"I said thirty-one nineteen"— she just needed to hand over another twenty. She shoved change into her purse without counting it.

Her laughter was a fortification against a growing terror. She knew what was happening to her. Her fear must have been immense, but if someone asked her a question, she made a joke about politics or the weather. None of us pressed her to elaborate. Why make a fuss? But one day we found silverware in the downstairs bathroom medicine cabinet. We found her earrings in the toilet. And she had no good explanation for why the shower curtain was torn off its rings and thrown across the backseat of her car.

We couldn't overlook it any longer. When we finally acknowledged the situation, we understood that we'd been ignoring the signs for months. We had turned denial into an art form. Like any good American family, we pretended that unforeseen things couldn't happen to us—until they did. Again.

On the last Thanksgiving my parents hosted in our house, Mom put a twenty-five-pound turkey upside down in a cold oven and left it there for three hours before Rodney noticed the mistake. There were eighteen hungry people in the house. That night they ate mashed potatoes and cranberry sauce and pretended everything was fine. Less than a month later, Ellen wrote fifty Christmas cards to friends and colleagues, wishing them a safe and happy holiday, but she wrote her own address on all the envelopes. She was surprised to receive fifty Christmas cards from herself in the mail.

Five months later, on an April morning, while my father shopped for groceries and brought his shirts to the dry cleaner's, taking a needed break, I entertained my mother in the family room. "It's nice out today," I told her. "I'd say it's up around forty degrees. Are you warm enough? Do you want your blanket?"

"It wasn't . . . On the steps," she said, and smiled. "Bell ding."

Ellen was trying to be clever for me. She once had a lively sense of humor, an appreciation for jokes and wordplay. But now her wit was lost, like a coin dropped into slush, and this "bell ding" joke was as incomprehensible as everything else she said. With great concentration she folded a Kleenex into halves, quarters, eighths. Then, very carefully, she unfolded the Kleenex and started over. This was a project that seemed to be crucial to her. Everything depended on getting that tissue folded.

"It's just . . . tucky," she said, focused on her task. Her brow knitted. "Tucky snaps." Hearing herself, she waved her hand as though erasing a blackboard. "It's not. . . . It's trucky."

"Did trucks come by today?" I asked, trying to understand. "Were they plowing the street?"

"No, it's not." She threw the Kleenex on the floor and attempted to stand.

At times she found it difficult to stand on her own. She rocked her torso forward and back, trying to build momentum. Finally she heaved herself up off the couch and took unsteady toddler steps across the room, as though each move might plunge her through the hardwood floor. Her diaper crinkled audibly. Roaming was something she needed to do, and I let her go without trailing behind her. She had lost so much already. No need to prohibit this urge. Just so long as she didn't wander out into the attached garage, I knew she'd be fine.

Ten minutes later, after a thorough tour of the ground floor—dining room, kitchen, coat closet—she reentered the family room. The pockets of her sweatpants were crammed full of small, smooth objects that had appealed to her along the way: coins, keys, colorful paper clips, baby carrots.

"Well, what a surprise," I said. "It's great to see you, Mom. When did you get into town?"

With both hands she held an empty bottle of Windex,

which she must have found in the recycling bin. "Well, hello." Smiling at me, she staggered toward the couch holding the Windex bottle to her chest, like a child with her favorite doll. My mother plopped down beside me again, the cycle complete: departure, return.

"Allow me to fetch your favorite blanket, madam." I stood, flipped the red afghan off the back of the couch and, with a flourish, spread it across her lap. "Will that be all for the moment?" I said. "Or will the lady be requiring a snack? I have a nice blueberry yogurt today."

She laughed at this. "Well, that's . . . ," she said, pleased.

the side effects of mercy

Enough screwing around. Get focused, I tell myself. Take a shower. Then send e-mails to Laffs and to my roommates in Brooklyn. Won't be back for a few more days yet. And after that? A roast beef on weck at Anderson's. Extra horseradish.

Instead, two hours pass in front of the computer. No socks on my feet. I haven't sent the e-mails yet. I haven't drunk or eaten anything. I'm too busy researching "assisted-suicide doctors." There's a man in Oregon who claims to have experience in this area. No photograph appears on the Web site. His address is not listed. His personal information has been concealed, it says, for his safety and the safety of his family. According to the bio on the home page, "Dr. Barry is a physician who has received the highest awards in the field of plastic surgery. After twenty successful years in the business, he had everything a man could need: a mansion, a new Ferrari, and a Danish supermodel wife. But when Dr. Barry's aunt came down with inoperable cancer in 1983, he watched her suffer horribly for a full decade before her death. There was nothing he could do for her. She begged him to prescribe a lethal dose of barbiturates, but the law restricted him. Dr. Barry knew, then, what his life's work would and should be. He turned his back on plastic surgery forever. He sacrificed millions of dollars for his dream. Eventually his hard work paid off. After years of grassroots work—including petitions, phone campaigns and door-to-door appeals—Dr. Barry was instrumental in getting Oregon's 'Death With Dignity Act' passed."

The Web site boasts testimonials from satisfied customers: "I have no complaints about Dr. Barry's performance. He was a true professional from start to finish. I couldn't recommend him more highly. One thing's for certain. If somebody else ever gets sick in my family, I know who we'll call!—*Phyllis T., Eau Claire, Wisconsin.*"

Creepy.

Still, I'm tempted to send him an e-mail, just out of morbid curiosity.

My mother's position on assisted suicide was unambiguous. In fact, in March of 1988, she became embroiled in a public controversy. Thomas Brill, a doctor living in Syracuse, published an article in a medical journal describing how he'd helped a female patient with a severe form of leukemia to commit suicide. The terminally ill patient, whom Brill referred to only as Linda, was already in excruciating pain, and did not want to undergo an extensive and painful bone marrow treatment that would have given her only a 10 percent chance of survival. Linda had been Dr. Brill's patient for over eight years. In the January 8 edition of *JAMA*, Dr. Brill detailed how he prescribed barbiturates for her and then told her how many pills were necessary for her to commit suicide.

The antiabortion group Christians in Action attacked the ethics of Brill's decision. They wondered publicly how police could arrest antiabortion protestors when they broke the law, but over a month had passed and Brill hadn't even been questioned about his direct role in a woman's death. His confession was in print, they argued, his guilt displayed for all to see in a national forum. They wanted him charged with murder.

My mother had no direct connection to the case, but she supported the patient's right to choose. Why force someone to undergo a long, drawn-out death simply because medicine had devised clever ways to keep sick people alive? She knew that doctors and ethicists rarely considered the degree of suffering that people with terminal illnesses actually experienced. The Brill case, which became front-page news in many newspapers, afforded Ellen an opportunity to share her views. She wrote an op-ed piece for the *Buffalo News* in which she cautioned people about condemning Dr. Brill without considering the plight of the patient. Shortly after the publication of her piece, she was interviewed by a local television news reporter and was quoted as saying that, yes, she supported Dr. Brill's efforts to ease a woman's suffering. At the time of the interview, she was employed as a nurse practitioner at St. Mary's Hospital, which was closely affiliated with the Catholic Church. A controversy erupted. A week later, protestors from the Christians in Action group appeared on the sidewalk outside our house in

Buffalo. My mother drove down the driveway in her Dodge minivan, ignoring the taunts and condemnations. These were the same sadists who stood outside the abortion clinic on Main Street with their pornographic placards of bloody fetuses.

I rode shotgun. Earlier that year, Mom had begun driving me to school every morning because I had a history of ending up on Elmwood Avenue and hanging out with miscreants. When written threats appeared in our mailbox, Mom explained to me that a lot of people in Buffalo were mad at her and that she would probably lose her job because of what she had said and written, but a good doctor was in danger of going to prison for an act of mercy.

I wish I could call Dr. Brill now, to pick his brain about this dilemma, but he died in 2004 of natural causes.

After a few moments of deliberation, I decide to e-mail this man in Oregon: "Dear Dr. Barry, I am interested in your advertised services. Can you give me a little information on how one might begin down this road? I'd appreciate it. Time is of the essence here, as I'm sure you'll understand, so please reply ASAP. Kind regards, James Fitzroy."

there is no place
that does not see you

Teetering on a snow-rutted Allen Street sidewalk, I avoid eye contact with other pedestrians. I walk alone past well-lighted bars and clothing shops and pizzerias, glancing in at all the untroubled faces. I imagine they are untroubled. Snow crunches under the worn soles of my boots. In Cybele's, a new waitress is reeling off the daily specials. I keep walking. Rust Belt Books glows warm inside. The owner, Brian, is seated on a wooden stool behind the counter, staring into the computer screen. I thought Brian had moved to North Carolina a few years ago. Somebody told me that. Maybe he's moved back. Just inside the front window of Jim's SteakOut, a biker with a Fu Manchu mustache feeds a taco into his mouth. All these places in the city, once so familiar and benign to me, will change if I decide to do this. My whole life will change.

If I kill my own mother, I might end up killing myself in the process. What will life be like for somebody who has murdered his mother? My fear that I will back down from this decision is not as strong as my fear that I will not back down from it.

I turn left on Elmwood and walk six or seven bone-chilling blocks, my head down, bare hands in my pockets. The snow-dusted trees stand rigid and brittle alongside the road, holding up their naked arms in protest. What can I tell you, guys? It happens every year.

When I was a teenager, I believed that the eighteen-block strip of Elmwood from Allen to Forest was the center of the world. Sometimes, on weekends, I traveled with a frothing pack of adolescents, but more often than not, on weekdays—when I was supposed to be in school—I walked alone down the Strip. It took nearly two hours to cover my Elmwood beat, one way. There was so much to see! Dozens of dangerous people lounged on car hoods and porch steps drinking from bagged bottles, with nowhere in particular to go. Hardcore punk music blared from open second-floor windows. Street vendors peddled their wares. Hours passed in seconds.

The sudden sunsets always halted me. I gaped. Standing alone on a street corner, I stared up at a toxic orange sky. The shake I'd smoked enhanced my appreciation. When I turned my attention back to the earth, I watched workers trailing their slack shadows thirty feet behind them. They had dragged themselves through another day. After the passage of the gainfully employed, the sidewalks came alive with shamans and scarred prodigies, the out-of-work, the drug dealers and prostitutes, the crackheads with their nasty-dog faces. It seemed to me that everybody was about eight minutes away from a full-scale meltdown. They all terrified me, and I avoided making eye contact with any of them, and sometimes even crossed the street to elude some of the more rapturous, but I deeply admired them, too.

It seemed a failure of imagination not to attempt to become one of them.

Weekday mornings, in the purple-dark hours before any of us got up, Mom headed downstairs in her bathrobe, cleaned up the piss-wet newspapers. She fed Bonkers, refilled his water bowl. He slept by the heating duct in the kitchen. On cold mornings she put a bath towel over his back. She squatted beside him and ran her fingers through the short brown hairs on his back. Then she drank a cup of coffee by the kitchen window, gazing out at the brick garage and the snow-buried backyard, before the house came alive with the drumbeat of footsteps.

Poor Bonkers was a marvel of ailments, a paragon of ill health. He had more problems than any other young dog in America. Bonkers was what my father called "a troubled case." Mom and Dad allowed me to name him—I was eight years old—and I decided on Bonkers McGillicudy. Years later I learned that most people don't give their pets last names.

Bonkers had asthma, kidney stones and chronic diarrhea. One winter he threw his back out by jumping in the snow. He had sores in his face wrinkles, sores on his legs. Mom used a Q-tip to apply the prescription meds. Dad said he was a pedigree.

One day I was on Ashland Avenue, walking Bonkers on a chain, when an old man in a satin baseball jacket called out, "Hey, kid! Come here!" I yanked on the chain whenever Bonkers tried to eat pinecones or dropped coins. The man who was now approaching was a tall and humorless person who shook his head and clucked his tongue at my dog. He told me that I was an awful person for owning such a dog. Couldn't I see how hard it was for my dog to breathe? This was due to the centuries of inhumane breeding the English bulldog had experienced. Didn't I have any compassion for living things?

I started to protest, but he raised his hands as if in surrender. "Say no more. But think about what I've told you."

"Okay," I murmured, eyes lowered.

I knew all the dogs on my street. Rocky and Rumples and Jessica and Mandy and Rafferty. Sometimes a group of dogs met at the corner of the street. Bonkers hobbled up to join them. He was respected. He wasn't the strongest or the most handsome of the boys, but he was an English bulldog, and that still carried some weight in the dog world. He had a deep, resonant bark. He ate anything: SuperBalls, dead birds, chicken wing bones. He could not distinguish between food and nonfood.

I loved Bonkers. I would never have hurt him. It made me sad that people thought that I was a bad person when I walked Bonkers around the neighborhood. For weeks after my meeting with that old man, I devised stinging comebacks, put-downs, insults, longing for the day I would see him again. Of course I never did.

Back at my father's house, I check e-mail. Amazingly, a response has come from Dr. Barry. "Thank you for your interest in my services. There are a number of things that any prospective client must know from the beginning. I work only within the state lines of Oregon, where PAS is legal. Therefore, the client must be able to travel to my offices in Eugene. Of course, this stipulation reduces my clientele substantially, but it does allow me to stay in business. ☺ I require full payment in advance. Prices vary according to the case. I do not offer group rates. Once we have agreed on a fee, which can range anywhere from five thousand to fifty thousand dollars, family members must sign numerous documents absolving me of any malfeasance in the death of their loved one. Not to worry, though. I have a hundred percent success rate. I am number one worldwide, according to the Hemlock Society's latest poll. Nobody matches Dr. Barry for customer satisfaction. Nobody! Now, if you agree to these conditions, please feel free to respond. I am at your service. If you choose not to respond, I appreciate your interest and wish you (and your loved one) peace and happiness. All best, Dr. Barry."

I write back: "Interesting! But how do you actually kill people? Regards, James."

The response comes back almost instantly. He must be sitting at his computer right now. "I'm afraid you misunderstand my métier. Dr. Barry doesn't 'kill' anyone. I merely provide the means for death. This is accomplished in a number of ways. In most cases, I prescribe palliative medicines. I give detailed instructions on how to take the meds. Death is a probable side effect. (I put it this way for legal reasons.) But that is a common misapprehension. I do not 'kill' or 'murder' anyone."

"So there's no machine?"

Twelve minutes later: "There is no machine. Correct. That went out with Kevorkian. It was a terribly sloppy and insensitive way to proceed."

My next question: "Do you ever feel remorse or regret because of what you do?"

His response: "No, I don't. Quite the opposite. I feel pride. I'm not locked inside an archaic paradigm. The aversion to assisted suicide is naïve and childish, a superstition based solely on Judeo-Christian beliefs that only God should determine when life should end. That's a cute sentiment but what happens when you're face-to-face with someone who's in agony and begs for relief? I would feel regret if I didn't help them."

last christmas

You hold a gift-wrapped box in your hands. You turn it over, looking at the bright red bow and shiny green wrapping paper, trying to fashion an appropriate response.

"Can I help you with that?" says Rodney's kid brother, David, now fifty years old. He opens the box and shows you what's inside. It's a cashmere sweater from Rodney. The two brothers help you to put it on.

Soft.

"It's Christmas," people keep telling you, "Merry Christmas," and everybody wants you to be happy about it. Crumpled balls of wrapping paper rest at your feet.

"Do you need to use the bathroom?"

Big windows behind the couch glow with the faint blue light of snow. Hours have passed. Your brother-in-law David has gone home. Your husband looms above you now. "Ellen?" he says. "Do you need to go to the bathroom?"

You look down and brush invisible lint off your jeans. "I could do that," you say.

"Okay then, give me your hand." His big, fingery hand reaches down and claws at your sleeve, touching the area where you've tucked your tissue. "Hold out your hand, honey."

You look up at him, scared. "What?" you say. "What happened?"

"Bathroom time," he says with a smile.

"Okay," you say, remaining seated, hoping that you've given the right answer, hoping that he'll leave you alone. Why is he touching your wrist? Does he want your tissue? Does he need to blow his nose? You reach for the empty sweater box beside you. You try to say, "Whose is this?" but instead you say, "Snoosis twis?"

"Ellen." His voice is tired now, aggressive and tinged with anger. "Come on."

After a brief struggle, he helps you to your feet. You step cautiously on the rug, lifting and dropping your slippered feet with great care, as the room slides and tilts around you. Your son, James, watches you leave the room. You turn to look at him, you want to smile at him and wave, to let him know that you're doing fine and aren't going away forever, but the act of tilting your head throws off your equilibrium, and you stumble and almost fall. Your husband gasps and grips your arm. He accidentally pinches your skin. There will be a dark bruise there tomorrow. One of the volunteers at the day-care center will ask him about it, suspecting domestic abuse. The day-care center is the place with the ten-piece jigsaw puzzles and finger paints. The place you don't like.

Your husband pinches your arm. You don't remember having stumbled. You remember only this man's hand, pinching. The pain. Unaccountable. An attack.

"Help," you say to your son. "Help me."

The bathroom door closes behind you with a click. The bald man—Rodney, his name is Rodney, Dodney—reaches out with his big hands and unbuttons your jeans, tugs them down over your thighs, and— Wait! What is he doing now? No, it isn't nice, it's naughty and rough, and you press your hands against his shoulders. "Please, no, oh God, don't," you say, and he says, "It's okay, Ellen, you need to use the toilet before bed," and you say, "No!" and he says, "We don't want you to wet the bed."

Early morning, wet thighs itching and cold, and the bald man's muttering again and touching your arm, pulling you up, bedroom floor pitching like waves, and he leads you to the bathroom, cold bright porcelain tile floor toilet, you slump—"Now please just sit there and go pee!" he says—and he plucks the urine-soaked sheets off the bed and disappears down the hall, trailing words behind him like rudder-churned froth.

Soon it's time for the wetness again. He helps you into the shower, holding one of your elbows. The spitting blast of warm water explodes against your bare chest. Whimpering, you cower in the corner. Standing outside the glass door, he instructs: "Put the shampoo on your hand, honey. Okay, good. Put it on your hair now. On your head. The other hand, no, on your head, honey. Yes. Rub it in . . ."

Clean clothes will be laid out on the bed, and the soggy stuff taken away forever.

Dementia is a trickster. Fleet of foot, it baffles and changes shape. Disappears as quickly as it arrived, and one afternoon you find yourself standing in a kitchen, holding scissors and looking down at the cut-up mail and pot holders and magazines around you. Or you're yanking all the damn cushions off a couch and tossing them across the room. "I'm not . . . ," you say aloud. "Because it doesn't . . ." Or you're standing alone in the backyard and hugging a family-size jar of applesauce to your chest. Rain drizzles down your cheeks, your neck, your chest. Wet grass blades are stuck to your forehead. You start to cry because it doesn't seem to . . . And you can't figure out . . . And why didn't they . . . ?

maintenance

Rodney and I visit Ellen together today, one last trip before I return to Brooklyn. Sitting on opposite sides of her chair, we hold her hands. I brush her hair and joke about giving her pigtails, cornrows, etc. Rodney files her fingernails with an emery board. But this isn't enough. This is only body maintenance. We can polish up her quarter panels, fill her tires with air, replace the floor mats and cigarette lighter, while still refusing to admit that this car will never get back on the road.

How can I do more? Make a plan of action. I will sleep here, on a cot outside her door. The staff will grow accustomed to my presence. "Morning, James." "Morning, Marianne. How's your son Michael doing?" I will volunteer here, doing all the tasks people find most repugnant, like scraping bloody-brown gauze off a tile floor, or inserting an indwelling catheter. In my imagination I don't need any training. I just go to work tomorrow, a dynamo of productivity. Over a few weeks' time I earn the trust of the entire staff. They grow to love my positive mental attitude (PMA), my indefatigable work ethic. "There goes James. What a valuable workplace contributor." I bring in stacks of CDs because evidently D-Unit has only one in its entire collection. And then, slowly, once a month, I will kill off a resident. Not so you'd notice at first. I'd start with the oldest ones, the in-firm, the already corpselike. I will kill one of these people each month. This is how I will be useful to them and their families.

My father looks at his watch. "Well, what do you say?"

That means: *Let's go now.*

He stands and bends over his wife. "See you tomorrow, Ellen." He kisses her lips. "Love you, hon."

I kiss her forehead. "Bye, Mom. I love you."

Afterward, at the nurses' station, Rodney leans his elbow on the counter and chats with Marianne, Sheila and Tina, the new unit coordinator. "According to *Consumer Reports*," he tells them, "a Honda is basically as good as a BMW. So go ahead and buy the Accord."

I run back down to Ellen's room to retrieve my coat. She has turned on her side to face the wall. I pull her blanket up over her shoulders. I turn to leave D-116 when a mumbling, gray-haired woman steps into the room and pushes past me. She toddles over to the bed and picks up the stuffed green frog. I'm not sure whose room she belongs in, but I know for certain it's not this one.

"Excuse me," I say to her. "Can I help you?"

That old passive-aggressive classic. *Can I help you?* Often used when help is not really on offer. More accurate to say: *Can I be allowed to educate you as to why you're violating the rules of proper behavior?*

I try again. "I think you're in the wrong room," I say.

Think. There it is again. I know she's in the wrong room.

"Ma'am," I say, "that's not your frog."

"Papa, please help me, Papa," says the muddled woman. She's not speaking to me. She repeats it in a quiet voice, over and over. "Please help me, Papa. Please help me, Papa."

An unraveling gray braid hangs down over her humped back. Lavender pouches of sleeplessness underscore her eyes. The lenses of her glasses are thick and made of plastic. Her skeletal left arm is encased in a dirty, yellowing, plaster cast. Three bony fingers jut from the ragged opening. I've seen her before in the Common Room, but I don't know her name.

"Come on outside," I say warmly, trying to extricate Mom's stuffed animal from her grip in the friendliest manner possible. "I'll walk with you."

"I'm waiting for my parents." She surrenders the toy and follows me out. She is at least seventy-five years old. A red, heart-shaped pin is attached to the flared collar of her plum-colored blouse.

"Let's go this way," I suggest. "It's nice to take a stroll, isn't it?"

"That would be nice," she says. "Please help me, Papa. Please take me home."

Like everybody else here, she has the disease with no known cure. This is not like a car wreck or a stroke, an event that has a beginning and an end. With those you suffer great stress at the front end, but in short time you're in the aftermath, dead or in recovery. This is a slow-motion death. It's so rapacious, this curse, but you can't mourn her passing because she's not dead. She's still here. This holding pattern can last a decade or more. Cancer is a cruel killer, too, but at least—at least—an oncologist can say,

"There it is. We see it." And there are treatments, however invasive and ineffective. With Alzheimer's, everybody just shrugs. There's no conclusiveness at all. They can't even make a true diagnosis until the patient is dead. You hear, "Just wait it out." Or you hear, "Try to make her as comfortable as possible, but make sure you take care of yourself."

And how am I supposed to do that?

"Papa, please help me, Papa." This combination of words, this ubiquiterm, must comfort this old woman in some way. It is the only remaining tether to her past.

I walk slowly beside her, with one hand on her bent back. "Have you been to the Nature Room?"

"No," she says, "where is that?"

"Come on. I'll show you. They have a television in there."

"Really?"

"It might be nice to watch some television while you're waiting for your parents."

"That would be nice," she agrees.

With her good hand—the unbroken one—she takes my hand in hers. She holds it gently by the fingers. I slow my steps to match her geological pace. Walking beside her, I wonder who she was twenty years earlier. How did laughter sound coming from her mouth? But I know she can never tell me. Here she totters down the corridor, taking one tiny step after another. Her parents are not coming for her, yet every day she holds out that beautiful hope. Who knows if she has any children of her own? Some residents never have any visitors, as far as I can tell. Others receive five visits a day and can't remember a single occurrence of camaraderie.

The old woman holds my hand the entire time. Outside the Nature Room, she halts. Says, "Oh no. I've been in there before. No, I'm not allowed."

"Okay, that's okay, you don't have to go in there."

"Yes," she says, relieved. She keeps a firm hold of my hand.

As we approach the nurses' station, I hold up my finger to my father in the universal signal for *Hold on, I'll be with you in one minute*. Smiling, the nurses and aides watch me promenade with my companion. We turn and walk back up the same corridor, retracing our steps, holding hands.

This nameless woman stops at each Memory Box along the way, pointing out children and couples. "Aren't they nice looking?" she says, turning her head up to look at me.

"Yes, they sure are," I say.

"I just want to go home and get into bed, I think. Oh, wedding photos. Who do you think he is? Can you take me home? I want to get in bed and take a nice half-hour nap. He will be here soon."

"I'm sorry," I tell her, "but I can't."

"Oooh, look at her. She reminds me of Janet—when she was little. Gotta get home. . . . How is Janet, by the way?"

I decide to bluff. "She's doing great, I think."

She squeezes my fingers together, her whole hand wrapped around two of my fingers. "Such a nice little girl," she says. "You're free to take the car if you need it. Dad and I think it's okay."

"That's nice of you to offer. Thank you."

An LPN passes in the opposite direction. She's a tall, slender blonde in her late thirties with large masculine hands. Carrying a clump of blankets, she winks at me. I smile back at her.

Perry Como sings, "Zing Zing Zoom Zoom."

"I just wish they would put names and dates under these photographs." The old woman pinches my fingers together to elicit a response.

"That would be helpful," I say.

"Wouldn't it?"

"Yes."

We reach Ellen's room again. Sunlight streams through the window, making the floor shine. Her bedside table is cluttered with holiday greeting cards, a CD player, a white cup with a bent straw poking out and a donated *People* magazine. Her head is turned toward us, but she doesn't seem to recognize me or the strange woman standing beside me. We stand framed in the doorway, holding hands.

"Is that a shortcut?" the old woman asks, pointing her tapered finger.

"No, it's a . . . dead end." I snort through my nostrils at this morbid answer—a miserable laugh. An exhalation of breath.

"They should hold dances in there," she says. "I'm tired of walking. I'd just as soon go home and take a nap. I didn't intend to be here this long. It's nice of you to be here with me."

"My pleasure."

I continue walking along beside her. Somehow she senses that I am not an enemy, that I will not hurt her. Who knows why we choose the people we do? We embrace some and recoil from others. Often, we decide in less than a second.

And we might stay with someone for years based on that momentary impression.

"I'm going in here now," the woman says. She releases my fingers and pushes open a half-closed door. "It was so nice to see you, David."

"Likewise," I say. "Have a good day."

"It's time for my nap."

"I understand."

She shuts the door quietly behind her. For a moment I stand outside, listening. This might not be her room. I wonder if there will be a commotion.

Will she need my help?

Soon I hear her murmuring to herself, "Please help me, Papa. Please take me home, Papa." The bedsprings creak beneath her weight. "I promise I'll be good."

merriment

On my last night in town, Rodney invites me to the Greenfield Club for dinner. I know he's proud of me. I'm conscious and ambulatory, everything a son should be. And at the club he can show me off to his friends. I'm happy to provide evidence that our family is still strong, despite our losses.

Strapped into the passenger seat, he stares out the snow-framed windshield. White breath. Brimmed hat. Leather gloves. "Thanks for driving again, James," he says.

In his presence I keep both hands on the wheel, nine o'clock and three o'clock. "No problem," I say. "Glad to do it."

I'm imprinting this moment in my memory. The two Fitzroy men, still alive and healthy, slicing through the streets of Buffalo.

The decaying mansions on Delaware are imposing hulks, some unlit and unheated, sitting in the darkness three hundred feet from the curb, evidence of Buffalo's glorious past, eighth largest city in the country in 1900, an industrial metropolis on the rise, a steel town and a cosmopolitan city, boasting some of the best shit that Frederick Law Olmsted ever designed. But it's time to face reality. We've fallen out of grace. Cleveland has surpassed us. Pittsburgh won't even look at us. And we're dead to Chicago. I stare through the windshield, both hands on the wheel. The snow humped alongside the road looks like rhinos trying to hide beneath a white shag rug. I imagine penguins waddling and teetering on the snowdrifts, bathed in silver light. I see glacial shelves of ice tumbling from the roofs of silent factories. I hear a homeless man's snow-muffled footsteps, and—

"Slow down," my dad says.

I glance at the speedometer. "I'm going twenty-four miles an hour."

"Pull in here," he says, pointing. "Here!"

"Relax, fella. I know where it is."

Under the weathered skin of his face, tectonic plates shift slightly. The resultant frown is brief. "Don't start," he says. "Just park over there, under that tree."

As per usual in his presence, I feel like I'm eight years old again. This is unnatural, I realize, a moral failing, and this tentativeness must end, because I am the stronger man here, young, powerful, intelligent, a representative of the future, and he's old, decrepit and doddering—he's literally riding in the passenger seat of life—and it's my job to worry about him now that he lives alone. What if he falls down and breaks his hip in his bachelor pad? What if he chokes on a TV dinner? It's time for me to step up and assume my new role in this family. This is my responsibility. Nobody else will do this. Time to become a grown man. But how does one begin? Can I read a book on this topic or audit a class in adult behavior at the community college?

I've been thinking about this for months now. When I told two of my associates in the Laffs division that I was taking a vacation in Buffalo, they thought I was joking. A vacation in Buffalo? Fuck off, they said. That's not even funny. I assured them that I was going back to Buffalo for one noble purpose: to assume a new role in my family. No more hiding in bars. I would visit my mother twice a day, making sure she got the best treatment available—clean sheets and blankets, decent food, regular dental care and physical therapy. I did not mention matricide. And I would also spend many hours with my father in his now-oversized house. We would play cards together and rent DVDs and pass our nights in rueful laughter, each made stronger by a shared experience, a couple of grown men commiserating, smoking cigars and eating bacon, whatever the hell grown men do together. I would advise him to buy stocks in water, gold and wheat. He would tell me to Turtle Wax a car using concentric circles, to cover more area and minimize streaking. Grown men stuff. In my imagination I was selfless and generous. The mental image of my sacrifice brought long-repressed tears to my eyes. I would atone and grow and learn. At the age of twenty-eight, I would finally be at one with my family. My coworkers shied away from me after this confession. They changed the subject. It was too much truth. They wanted zingers, one-liners, jokes about tits and dicks. They didn't deal with dying mothers and estranged sons. That was a different division's job.

Parked beneath the designated tree, I cut the engine and turn to my father, my seat belt still strapped across my chest. Operation Male Bonding was in effect. "So what are you doing with your life?" I ask him.

"Excuse me?"

Awkward attempt. Rephrase the question. "What do you

do for fun, Dad? Do you have any hobbies or favorite activities?"

"I serve on a few boards."

"But I mean for fun. How do you feel about bingo?" I say, raising my eyebrows. "Or we could sign you up for a Tai Chi for Seniors class."

"I'm fine, James. Let's go inside. It's cold out here."

"Meals on Wheels? They're always looking for drivers. You love to drive. But maybe you'd like something a little less depressing. Am I right? How about speed-walking in the mall?"

"Give me a break," he says, opening his door.

The dome light illuminates the car's interior. "Bowling?" I say. "Bocce?"

"Not interested. Let's go in." His door slams behind him.

Rodney lives by an unspoken code of manhood. A real man works hard every day, Monday through Friday, and he doesn't complain or speak ill of his employers, even if the workplace doesn't please him, because a real man suits up and shows up and arrives on time, nine o'clock means nine o'clock, and I admire him for this stiff-backed discipline, because I just can't get fired up about most mundane tasks. I once asked Rodney how many times he had called in sick over the years and he thought about it for a minute. "Well, I had appendicitis in 1983 or 1984," he began. I said no, come on, you know what I mean, how many times did you just call in, maybe even coughing a little to sell it, because you simply didn't want to be there, and he said he'd missed fewer than five days of work in thirty-four years with the same company. It's either beautiful or depressing.

Mara Coursey's mom stayed over one weekend, and said later that Rodney reminded her of *her* long-deceased father. It shouldn't be surprising to me, then, that he never talks about Mom's illness. In Rodney's world, a real man doesn't burden other people with his miseries. If you're a man, you don't whine or bellyache. You don't ask for help unless it's absolutely necessary. You simply take your lumps and keep moving forward.

My father and I trudge across the parking lot together. Even the stars are buried under snow tonight. It's a silent winter's night in Buffalo—the new snow falling through crowns of yellow light. Buses and cars are shushing down Delaware Avenue.

Snow: the quietest thing in nature.

"Nice night," I say.

"Freezing."

In the Grill Room of the Greenfield Club, a long wooden table—a Last Supper table—occupies the center of the room. Ten men sit around it smoking cigarettes and cigars. The Grill Room is the one place in the club where they can smoke without reprisal. Many have adopted the habit on principle. They're drinking gin, bourbon, vodka and Scotch. This is not the main Dining Room or the Piano Room or any of the other formal areas. Here they can take off their coats and loosen their ties. Some men even remove their shoes. They gamble to determine who buys the next round of drinks. Here the women curse and smoke cigarettes. They sit at smaller tables arranged on the perimeter of the room. They seem pleased to be segregated from the boisterous men at the center table.

The moment we enter the room, a man shouts out, "Hey, Rodney!"

Another joins the chorus. "It's the high roller."

A third says, "Are you gonna sit with us tonight, Lucky?"

They begin making space at the main table, pushing aside a battalion of empty glasses and bottles, a few folded newspapers, their cell phones and PalmPilots, a bowl of mixed nuts and a rattling plastic cup filled with dice.

"Not tonight, gentlemen," Rodney tells him. "Got a table for two. I even made reservations in advance."

"Fancy!"

"You must have connections here."

Billy Meadows smiles up at me from a sea of white heads. He's grinning. "Well, look who's here," he says. "The prodigal son."

"Hey, Bill," I call out, matching his amplitude. I want to play along here, make Rodney proud. "What's up, Captain?"

"*Nada*, kiddo," he says. "Just staying out of trouble."

This elicits a hearty guffaw from most of the old men at the table. Billy swings his head, mugging for them. "Wha'?" He smirks. "I've been a good boy."

"A good boy!" repeats one of the men. "That'll be the day."

Rodney joins right in and banters with his buddies. I stand behind him, smiling. Once he told me that he joined the Greenfield Club because he wanted to give Kate and me exposure to a life that he'd never experienced as a child. He wanted his children to be at home in this world of comfort.

"Good to see you, Billy," I say, trying to break in on the merriment, the locker room chatter. "I hope you're not giving out any tax tips."

The old men laugh charitably. My father smiles at me. A week from now they won't remember this joke specifically, but they might think: *He seemed like a good kid*.

A good son.

Soon we're seated at the back corner table, by the stone fireplace.

"You want to get that artichoke appetizer?" Rodney smiles at me. "You discovered that one."

Before I can answer, an attractive middle-aged woman in a snug business suit appears beside the table. Her face is perfectly symmetrical, a masterpiece of counterbalance. My eyes travel straight down the center of her face, straight nose, soft full lips, her beauty only slightly blurred by four or five decades of life. She hands Rodney an envelope. "You're invited to my birthday party," she says, and for an instant I can imagine her as an eight-year-old, an eighteen-year-old. "You've got all the details right there, mister, except my real age." She turns her attention to me. "I'm Celeste Matthews."

I stand. I should have stood when she first approached the table.

"I'm James," I say, shaking her hand. "Pleased to meet you."

"Sit, sit, sit," she says. "You've trained him well, Rodney." She winks at me. "We don't worry about that stuff here. Your dad would be jumping to his feet every ten seconds if that weren't the case. Are you going to be in town next weekend?"

"I'm heading back to New York tomorrow morning," I tell her.

"Oh, I was going to invite you to my party. . . . I was born on December twenty-second a thousand years ago, and when I was a kid it was terrible to have a birthday so close to Christmas. So a few years back I decided to throw a party at my house every year in early December. Took me a long time to come up with that solution. Now everybody thinks my birthday is December third. Not that it matters much anymore." Turning back to Rodney, she says: "No presents. Bring booze."

"I'll be there," he says and tucks the envelope into an inside pocket of his sport coat. "If it's anything like your party last year—"

"This one will be even better," she says. "David Cartwright is catering it."

A tall gray-haired man with extremely fine features— glittering blue eyes and a straight nose—sidles up next to Celeste and lays a proprietary hand on her shoulder. They look so much alike that you'd be tempted to think their relationship is incestuous. "Is she psyching you guys up about her birthday bash?" he asks.

Nodding, I say, "I hear that David Cartwright is catering it."

"Let me tell you something," he says, and leans in closer, as if sharing a secret with me. "Your father is a great man. I mean that sincerely. I keep trying to elect him dean of the club, but he won't accept the nomination. Will you work on him and try to change his mind?"

"I'll do my best."

"Good man. Talk some sense into him. He's a natural for the position. Now, what say we head back to our own table, dear?"

"Nice meeting you," she says to me. "And I'll see you next week, Rodney."

Smiling, Rodney watches them cross the room to their table. I'm tempted to say that they married each other because it was the closest thing to making love to themselves. They can stare into their own reflections across the table.

"So why won't you be dean of the club?" I ask him.

"Ah, no way. Being the dean is like being a church president: it sounds like a good idea until you actually do it. I don't need that type of complication."

"Were you ever a church president?"

"Unfortunately, yes." He smiles. "Twice. And treasurer."

He's in a festive mood, and I can see that being here pleases him. This is a safe province, one of the few places in his world where the laws actually make sense. Rodney can make eye contact with someone over my shoulder, nod, and within sixty seconds his empty glass is replaced by a new one, filled to the brim. He nods and smiles at a waitress and the leather-bound menus appear. His friends visit the table because they like and respect him. Seeing him makes them happy.

Reaching for my water glass, I say, "Must be nice to have a place you can go to and feel so welcome."

"I like it," he says. "Do you like it here?"

"Yes."

"Good. I'm glad." He surveys the Grill Room. "My friends look after me. Alice Dutton brought me a vegetable lasagna last week. In fact, there's still a big piece in the fridge if you want a midnight snack. And Larry Meadows is threatening to drag me down to Florida next week. He's got a winter home there."

I do not have an Alice Dutton or a Larry Meadows in my life.

"And I thought you were just sitting at home, brooding."

"I wish." He laughs. "They won't leave me alone."

From our strategic position in the corner, we watch the waitresses glide through the room, their trays overloaded with food and drinks. Whoever does the hiring in this place should be commended for his choices. All the female employees are pretty; some are stunning.

"Excuse me for a minute," I say, pushing back my chair. "I need to go to the men's room."

"Having trouble with your bowels again?" he asks in a loud voice.

"No." I glance around. "My bowels are fine, thanks."

"How are those Lactaids working?" he says. "Doing the trick?"

Rodney looks up at me with wet joyful eyes, an expression of buzzed amiability on his face. He means no harm. He's trying to connect with me. Nothing can hurt us in the Greenfield Club, where the cocktails arrive trembling to the brim, and where Rodney merely signs for everything before we leave. He settles his accounts by writing a personal check at the end of each month. Nobody steals stuffed animals in the Greenfield Club.

"I'll be right back," I say.

In the men's room, I shut the stall door behind me. I

unbuckle my belt and sit on the can, overwhelmed again by childish rage. Why Ellen? Why not me? I would take this burden from her if I could, trade my life for hers right now, because I know that she would do more with the opportunity.

Think about him, I tell myself. *He has lost a wife.* Over thirty years of marriage! I don't know what that means. Mara and I lasted almost four years. We almost got engaged. Does that count? We were engaged to be engaged. Well, no, I guess it's not quite the same. What does Rodney think about? What does he remember about his wife? Years later, I recall trivial and ridiculous things about Mara: how in an effort to save money she'd slice the toothpaste tube open with an X-Acto blade and run her brush around in the gaping maw of the split, getting a few more days of use out of the dissected tube. Or how she unhooked her bra underneath her T-shirt and pulled the strap through the sleeve. A deft little maneuver, I thought. But I don't want these to be my memories of her. Why can't I choose the images, like a parent who visits a bakery and picks a birthday cake from a three-ring binder? *Yes. This one*, I'd say, pointing. *This one is Mara.*

A few years ago, Rodney believed he would retire and travel the globe with his retired wife. He desperately wanted that experience: the gray-haired, financially solvent Americans in Europe life, blowing through Rome and Berlin and Paris in ten days, wearing their sunglasses and SPF 40 sunblock, or maybe kicking back and reading a *Sports Illustrated* on the scrubbed deck of an Alaskan cruise liner, a digital camera suspended from his neck. He had earned the right. Over thirty years with the same company. Loyalty. Hard work. Over thirty years with the same woman. Patience. Endurance. How could he have guessed that *this* would be his future? When Ellen fell ill, he tried everything, no matter how unconventional: assorted vitamin packets, chelated drips. On the kitchen counter, he crisply divided her meds with the skill of an amateur pharmacist: Depakote, Prempro, HCTZ. Every Monday morning he filled three plastic pill cases. They stacked on top of each other like children's building blocks. On the sides were strips of masking tape marked, in his precise penmanship, MORNING, NOON, NIGHT.

Start living, I tell myself. That seems to be the only moral in this fable. *Live now.* Don't wait for a future that might never come. Don't trade this moment for a false promise of security, or a pension, or an afterlife. But saying "live now" is about as practical as telling a depressive to "just be happy." How do you actually do it? Maybe what it requires is a shift of perception. Okay, fine. And how do you bring that about? Because if you're thinking about being in the moment, you're not in it.

These white tiles are inlaid with gold fleurs-de-lis. I count seven of them—no, eight. Nine. How long have I been sitting here?

I flush the toilet. Wash my hands. Stare at my face in the mirror.

The simplest tasks completed with no thought or effort at all.

These are things she can no longer do.

"I thought you'd fallen in," Rodney says when I return to

the table. He has a lowball glass of gin before him. "I was going to send out a search party."

I look across the table at him. His suit is tailored, his shirt and collar pressed. He sits bolt upright, his back straight. Military posture. His still-young wife is demented. The orderly world he once believed in is now gone, a shattered memory. Yet he continues to smile and nod at his friends.

I don't want this man to die without knowing that I care for and admire him. "I know this hasn't been easy for you, Dad," I say. "And if you ever want to talk . . ."

He pats my hand. "Order whatever you want, James. Whatever looks good."

My father does not even bother to open his menu. Outside of Lent-required sacrifices and the occasional whim, he's been ordering the same thing for thirty years: mixed green salad, baked potato and an eight-ounce sirloin steak, rare.

"I've got your back," I tell him. "I mean that. You ever want to talk, give me a call. If you ever want to talk about Mom, or anything else, I'm here for you."

"Thank you," he says. "There's also the shrimp cocktail. You liked that when you were a kid."

"I'll split one with you. I don't think I can eat the whole thing myself."

"Yeah, right," he says. "I've seen you eat an entire cow. You're a bottomless pit."

Rodney nods at someone, and a pretty waitress in her early twenties materializes next to me. Gelled black hair chopped short. Gray-green eyes. Slender legs and miraculous breasts, but I fixate on her muscular arms, the forearms solid and strong, three distinct veins standing out (as you'll often see in waitresses and young single mothers who have to carry strollers up and down stairs), and the hint of a tattoo underneath her sleeve.

She says, "Are you ready to order?"

MARY SHEEHAN,
radiologist

They were called the Track Team. Every year, in the dead of winter, these men jogged for miles through the snow, naked. They wore boots and winter caps, nothing more. . . . At first, I thought it was an old wives' tale, a local yarn, until I saw them myself. After a massive winter storm, a record snowfall, I took a walk with my boyfriend in our neighborhood. On the sides of the road, frozen snow was banked up about twelve or thirteen feet high. There had been a complete whiteout earlier that day. No tire tracks on the road. No human presence at all. My boyfriend—Clark—and I were both dressed in ski gear: goggles, gloves, the whole nine. I felt like an astronaut on the moon. We trudged maybe three blocks and then turned back, trying to locate our previous bootprints. Nature had already erased us, not ten minutes later. Snow blew horizontally into our burning faces. My cheeks tingling, I shouted into the wind, "Isn't this great?"

In our neighborhood, people put snow markers on either side of their driveways—wooden stakes with fluorescent green tips, forty-eight inches tall—so that the plow drivers didn't veer off course and tear up anybody's lawn. At that moment, though, nobody's driveway marker was visible. We saw no green at all. Buffalo had just topped sixty inches of snow in one great storm. We might as well have been on the moon. And that's when they appeared. The Track Team. We had just turned onto our street when the Track Team burst through a wall of snow at the end of the block. Sixteen men, buck naked, ran toward us at a nice leisurely pace, their forearms pumping. They might have been ghosts, white-skinned against the white snow. Clark and I stood there watching them, silent, our mouths agape. Finally, he said, "Holy shit! Look at that." And I was like, "That's the Track Team! Oh, my God." We couldn't stop laughing. I said, "I didn't know they really existed." We slapped high fives and hugged. It was just an incredible sight. "Only in Buffalo," I said. Clark agreed. "Only in Buffalo."

no worries

Evening. I circle her block a few times. She probably thinks I'm a creep. And there's also Regis and Granger to consider. All night I've been glancing over my shoulder, expecting them to appear. As cheesy as their bullying techniques are, I have to admit they are making me doubt myself. Following a repetitive five-block loop, I'm approaching Niagara Street now and I can't decide what to do.

They have choices, Regis and Granger. They can kick my ass individually, or they can do it together, as a tag team. That's the frustrating part of this. I can't call one of them out and stomp him into the dirty snow. I've been in fistfights before, and I'm reasonably strong and crafty, but I understand my limits: These guys will hurt me and enjoy it. I'm 2–4 lifetime in fights. If I practiced more, I'm sure I'd be better at it. Tonight's not the night to begin. The problem is, I always start laughing uncontrollably, and that only antagonizes my opponent. I never take it seriously enough.

"Fuck it," I say aloud. No guts, no glory.

I park outside Corinne's studio, watching her shadow play across the illuminated third-story windows.

Standing on her snowy stoop, I press the glowing orange doorbell, listen for the distant chimes and wait for her to descend. Moments later, I hear her trampling down the stairs.

"James," she says, peering out a partially opened door, "I didn't expect you."

"Hi, Corinne."

We stand on opposite sides of her doorway, the threshold to her privacy. She makes no effort to hug me, but she doesn't push me away, either. I say nothing, having learned long ago that silence is a wise, timeless skill practiced by the greats.

"What do you want?" she says at last.

"I'm leaving town tomorrow."

"Okay."

"Can I come up?" I hold up the greasy white paper bag I brought along as a peace offering. "I have pizza. Are you hungry?"

"Okay. Come on in." Corinne shuts and locks the door behind me. "You can come up for a little while," she says, "but I have work to do. I'm working."

On the third floor, I settle into the armchair and pull a plain slice from the bag. "You want one?"

"Nope," she says. "I had dinner already."

"How's the painting coming along?"

"Not great. I don't want to talk about it."

"Have you begun looking for a new place yet?"

"Ahhh, man. I don't want to think about that right now." She presses her fingertip to the tip of her nose. "This place is home to me. I've been through so much up here."

I eat my slice in silence. I feel like I owe her something,

some explanation or act of kindness, but the truth is probably more simple and obvious: I'm not that important.

Corinne turns her back to me. Gnawing her dirty thumbnail, she stares at the canvas. Her neighbors probably think she's crazy. She paints and prays and laughs and screams up here. She mentioned once that some mornings she walks to the bodega in her pink bathrobe. She doesn't seem to care what people think of her.

"What do you do with yourself when you're not painting?" I say.

"Not much. I've been going to Narcotics Anonymous meetings for over a year now. I have a sponsor and a home group."

Wasn't she slamming down drinks in McGlennon's with me? But then again, I don't ever last long on the wagon myself.

"For years I just thought I was cursed." She laughs. "I was the drama *queen*."

"Maybe you were just in a lot of pain."

"Oh, I was." She laughs again. "Most definitely. But the only problem was that I had created all of it. Nobody was making me act that way. It was so much easier to be a scrub, better to be too drunk or high to actually finish anything I had started. Better to wake up and not remember anything and act like nothing mattered and *fuck you* if you thought it did, because God was dead and love was a lie, and I'll slash this fucking canvas right now if you tell me it's any good. . . . Yeah, I played that role for years. It was an affectation like any other. Self-destruction and sabotage. And really I just wanted to *make* something, and

I was scared that I would fail. So I *made* myself fail. You see?"

"Yes."

She drops another CD in her boom box. "But nothing honest came out of me because I wasn't honest. My work was awful then. Just awful. When I stopped hanging out every night at the Old Pink, that pissed Regis and them off. He used to call me at night: 'Where are you?' And I'd tell him the truth: 'I'm working.' And he'd laugh at me, tell me I was bullshitting myself."

"That guy's a madman," I say. "Am I the only one who recognizes this?"

"You know, I've seen a different side of him. Regis is just a sick guy trying to get well. You have to treat people like that with patience and compassion."

"Whatever."

"Some people are more complicated than others."

"He's stalking you."

"It's not that simple."

"Have you told him to stop? Have you made it clear that you don't want him in your life?"

"Mind your own business, James."

She resumes painting. With her back turned to me, she makes odd noises in her throat. At first I think she's crying, and I try to think of something comforting to say to her, but she isn't crying. She's laughing. In a flash of recognition I realize that Corinne might be as crazy as Regis and Granger are. They could be kindred spirits.

"You know, I pity the planets," she says. "Just think of them out there, rotating around the sun, the same routine

day after day, year after year, so close to one another, neighbors for so many millennia, unable to communicate."

"Do we know they can't communicate?"

"Yes. We do." She laughs again in a way that now concerns me. It's the laugh of someone not taking her meds. It
isn't freedom that I hear, or contentment, the sound of
someone enjoying her life. It's a brutal taunting noise that
comes from deep within her, a laugh that indicates that she
alone sees through all the world's myriad duplicities, that
she alone has the truth. Humanity is screwed and only
damn fools fail to recognize it.

She says, "I have answers to so many questions that most
people have never even asked."

"Right," I say, ready to leave. I toss my napkins in the
bag. "I'm sorry for bothering you. I'm just—"

"Let's play a game," she says and turns toward me. "Shut
your eyes. Go ahead. Shut them."

"Don't put anything in my mouth," I say.

"This isn't kindergarten," she says.

I shut my eyes.

"Now. I want you to imagine a gray day in October. A
cold, steel gray October day. You're walking down a city
street, walking down the sidewalk, and you look up and see
a human brain snagged in the thin branches of a tree.
Okay? Are you thinking about it?"

"Yes." I see a brain impaled by a branch. "And why am I
doing this?"

"Oh, no reason," she says. "I just wanted to put an image
in your head."

"You're a nut." Now I'm stuck with a stabbed cerebellum.

"Okay, fine. I got it," I say, playing along. "Now I want you to shut your eyes. Go ahead. Shut 'em. . . . Okay. Picture a ripe mango lying in the street. See the blacktop, the melting snow, and the double yellow lines down the center of the road? Now watch that mango get crushed under the rear tires of a pickup truck with Yosemite Sam mud flaps. Crushed. Splurting orange goo."

"Good one." She laughs. "I can see that."

She plucks an oversized hardcover book off of the stack on the floor. She flips through it until she finds the page she's looking for. "Hey, read this." She turns to "Content Is a Glimpse," an essay by Willem de Kooning.

I hold the book in my lap. She stands just behind my left shoulder. "I want to share this with you. There," she says, pointing. "That is my favorite line in all of literature. A painter wrote it. A painter whose first language wasn't even English." She jabs the book with her finger. "Read this line."

I thought everything ought to have a mouth.

Confused, I look up from the page. "That's your favorite line of all time?"

"Isn't that so beautiful and strange? Everything ought to have a mouth. That sentence haunts me." She grabs the book from my hands and slaps it shut. "I agree with de Kooning. Everything ought to. Yes. Of course. The grass, the trees, the air. Your mom. You. A mouth."

I'm uncomfortable. Now I imagine wet mouths, lips on trees, teeth in pudding. It's horrible. Mouths everywhere.

"Everything should be able to express itself," she says. "At the very least I think everything ought to be able to say when it's in pain. You know? Everything ought to be able to say, 'Help me.'"

Is she just riffing, or is she actually speaking about herself?

"Do you need help?" I ask her.

"With what?"

"I don't know," I say. "Anything?"

I look down and see a mouth opening up on my thigh. Lips curling into a sadistic grin. I see mouths cracking the walls, splitting the floorboards. There are enough mouths in the world already, I think, and if anything we probably need a billion or two fewer, but I would never admit that to her. She seems so fragile tonight. I want to agree with her and tell her that I love de Kooning, because I do. But my mouth never says what I want it to say.

"Speaking of favorite lines," I say. "Here's one that I like: 'Talking about oneself can also be a means to conceal oneself.'"

"Who said that?"

"Nietzsche."

"Oh, fuck him. He was crazier than anybody."

My phone vibrates in my pocket. I glance at the number but don't even bother to answer. These guys are too much. I grab the Black Magic baseball bat and stomp down the stairs. Standing in the middle of the street, I shout up at the windows of the building across from Corinne's attic. "Come down here!" I shout and swing the bat a few times. "Come on, you pussies! I'm waiting for you."

The building across the way is dark, abandoned. They don't come down.

Corinne's shadow looms behind the broken glass and the taped plastic sheet. I see her cupping her hands to the window and looking out.

I'm breathing hard, alone, in the street.

Who is the insane one here? Who can arbitrate in this case? I know one thing: After tonight, I'm not going back upstairs. Corinne has enough inconsiderate men in her life. She'll be better off without me.

I'm sure I'll pine for her three months from now, alone in my Brooklyn bedroom, inaccurately remembering her deep passion for me.

I climb the stairs and return the bat to its rightful place. "I'm gonna take off," I tell her.

"No worries," she says, without turning. "I've got to finish this."

MIKE SCHWEIZER,
chef & actor

One morning I woke up on a grassy knoll outside a bus station in Oswego. I had a backpack full of switchblade knives and a map of British Columbia. Confused the hell out of me. So I limped to a nearby bar, tried to make sense of it all. Ordered a few whiskeys, got to chatting with the bums at the rail and bam! Next thing I know, I wake up chained to a brick wall. Swear to God. I was so scared.

There was a square slot in the metal door. Every now and then a hand appeared with food in it. For weeks I ate like an animal at a petting zoo. The hand fed me a stale roll every day and ten dripping spoonfuls of lumpy soup. Every day at the same time it was the hairy hand and the soup/sandwich deal. You want to know hungry? I licked that spoon so clean you could see your reflection in it. And I'm not ashamed to admit: After the slot was shut again, I lapped up soup right off the gritty floor. Well, that was a turning point in my life. I knew I had to make a few changes. It was time for a new strategy. I said to myself, "Okay, Mikey. You can't keep getting into these situations." But then the damnedest thing happened.

I befriended my captors! Well, I began to see their point of view. They were actually pretty nice guys when you got to know 'em. We didn't speak the same language. Our religious beliefs differed enormously. But we were men. Human beings. And that counts for something. It started with us playing blackjack through the slot in the door. Sometimes I played double or nothing for my lunch. Pretty soon they were in the cell with me, sittin' on the floor, sharin' their smokes and jokes. And together, with some of their friends from the compound, we made these Super 8 films of a gritty black-and-white underground variety.

I wouldn't show them to my kids. They were pretty raw and physical. High-energy features. I sweated a good deal and the bathrobe they gave me reeked something awful, but those films were good for me. No matter what my wife says about my film career! I felt glorious. Liberated. But I suppose any change of scenery after eight months in a musty dungeon is pretty nice. I put on some healthy girth, the dark rings under my eyes vanished, the open sores on my coccyx healed up completely.

I said, "God, if this is Your will for me, I will do my best to serve You." And I was in great demand then because . . . Although I am only averagely handsome, as you can attest, nobody there had ever seen the likes of my physical endurance before. And they all wanted to get it on film. I was making five or six features a day. Hell, they gave me cocaine, caffeine and these crazy speeders that made me want to sing Broadway show tunes in falsetto. Those films—well, they were really something. Soft focus, slo-mo close-ups. All the fixin's. We used a lot of backlighting, suggesting spiritual relationships. And I met many new friends in the process. There was Tootie and Electra and Mommie Terwilliger, just to name a few. And soon I had my own apartment overlooking the lake. Women and men of many nationalities were calling me Daddums and El Matador.

Now at this time in my life, I was drinking two or three quarts of vodka a day, in addition to all the pills I was popping. It was almost becoming a problem. And then it got so bad I didn't want to make any more of their stupid movies, and I didn't want to eat or sleep, and the directors started whipping my naked back with extension cords, shouting, "Act! Act, you mule!" One day I just fell backward on the cement floor with a plop, weeping like a baby with a soiled diaper. Blood puddled around me. I thought I'd sunk as low as a man could go! But little did I know that it would only get worse. I'll spare you the gory details, but I realized there was always another bottom right beneath your last bottom.

"God, please," I begged. "Most merciful creator. Save me from this hell." Well, after that, my life was totally different. This is a tale of redemption, I suppose. When I escaped, thanks to seven kind acts by perfect strangers, I returned to my wife Claire and she gave me unrelenting grief every day. That pained me more than anything. Before I was kidnapped, Claire was the sweetest woman in the world. Sweet as pie. Kind. Gentle. Always smiling. But after I returned from captivity and told my broken-hearted wife about my adventures in such vivid detail, she left me and moved to her mother's house. Claire didn't believe I was telling the truth. A private detective told her I'd been holed up in a Quality Inn smoking crack with a prostitute. Now that was a bald-faced lie! After that, I tried to better myself. I even took elocution courses. I spoke like a goddamn Brit for years. Claire took me back, but she never forgave me. And I learned a valuable lesson. I have debated this with my spiritual advisor. He doesn't quite see it my way, but I know it to be wisdom.

Here's what I know. Never tell a woman the entire truth. Tell her only what she wants to hear, and save the rest for the fellas at the bowling alley. Trust me. Why make a fuss? The mind is so complicated. Some things it doesn't need to imagine. If you remember nothing else, remember that. Don't give her something to dwell on. Because she will remember for decades. Like an elephant. She will manage to personalize it somehow. And why do you want to torture her with that?

out on the weekend

Parked outside Mara and Cathy's old apartment, I look up at that window and see the back of a man's head silhouetted. The blue glow of his TV ignites his hair. He doesn't know or care that she and I fell in love in that very room. But I care. Somebody should do an ethnography of that house. We should document its history from the day of its construction. I would like to know who lived there and what happened to them.

Buffalo summers are among the best in the world—better than Florida, better than Jamaica—not only because of all the clement eighty-degree days with low humidity, but because everybody in town has just survived the shitstorm of winter. Pain prepares us to appreciate pleasure.

It's June and you drink six or seven beers in your apartment, waiting for it to get late enough to head out and drink six or seven beers in public. You listen to Neil Young or Tom Waits for an hour or two, the type of music that makes you feel both thoughtful and tragic, and finally it's time. You head out into a warm buzzing summer night, the sidewalks crowded—music blasts from passing cars, tattooed girls ride past on bicycles tricked out with banana seats and U-shaped handlebars—and you stroll into a bar at midnight. You're wearing boots and jeans and a ratty T-shirt.

You're twenty-three years old and decent looking. The alcohol hasn't taken its toll yet. You've been arrested a few times for minor offenses and you have a DWI under your belt, but so does everybody else you know. Relief washes over you when you hear all the upraised voices, the laughter. You take in the entire room in a glance and someone you know waves from the bar. "Jim!" This new best friend hands you a beer with the implicit knowledge that you will reciprocate fifteen minutes from now.

You drink, knowing your girlfriend, Mara, the choreographer, is working late in the studio, bossing around other dancers, other sweaty young athletic women who have changed their clothes in front of you, stripped off underwear as if you weren't even there, as if you weren't a young man with a functional penis, peering goggle-eyed over your Vonnegut paperback. You were expected to be above that typical macho bullshit. You were supposed to be enlightened, artistic, like them. Sure. But you weren't. Not really. That girl is naked! And didn't they know that you were addicted to everything, addicted to more?

You drink until last call, knowing that hours earlier your girlfriend came home, exhilarated from a night of physical and creative exertion, her eyes bright, her body strong, and she went to bed alone. In the morning she'll find you passed out on the living room floor, half naked and drooling.

Mara knows and loves your mom, the real version and not the future monster in the wheelchair. No other woman you date will have this power over you. No other woman will harbor her own memories of your family, her own mental images. Future girlfriends will know only what you decide to tell them.

According to Ellen, Mara Coursey is "a keeper, a catch." Rodney calls her "a bright gal." They consider her part of the family already. They buy her Christmas and birthday gifts. Ellen says, "Are you going to marry her?" Rodney says, "Your mother had great legs, too." This incredible summer will be notable in many ways, thrilling and haunting, for both its beginnings and its ends.

You're still under the illusion that your girlfriend will put up with endless amounts of bullshit if you act contrite enough after yet another mess. Just smile and apologize after fucking up yet again. Soon, very soon, you will learn a harsh lesson. Some women don't want to marry a selfish drunk. They don't want to get drunk every night. They don't want to watch you do that to yourself.

But an even harsher lesson, the most difficult to face, will come when you finally acknowledge that you made the decision, not her. She did not break up with you. You chose one love over the other, and Mara Coursey accepted her defeat and walked away.

thank you

Three hours before my flight, I'm back on the D-Unit, sitting by my mother's bed. Rodney believes I'm at the airport already. Nobody has entered D-116 in the entire time I've been here. The corridors are quiet, deserted.

The metal rails hold her in. I sit beside her in the chair, the stuffed frog in my lap. She has managed to turn onto her side so she can face me. Her legs are twisted. "Please," she wheezes.

"Hang in there," I say. "You're doing fine."

Her geranium is wilting already. The pink flowers hang limply on the buckling stems.

"Please," she repeats.

"What?" I say, standing over her. "Please *what*, Mom?"

"Wuh-wuh-wuh," she says.

I pull the pillow out from underneath her head. "I'll do it. What are you asking me to do?"

Nobody enters the room.

"I'll do whatever you want me to do," I say. "I swear to God."

She says nothing. She looks at me with unblinking eyes.

I hold the pillow before her face. "But you have to tell me to do it," I whisper. "Tell me yes or no. I need your permission."

She continues to stare at me.

I imagine pressing the pillow down on her face. Five seconds pass. She does not fight. In fact, she holds my wrist companionably. The quality of light in the room does not change. Nothing in the world changes. I remove the pillow from her face. My mother blinks. She is deep inside her body looking out at me, a young Baha'i, a nurse at Buffalo General, a smiling mother holding her first baby in her arms. All those Ellens are inside her, looking out at me. What does she want me to do?

In my imagination I try again, again, again. Each time I pull the murderous pillow away she stares up at me, blinking those intensely vacant blue eyes. With both hands I press the pillow down forcefully for four minutes, for thirty-five minutes, for an entire day. The sun sets, rises again. Weeks pass. Next month's rent is due. She might live as long as I will, maybe longer. She might outlive everybody in the family, unaware of the passing of time. She will follow me from city to city, riding in an oversized papoose on my back, murmuring, "Please, please."

"I can't do this, Mom," I say, low. I replace the pillow beneath her head. "I'm sorry. I can't."

"Haldo," my mother says to me. She smiles radiantly. "Haldo."

Maybe she thinks we're playing a game together. I lean over her and listen. "F-f-f-fitto," she says. She's not speaking a comprehensible language. But it's not a game, I realize. Recognizing my unease, she is still willing to come to my aid, to help me out of this trouble, even though her words no longer make any sense to me. Shouldn't I know by now what she might say?

Before leaving, I place the frog in her arms. "Here you go, Mom," I say. "I can't do what you want me to do," I say. "I'm sorry. I can't."

My mother smiles up at me. As guileless as an infant, she doesn't seem to be experiencing any of the emotions and pain I have attributed to her. She simply smiles, and then, for one shining moment, she surfaces from the sludge of her disease, and offers me a gift. "I'm . . . okay," she says in a small voice. And in saying it, she seems to believe it herself. Squeezing my hand, she sets me free. "I'm okay," she says again, her voice barely audible.

How amazing. A few days ago I wondered why anyone would choose a life of humility over a debauched, selfish one, and here's my mother smiling in hell, offering me an answer. Maybe a nurse who actually enjoys her work derives from service more pleasure than one could find in decades of straight-up hedonism. If that's the case, then the question of an afterlife is moot. If you find your contentment here, anything good that comes afterward is a bonus.

Before leaving, I pull my mother's glasses off her face. She opens her eyes and glares at me, confused. Now, in addition to everything else, I've stolen her clear vision. Rubbing the flecked lenses on my T-shirt, I whisper, "I'll clean these up for you. Because maybe you'll want to look out the window later, or watch some TV."

Wishful thinking. In a perfect world, I imagine Mom and the rest of the demented gang lounging in the Nature Room, enjoying a program on Animal Planet, passing the popcorn bowl and gossiping. "Dementia's a bitch, huh?" They laugh.

I slide her glasses back on her face, hook them gently over her ears. "How does that feel, Mom? Is that better?"

She says nothing.

welcome home

"My son Dale lives in Wisconsin." The woman beside me wears a beige belted trench coat, lime green slacks and flat black dancer's shoes. "Madison, Wisconsin."

Is she addressing me? Hard to tell. She's staring straight ahead. Is a response desired or expected? Headphones around my neck, I'm holding a copy of Hemingway's *The Sun Also Rises*, an airport impulse purchase.

"Does he?" I say tentatively. The way she clutches her boarding pass, like a child with a permission note from Mother, endears her to me. Hopefully somebody in JFK will be glad to see her. The arrivals gate can be a forlorn place.

"Yes," she says with a nod, still holding her pass. Her fingers are so delicate and gnarled, the tips of them wrinkled and glossy, as though she's been soaking them in water for days. She must be close to eighty years old. "He was out there visiting Cassie, my oldest, and when he took a walk around her neighborhood, Dale saw a house for sale and"—she chuckles, still amazed—"he up and bought the house." Snaps her fingertips noiselessly. "Just like that! Now they're neighbors. After all these years."

"How did Cassie feel about him moving so close?" I say, grinning conspiratorially.

"I think she thought it was a hoot. They get along so well, you know."

"In-flight crew members," the captain booms like a god, "prepare for takeoff."

I say, "Are you a dancer?"

"Me? A dancer?" She laughs. "Why do you ask?"

"You seem like you could be one. And your shoes . . ."

"Oh. These? My husband bought me these years ago. In San Francisco. I should throw them out, they're so worn."

"Ladies and gentlemen, we are number one for takeoff," the captain says.

My new friend turns her head and stares out the oval window, like a Thomas Eakins painting of a woman gazing into a mirror. She pokes her puffed white hair with her fingers. I fold the little blue pillow behind my neck and shut my eyes. I'm asleep before the plane hits cruising altitude.

At the luggage carousel in JFK, a well-dressed couple stand next to me. They both hold slender briefcases in their leather-sheathed hands. "Carl's with a voice-recognition software company that went public last month," the woman says. "They're based in Boston."

"Oh, really," the man says. "And how are they doing?"

"Very hot," she says solemnly. "A real winner. Solid performers."

"That's good to hear."

"I'm just thrilled for him. He was in torn earlobe repair for the longest time."

"I remember that."

She laughs. "Now that's a trend that won't last."

"Where you all coming from?" says a man behind them. He smoothes down his auburn mustache with the side of his forefinger, like he's petting a hamster. He coughs dryly into his fist.

"Uh, Buffalo," the woman tells him. "Like you. We were all on the same plane."

"Did you like it there?"

"We were in the Hyatt the whole time," she says.

"Nice hotel, the Hyatt. The one downtown?"

"Yes." She turns away from him. "Carl doesn't know his head from his ass most of the time. You remember that credit card debacle last year?"

"Oh, man. I tried to warn him about that."

"So did I! But it shouldn't even have been an issue. You can re-age your account if it's a matter of past-due credit."

"Obviously. But Carl steps in shit all the time. We all do, but the difference is he manages to smear it all over himself."

The mustached guy sees that I've been observing his interaction with the cosmopolitans. "Hey, buddy," he says and flips his chin up at me. "How's it going?"

"Pretty good," I say. "How are you?"

He nods confidently. "Solid."

A black Lincoln chariots me back to my apartment in Brooklyn. Big-bellied, the driver sits a great distance from the steering wheel. He appears to be steering with his crotch. On Atlantic Avenue he swings the Lincoln possessively between all three lanes and pounds his horn often, even shakes his gloved fist at another driver, like a cartoon of a New York City cabdriver. At this hour the road is lousy with warring Lincolns, the Brooklyn car service vehicle of choice. We're all slooshing under yellow traffic lights just before they turn red.

"So where you coming from, guy?" he says, ending a contemplative silence.

"Buffalo."

"Yeah? Sorry to hear that." Big toothy grin in the rearview. "What's doing up there?"

"Not much," I tell him. "I have family there."

Outside, one version of Brooklyn rolls by. Subsidized housing. Auto parts stores. Bodegas. Barbed wire.

"Went up to the old farm, eh?" Grinning again, he lifts his chin so I can see all his teeth in the rearview mirror. He steers serenely with his thumb. "What a big difference between the City of New York and upstate," he says in a loud voice, as if I'm now seated in the back row of an amphitheater. "I go up to Saratoga a few times a year, and I'll tell ya: I get homesick."

I turn my attention to the landscape. Junked cars on almost every block, crumpled like aluminum cans by the side of the road. Abandoned buildings. Some areas of Brooklyn could be Beirut.

"What airline?" he says.

"JetBlue."

"I never flown them before," he says thoughtfully. "JetBlue. They bought up all the other airlines and took over terminal six, didn't they?"

"I'm not sure."

"Yes, they did," he says, nodding. "It was wise of them."

Some people like to chat with the driver; others like to stare out the window and daydream the whole way.

Another trip to Buffalo, New York, and all I have to show for it is a resilient hangover and a pocketful of Canadian quarters. The cashiers at Wilson Farms and B-Kwik slip these impostors into your change when you're not looking. You might as well scatter them on the sidewalks of Brooklyn. They're no more valuable than the lint attached to them.

"Frankly, I get homesick when I go upstate," he says. "I miss the traffic, the pollution. You know what I'm saying? Son of a bitch," he curses the driver of a yellow taxi, then turns onto Eastern Parkway. We say nothing to each other for fifteen minutes. I'd like to be a good sport, to chitchat with this guy, but really I have nothing to say.

Outside my window, the landscape changes again. A different Brooklyn rolls by in its proud, crumbling senility. Brick buildings and tall, gnarled trees. The avenue widens to become a parkway. Three competitive, crowded lanes on each side. The genius of service roads, clogged with delivery trucks. For a few blocks the sidewalks along Eastern Parkway become a medley of cultures. I stare out my window. At the Utica Avenue intersection, three Hasidim are sharing a corner with four West Indians. Everybody's waiting for the light to change. Across the street, paper trash swirls in front of a twenty-four-hour McDonald's.

Blasting past the Brooklyn Museum, we continue to battle other cars, daring them to sideswipe us. In Park Slope we hit yet another version of Brooklyn. Brownstones and row houses. Trust-fund hipsters and tattooed lesbians. West Indian nannies and double-wide baby strollers. The women come and go, talking of real estate bubbles. Finally we roll to a stop in front of my apartment on Carroll Street. The driver pops the trunk with a push of a button.

"Take a card now," he says, handing one back to me. "Call us if you need to be picked up again. Call the day before, or at least ten hours ahead of time to be sure. It will be wise of you to do that." He rests his elbow on the seat back. "And that'll be thirty bucks."

I have two twenties and a ten. I hand over forty, ask for four back.

"Thanks, my friend," he says. "Welcome home."

words

In bed, I fight to silence my mind. I punch my pillow.
Enough is enough. I need to fall asleep tonight. No more
playing around. Time for sleep! Let's get focused here. . . .

It's no use. I'm wide awake. Is it any wonder so many
people get drunk or high before facing their tormenting
beds? Many residents of the Elms no longer seem to feel
this anxiety. They drift off to sleep in their wheelchairs like
infants buzzed on breast milk. They take two naps a day
and still sleep soundly through the night.

Maybe their lives aren't so bad, after all. Maybe they've
got it made.

The worst hour of the day is four a.m. Lying on your
back, sober, staring at a hairline fracture in the ceiling,
haunted and shaken by ghosts, you just want to cut your
own head off. You have a full day tomorrow and this awful
brain won't shut off. Enough! No more words. No more language. No more meanings and interpretations. The two
girls from the gas station are coming over. How are ya, Mr.
Roszak? Best day of my life so far. The poverty of language.
Impossible to convey truth, suffering, beauty. We're getting
closer to victory in our war against terror. Is that a shortcut?
I promise I'll be good. Just sleep. Flick the switch. Shut it
off. The day is over.

Four thirteen a.m. Four fourteen a.m. Assaulted by memories. Weapons of guilt. I'm over at their house, entrusted with the task of babysitting my mother. After having just shaved my face, I sit on the living room couch, reading a magazine, and Ellen comes up behind me, her diaper crinkling, and pokes me forcefully behind the ear with her finger. Recoiling, I say in an angry voice, "What the hell are you doing?" She becomes frightened and stammers, "But you—you have the—" and with a sigh I watch my mother's crazy pantomime and attempt to understand what she is unable to say. Again she points at my head. Exploring with two fingers, I locate a glob of white shaving cream behind my left ear. She was only trying to be helpful, motherly. "I'm sorry," I say, and Ellen shakes her head, still frightened by my response, and says, "No, it's not a sorry— It's never a sorry," but I am really apologizing for having overreacted this way, apologizing too for my horror at my mother's touch, as though I feared her dementia could be contracted through physical contact.

No more. Enough. Sleep.

It's some kind of moral failing to etch only the punishing moments into your brain, making those visions true and inviolable and definite, while abandoning the positive moments as orphans, aberrations. If my thoughts have the power to create my future, as I once read somewhere, and if it's true that what I will become tomorrow is determined by what I think today, then I should choose to protect more pleasant memories. Once, when I was babysitting her, I asked her if I could read her a short story, and she agreed, and we sat out on the back porch, where the ducks sometimes dared to join us, which always thrilled her—she had given them all names—and I began to read from one of her books, *Women and Fiction*. The story I chose was Tillie Olsen's "I Stand Here Ironing." Mom sat next to me, listening, her head bowed, a half smile on her face. I stopped reading after two pages and said, "Is this okay? Should I continue?" because I didn't know if she could follow the flow of words anymore, and actually I was getting lost myself, unable to concentrate, too busy imagining her confusion. When I asked her if I should keep reading, she raised her head and looked at me, as if she had returned from a long-distance journey. "Yes," she said. "It's very good." She had been transported by the fictional dream. Despite the encroaching dementia, she understood Olsen's words better than I ever could. She was both the daughter and the mother in the story. "Go on," she said. "It's perfect."

Four twenty-one a.m. I don't think I'll ever get to sleep tonight.

But at four thirty or so, I drift off to sleep and remain free of torment, free of suffering for almost an hour. Yet just before the sun rises, I hear them gathering again in my mind, those immaculate words spooling out . . . trailing multicolored threads. Mother, euthanasia, death, Brooklyn, snow.

help

They're partying hard in Bogotá tonight.

Cynthia, a paralegal who lives in my building, turns thirty tomorrow, and she's rented out Bogotá, a Colombian restaurant in Brooklyn, to commemorate the event. Wedged up against the bar, I'm sweating like Nixon debating Kennedy, which makes my hair look even thinner. I can't figure out why no single women are talking to me: I'm a balding twenty-eight-year-old making archaic political references to myself. I'm a catch. The blaring salsa music, a 4/4 assault of horns and percussion, demands movement and gaiety. Presently a trombone and a cowbell are battling for supremacy. Everybody is shouting. I don't feel like drinking tonight.

"Hey, James, why aren't you dancing?" Pretty Michelle sidles through the crowd. One of Cynthia's three roommates, Michelle walks other people's dogs for a living. She's twenty-five. Last year she cleared sixty grand dogwalking in Park Slope and Cobble Hill. She pays only eight hundred a month in rent. "Too cool to dance?" she says, smiling.

Michelle and I have had sex a dozen times in the last year. We both agree that it's a bad idea. We both agree that we should stop.

She looks amazing tonight. When men talk about being a

leg or an ass man, I always say I'm a face man. Old school. Michelle has a lovely, thoughtful face. And she has a kickass body. Her black cocktail dress fits so snugly I imagine I can see her appendectomy scar through it. Her arms and legs are long and lean and tanned, glistening with some kind of lotion. She's wearing kitten heel shoes. The bartender, a dude with one of those thin chinstrap beards, is staring openly at her.

My phone vibrates. When I finally fish it out of my pocket, I'm surprised to see that it's my father. He never calls me after cocktail hour. He's usually in bed by ten o'clock at night. I hold my finger up to Michelle, asking her to wait a second, but she scoffs at me and plunges into the party again. Rodney says, "How are you doing?"

"Um, good," I say, the phone pressed to my right ear. I plug a finger into my left ear. "How are things with you, Dad? Everything okay?"

"Oh, sure." Standing in his kitchen, I imagine, staring out at the snow-covered street, my father sighs into the mouthpiece and a tornado hits my ear four hundred miles away in Brooklyn. He's alone in an empty house. "Just thought I'd see how you were feeling," he says. "Did you have a good time at dinner the other night?"

"It was great," I say in a loud voice. "Are you sure everything's okay? How's Mom doing?"

He says something I can't hear. Then: ". . . scratched somebody again yesterday."

I push my finger deeper into my ear. "A staff member?"

"Another client."

The music stops suddenly. My father coughs. I hear him unwrap a cough drop. Hall's Menthol. Same as always. After another lengthy pause, he says, "Okay, you have a good night, son. I love you."

Before I can respond, Rodney hangs up.

pamplona

Early, too early, Michelle sits up in my bed, hugs her thighs to her chest. "What a wild dream." When I don't respond, she says it again: "What a wild dream I just had. Do you want to hear it, James?" She shakes my shoulder to rouse me, though I'm already awake. How could I possibly be asleep when all night long she thrashed around like a spastic, elbowing me in the neck? I'm sure it was a wild dream. Of course it was. All of her dreams are wild.

After stumbling out of Bogotá, about ten of us all piled into Southpaw, including the staggering birthday girl. Michelle and I got home at around four in the morning, I think. Now it's not even ten o'clock on a Sunday morning. The day of rest and football.

Three weeks ago we vowed to stop doing this. No more sleepovers, we said. No more sex. We agreed that we were holding each other back, preventing ourselves from forming committed relationships with other people. Now, after a late night in Bogotá, here she is again. We're both to blame for this backslide. A few months ago, when this began, we had a serious talk about how neither of us wanted a relationship. We would just hang out with each other from time to time. It all seemed peaceful and democratic. It was just sex, we said. An arrangement. No problem.

The blankets are on the floor. I'm freezing now. In an excited voice she's telling me about her latest dream . . . subterranean caves, fanciful animals, a chase, very frightening. I'm barely listening. I just want to sleep. Rodney's call was strange. I can't put my finger on it. He seemed so glum and distant. And I had a bad night's sleep because Michelle woke me up every two hours with her twitching and bucking. "Put the skates on the kitty, General!" she called out in her sleep.

Last night I dreamed a little, too. I dreamed about Pamplona. The sun hammered down on my oiled black hair. I stood triumphantly over a bloody bull, a thousand-pound beast slain by my sword. Victorious yet humble, I stood in the ring with dignity and ignored the standing ovation. Then I bowed to a tanned señorita in the stands. She blushed and dropped her handkerchief over the railing. I lunged forward to retrieve it.

"Make coffee," Michelle says, gouging me with her fingernail.

"Cut it out, Shell. I'm sleeping."

"Make coffee," she says and picks at the dry skin on my forehead.

I cover my face with the pillow. "No. You."

"But mine never turns out as good as yours. It's too weak when I make it."

"Put more in."

"Fine." She shrugs. "Forget it." Now she's examining a large freckle on her shoulder. "Was this *always* here?" she asks in a soft voice.

She's beautiful when she looks like this: messy hair, pillow marks on her face.

"Please," she says and flicks my earlobe. "Coffee."

I roll over and look up at her. "If coffee will make you happy, I'll do it. But I don't think coffee will make you happy. You'll just want something else afterward."

"Café con leche," she says.

"Okay. I'm working up the motivation for this."

"Good," she says, pressing her face into my pillow. "Let's not fight today."

"You're right," I say. "No fighting today."

"Thank you."

"But if I do this, if I make coffee, you have to get up and get moving. No falling back asleep. Is it a deal?"

"Yes." She nods sleepily. "Promise."

"We'll have a cup or two and read the paper, but then I'm watching football."

"Deal," she says. "Get brewing, baby."

I climb over her and snatch my bathrobe off the floor. I walk through the cold dark hallway into the kitchen. I'm wide awake. The lights are all on now. I make a full pot and sit on the couch and continue reading my book.

Jake Barnes, the narrator of *The Sun Also Rises*, is not doing so hot. For one thing he's impotent and the woman he loves, Lady Brett Ashley, is a nymphomaniac. They're deeply in love but can't screw. Night after night Jake has to watch her traipse off with other men. That's rough.

While my roommates sleep, I bang through the final forty pages. On the last page, they're riding in a taxi together. Lady Brett says, "Oh, Jake, we could have had such a damned good time together." Before Jake replies, a policeman directing traffic lifts his baton. The taxi stops. The symbolism is pretty clear. Poor Jake can never get his own baton up. So these two can't possibly stay together. The end.

Brilliant. Hemingway is still the king. I toss the paperback aside.

Every Sunday I have this whole room to myself. Coffee, silence, peace. I live for it. My roommates, Murph and Samuels, don't crawl out of their caves before three in the afternoon.

Down the hall I hear Michelle moving around the bedroom. She's up. Oh, no. She's getting in the shower. That wasn't part of the deal.

"Michelle!"

"Just a quick one," she calls back.

Michelle always uses two of my clean towels. I have three in my collection. After her shower, she returns to my bedroom, uncaps my deodorant and dabs it in her shaved pits. I bring her a cup of hot coffee with milk, two sugars. She still has one of my towels wrapped around her head. "Thanks," she says, and sits on the edge of the bed.

"No problem."

"James, I've been thinking." She takes a deep breath and exhales. "I'm not coming down here anymore. This is it. Last time."

I can't tell if she's joking or not. "Really?" I say. "What brought this on?"

"Don't tell me you didn't expect it." She unwraps the towel from her head and, tilting her head to the side, scrunches some wet hair in her fist. She drops the towel on the floor. "I have my self-respect, you know." She takes one sip of coffee, nods in approval and then puts the mug on the nightstand.

Clearly she's trying to protect herself. Three weeks ago she said, "You know, you're hard to reach sometimes. You're like the middle of the lake."

I laughed. "What is that supposed to mean? I'm full of plankton?"

She glared at me. "Why is everything a joke to you?"

"Because it is," I said. "Life is a joke. We have no choice but to laugh at it. Otherwise, we'd be bawling all day long."

That pissed her off. "Oh, you're so profound. Why don't you put that in a greeting card?"

We'd been hanging out, no strings attached, for far too long at that point. The tension level was rising. We had reached security level orange. High risk.

Michelle stands and heads to the door. I guess she's not joking about this. "Give me a good-bye hug. I'm leaving."

I seem to have a knack for frustrating people.

Among the many great lines in Gregory Corso's poem "Marriage," one in particular speaks to me: *Because what if I'm sixty years old and not married, all alone in a furnished room with pee stains on my underwear.* That could easily be me. I know exactly how the old man arrived there. Like him, I have passed up hundreds of opportunities in my life, retreated into a safe and bloodless fantasy world, to avoid pain and inconvenience. But maybe that old man's truth is even more complex than I imagine. Maybe he took all the chances, made himself vulnerable and still his wife died, leaving him alone in that furnished room. If it is an immutable law that everyone we love will die—and I'd invite anyone to argue against this—shouldn't we then attempt to avoid attachments at all costs? If we already know the ending, why sit through the whole movie?

"This is a little dramatic, Michelle," I say to her. "We live in the same building. We're going to see each other."

She ignores me and hurriedly dresses. "I'll miss you, James," she says, wiggling into last night's dress. "I will really miss you. But it's for the best. We can't live this way anymore." Fully clothed, she turns to me and holds out her arms. "Now give me one last kiss before I leave."

We embrace. I kiss her warm neck just below her triple-pierced left ear. I run my hand through her wet, curly hair. She murmurs something in my ear. It sounds like *pajama* or *banana*. Whatever. It's exciting. It's new.

I lift the dress over her head, and soon we're in bed together again. "James," she says.

"I want you to stay," I tell her. "I do."

service

The following morning my father calls me, rouses me from shallow sleep. "She's gone," he says. Seven thirty-eight a.m., a bad connection. I move to the kitchen, where I get better reception. "Say again?"

"Ellen," he says, his voice ragged. "Your mom passed away this morning."

Six hours later I'm flying over New York State, head against the window, thinking, "At last."

Rodney meets me at the luggage carousel. He's wearing a fur-brimmed hat, beaver or muskrat, an enormous hairy astonishing thing, and an orange quilted parka the color of butternut squash. A lunatic. A *warm* lunatic. I ask him how he's holding up.

"Fine," he says. "You hungry?"

"A little. You?"

"I should eat," he says.

Soon we're sitting across from each other in a Bob Evans Restaurant, a few miles from the airport. Bob Evans is going for a down-home feel, but unless you grew up in a log cabin somewhere, this place does not feel like home. Baskets and rakes on the walls. Pornographic photographs of mashed potatoes and celery-studded stuffing on a sun-dappled wooden table. The place mat suggests: *Give a gift that shows you care. Bob Evans gift certificates.*

"I've drafted an obituary," Rodney tells me while inspecting the laminated menu. "I'd like you to look at it tonight when we get home."

"Of course. I'd be glad to. Was she in any pain?"

"No," he says, still not looking at me. "Nope, she passed away in her sleep. Easy."

"Were you with her?"

"No." He unfolds his napkin, lays it across his lap. "One of the staff nurses was there."

"That's good. Do you know which one?"

"Which one?" he repeats, staring at his menu again. "Her name is Tricia."

"Oh, I know her."

"Nice gal," Rodney says. His eyes are glistening. He tells this story to the menu: "Tricia told me. She got right into bed with Ellen. Held her. This was around ten o'clock at night. She saw it was the end—she heard it, she said, a rattling sound in your mom's throat—and she helped Ellen through it."

I push myself out of the booth. I attempt to put my arms around my father's shoulders, but it's hard to hug an old man sitting in a booth in a franchise restaurant. Especially when he won't turn toward you. I put my hand awkwardly on top of his head. "You did everything you could for her, Dad."

"Thanks. Thanks."

I return to my side of the table. My palm feels greasy

from touching my father's bald head. I need a moist tow-elette. Without drawing attention to the act, I rub my palms on the thighs of my jeans. "I didn't get a chance to see your new apartment last time I was here. Can we see it later to-night?"

"Tomorrow," he says.

"Great. I'm looking forward to it."

Now both of us are perusing the house copy of the news-paper. We've been waiting for this day for years, and now it's here. Mom's dead. What is there to say exactly? Maybe hugs are silly. They're showy, melodramatic. Ellen is at rest, we believe. She's at peace. We're grateful for this. This is how men show respect for the dead. This is how strong men be-have. They do not cry in Bob Evans. They endure. They prepare a face. Blinking back tears, I apply myself to the Sports section. Columnist Larry Felser thinks the Bills have a good chance of winning their last game. He offers a list of ten reasons to support his belief. Felser's making a convinc-ing case here, really walking me through the possibilities. I appreciate his optimism.

"Amazing," Rodney says suddenly. He's reading an article in the Local section. "This guy has given three hundred pints of blood."

"Who?"

"Some eighty-year-old man," Rodney says, showing me the picture. AREA MAN FINDS A REWARDING WAY TO BE OF SERVICE, reads the headline.

"And he's still alive?" I say with a laugh. "How many pints have you given over the years?"

"Oh, God, nowhere near that." He fishes his worn leather wallet out of his back pocket, flips it open and locates his Red Cross card. "Let's see," he says, reading the back of it. "Nine gallons."

"God damn," I say, appreciatively. "Eight pints to a gallon, right? So that's—what? Seventy-two pints? I think you can catch him, Dad."

He laughs. "I doubt it, Jim. I'll be dead long before that."

"Are you guys ready to order?" A smiling, gray-haired waitress is standing beside the table, a miniature golf pencil perched over her pad. "What're you having, sugar?" she asks me.

I'm not that hungry. My mom is dead. The Bills are in last place. Who's got an appetite? But *sugar.* Oh, I love that. That makes my day. Sugar blows *honey* and *doll* away. She recognizes that I'm a sweet treat. "I guess I'll have a BLT," I say.

"A Bob's BLT?" she asks.

This gives me pause. "Are there many different kinds of BLT?"

She nods. "The Bob's has a fried egg on it."

"An egg? But, but wouldn't that be a BELT, then?"

She looks up from her pad, purses her lips. Rodney rolls his eyes.

"I'll have a regular BLT," I say. "Traditional style."

"Fries with that?"

"Sure. Make it a deluxe."

She eyes me suspiciously. "Soup? Salad?"

"No, thanks."

She turns her attention to Rodney. "And for you?"

Rodney taps the stiff laminated menu with his knuckle. "Bowl of chili. Banana nut bread. Large birch beer."

Jesus. That's a solid order.

"You got it, sugar," she tells him with a smile.

After she leaves, Dad and I resume reading. The Bills do not have enough speed at the safety position, according to Felser.

On the way to the car, Rodney says, "She fought hard, didn't she?" He wipes his eyes with his gloved hands. Right in the middle of the parking lot, I grab his shoulders and pull him into a bear hug. He sobs on my shoulder. Snow falls around us. "It's over," I say.

My father's silver Buick rolls like a pinball through tunnels of banked ice. His high beams chop through the falling snow. Staring out the window, I imagine Ellen dying in another woman's arms: a stranger, a sister. A narrow hospital bed, creaking under their weight. I understand that this is heroism. How can it be anything else? No matador in the world shows that much courage. Give me a good RN over a fireman or a police officer any day. Every day a nurse sees truths that would crush a weaker person. And a good nurse resists the urge to lie, cheat and steal her way out of reality. She just stands in the ring and fights. There's puke on the wall. There's blood on the floor. Welcome to life, child. An old philosophy teacher of mine used to say: "If you've got one foot in the past and one foot in the future, you're pissing on the present." He was often drunk, but his message was sound. He stressed learning how to experience a moment. He talked about being present. Sounds easy until you actually try to do it.

whiteout

Rodney parks his car in the driveway outside his empty house. I love how the neighborhood looks after a light snowfall. Clean. White. Pristine. You feel that anything could happen. My native city at its finest. You go to sleep in one world and wake up in another. It's an enchantment only nature can provide. Although I imagine heroin produces similar results.

"Nothing for us today," Rodney says, shutting the mailbox. "No news is good news, I guess."

Across the street, two well-dressed men step out of a parked car. Wearing suits and overcoats, they approach us with hunched shoulders, their gloved hands buried in their pockets. The taller one leads the way, a thin man stepping gingerly through the fresh snow in his polished shoes. He says, "James Fitzroy?"

"Yeah."

"I'm Detective Carlson." Then he nods at a shorter, stockier guy who's pinching up his pleated slacks at the thighs to save the cuffs. "And this is Detective DiMatteo. We'd like to have a few words with you, if you have a moment."

My heart rate quickens. I always feel guilty, criminal,

even when I've done nothing wrong. Unfortunate remnant of my youth. "Why?" I say. "What do you want to talk to me about?"

"We'd like to ask you a few questions about your mother's death."

They both recognize my confusion—I can see it in their eyes—and I imagine my face clearly reveals my disorientation, as if I'd awakened from one dream only to realize that I am in another dream. Cops. Bosses. Judges. Men in authority make me uneasy. Right now I would probably fail a lie detector test. If somebody asked me my astrological sign, and I told the truth—"I am a Libra"—the machine would indicate that I was lying.

Rodney smiles at me. "Go ahead," he says casually, waving his hand. "It's just routine. They've already talked to me."

They have? Thanks for the heads-up, Dad.

I motion to the house. "You guys want to come inside?"

Detective DiMatteo fields this one. "No, that's not necessary. We'd rather talk to you in the car, if that's all right."

"This is strictly informal," Carlson says.

"Routine," DiMatteo adds. "Your father is right. Nothing to worry about."

Rodney has already gone into the house. The front door is ajar. As I follow them to the car, I think about what I'll say. I didn't kill her. Sorry, fellas. Thoughts are not actions. I don't have to explain anything to you.

The two men climb into the front seat. I take a seat in

the back. Carlson cranks up the engine with the twist of a key. Fleetwood Mac blasts from the speakers. "You Make Loving Fun." With one hand DiMatteo lowers the volume and turns up the heat with the other hand. Should I demand to see my lawyer right now? Or would that make me look even more guilty?

DiMatteo turns to me, his forearm resting on the seat back. "Thanks for chatting with us," he says.

"No problem," I say, folding my hands in my lap. "Why wouldn't I? I have nothing to hide."

"Agreed," he says. "Exactly right."

I cross my arms on my chest. "You know, I was out of town when she died."

"I think you misunderstand the purpose of this conversation," he says. "We have reason to believe that your father had something to do with your mother's death." He pauses to let that sink in. "Now, according to our records, he waived the autopsy almost two years ago, which is perfectly legal, of course, but we always investigate when there's—when there's reasonable doubt. And here it seems . . . There's a possibility your ma might have been smothered. What can you tell us about this?"

When I say nothing, Carlson gets into the action. "Now, as you know, we've already spoken to your dad. On the night your mom died, he claims he was having dinner at a friend's house, but one of the . . . the attendants . . ."

"The aides," says DiMatteo.

"One of the aides informs us that Mr. Fitzroy visited his wife's room on the night of her death, which was out of character for him. Strange. It raised some eyebrows. And then when she was found in her room . . ."

I can't believe this is happening.

DiMatteo flips open a notepad. "Understand that we're not accusing him of anything. We're just trying to get to the bottom of this. One of the nurses," he says, searching for her name, "a Tricia Vacanti, a night shift nurse, says that she was alone in the room with your mother when she died. She also says that your father was not at the nursing home on the night in question. So we have conflicting reports."

"I believe Tricia," I say, looking out the window. "I think she's a credible witness."

Carlson has me on the ropes still, and he's throwing a few body blows. "Here's the question, son," he says. He stares at me in the rearview mirror. "Do you believe that Mr. Fitzroy, your dad, might have had anything at all to do with your mom's death?"

"No, I don't. He's not capable of anything like that."

"You're sure about that?"

"One hundred percent. He'd never, ever do something like that." I open the door. "If you knew my dad, you'd know I was telling you the truth."

Carlson glances at DiMatteo, then finds me again in the rearview. "Okay, thanks for taking the time to speak with us."

Before shutting the door, I poke my head into the car. "You couldn't be more off base with this one, guys. Please just let my mother rest. We've been through enough already."

Carlson stares dead ahead, his thumbs hooked on the wheel at six o'clock. He says, "We tend to agree with you."

"Have a good day," says DiMatteo.

I shut the door on them.

don't quit

October 29

Dear James,

Hope the semester is going well. We haven't heard much from you since you moved away. We appreciated the call a month ago. Give your old folks a thrill sometime and ring us up again.

Warning: Unsolicited advice coming: Have you tried talking to the professor of your Literature course? I know you said that he's difficult and doesn't even "like" literature, which I find hard to believe, and that you want to drop the class, but maybe you can explain to him that you are a freshman. Admit to him that you're trying to get acclimated to a new way of life. You can also tell him how much you're working outside of class, that you have a job and you're not just loafing around the dorms. Now, that might help and it might not, but I think that is probably the step to take <u>before</u> quitting, which should be your last option. He may not give a damn and if that's the case, bully for him, but at least you tried. You don't want to have to take any makeup courses this summer. That's no fun!

Your friend Camille sounds like a lively gal. Dad

and I would love to meet her but we don't want to cramp your style. If she really does have as many tattoos as you say, I'd be sure to prep Dad beforehand so that he wouldn't gawk at her too much. We'd try to show her a good time and not embarrass you. I bet Camille would like to see the ducks. For some reason, they haven't migrated yet. They seem confused.

Anyway, enough out of me. I'm going for a walk around the block. I've put on a thousand pounds—you won't even recognize me at Thanksgiving.

Love,
Mom

a wake

Every room of Aunt Rita's big house is lit up, glowing yellow light. The dining room table is laden with pastries, cold cuts, fruit baskets, candies and chocolates. There are bright translucent glass bottles of honey mustard, mayonnaise and raspberry preserves. Rolls, doughnuts, loaves of bread. And there is booze. Irish whiskeys, Swedish vodka, red and white wines, green bottles of beer. I don't recognize half the people here, but everyone seems to know who I am. I have finally attained celebrity status. The motherless son. A pink-faced codger with toothpaste crusted in his white mustache grips my hand, hard, and says, "Sorry for your loss, guy."

A Trinidadian woman in a green velvet dress introduces me to her six-year-old son, Clancy. "Hiya, Clancy," I say, shaking his hot fat sticky hand. "Have you eaten yet?"

He shakes his head no. Powdered sugar covers his upper lip.

"Dig in, buddy," I say. "Look at all this good stuff."

I stalk around the food table, sampling everything, even dairy products. I have a Lactaid pill in my pocket. A small white dog, some kind of stumpy-legged terrier, nuzzles against my shin. Grazing, I cut a wedge of cheddar and then tear a clump of fat purple grapes off the vine. I thumb a sausage cube off its toothpick and it drops to the floor, a snack for the pooch. Then I walk into the adjoining room, chewing a paste of cheese and grapes, spitting the wet seeds into my cupped palm.

In the living room, my aunts, surrounded by well-wishers, trade stories about Ellen's childhood, how much they admired her; Ellen, the oldest, venturing off into the world first, getting an apartment and a job, alone, while they were still stuck in school. "She set such high standards for herself. I mean, she used to say to me, 'You're either part of the solution, Rita, or you're part of the problem.' Can you imagine? I was eleven years old!" The stories start lightly, punctuated by laughter and fond memories, inside jokes, and they begin to sound like tall tales, revisionist history, but each woman ends up sobbing, shoulders shaking. "Sorry, sorry," Aunt Rita says, dabbing her cheeks with a carnation of Kleenex. "This is a celebration, yes?"

I guess that's what you'd call it.

So what can I bring to this situation? I'm not the only one who's suffering here. If you asked Ellen the question *How can I be useful in a given situation?* she would probably offer a simple answer: *By moving a muscle.*

Not all of us find it so evident, though.

There they sit in the center of the room, the two remaining Lundgren sisters. Crushed Aunt Rita, with her child's eyes, the youngest and almost fifty herself. She looks down at her black wool skirt. Her slender face is sunburned from skiing and gardening. Her fists are clenched in her lap. Beside her presides Aunt Donna, the middle child, the arbitrator: Her plump arms are crossed on the shelf of her bosom, blocking any unwanted or insincere entreaties. She is one of those people who can only be angry at everything or pleased with everything—she lacks the ability or desire to choose. Her square white face is scrunched like a cauliflower. Furiously she drags a green paper napkin across her eyes. The napkin says YULETIDE BLESSINGS! on it. We know better than to try to jolly Donna along right now. She will not be diplomatic.

My sister and Allison have been joined by three of Kate's closest high school friends. They are in a supportive huddle, trading stories about Ellen.

By the fireplace, Rodney stands beside Father Brian. They're talking about professional football. Holding a plastic bottle of water, Father Brian mentions something about a "rebuilding year." I watch Rodney's face for a long time, a full minute, to see if I can recognize anything in his eyes. In one hand he holds a half-eaten croissant over a napkin. In his other hand, a bottled beer. His body language seems open, receptive and innocent. After a moment he turns his head toward me, as if sensing my surveillance, and my father meets my gaze with a steady, somber expression. I don't want to know the answer to my unasked question.

Talk about a Buffalo lockjaw. He could teach a master class.

Showcased under the track lighting, like aging debutantes surrounded by unacceptable suitors, the Lundgren sisters look truly devastated. They're holding hands and grieving privately now. A heavy silence falls over the living room. It's a tangible presence, the weight of absence. Ellen

set the standard by which many of us still measure ourselves. In this way, she gave birth to us all.

Growing up, Ellen and her two sisters drank oceans of
coffee. They began drinking it as children, six years old.
They claimed that all Swedes did. Their parents, the Lund-
grens, served it with every meal. Donna and Rita also agreed
that Ellen made the best coffee in the family. They bought
the same beans. They poured hot filtered water through the
grounds. They eschewed measuring and went on instinct.
They copied Ellen's methods in every particularity. Still,
they couldn't quite match the taste of her coffee.

One summer, when I was fifteen, my mother revealed
her coffee-making secret to me. It was simple. No big deal.
She used nutmeg and cinnamon, just a rumor of each, to
spice the grounds. Some mornings I beat her downstairs
and brewed coffee for her, as a surprise. That happened
only twice, maybe three times. More often than not, she
and Bonkers had the kitchen to themselves.

My mother's sisters have created an impenetrable shield of
sadness around themselves, as though they are the only ones
suffering. Mom's two brothers, restrained bald men in wrinkled suits, stand off to the side, ceding the starring roles to
their younger sisters.

Seated on a low ottoman, a glass of ginger ale between
my feet, I try to imagine what an unselfish person would do
in this situation. He would probably just move a muscle.

"Hey, who wants coffee?" I say, rising.

THANK YOU

Stephen Ames. SueAnn Ames. Kevi Ames. John Ames. Stuart and Simon Ames. Jack, Carol, Isa, Laurence and Jeremy Wooster. David Miller. Neil, Margaret and Taylor Schmitz. Tina, Arley and Chandler Lewis. Scott Moyers. Andrew Wylie. Emer Vaughn. Leslie Wells. Ellen Archer. Will Balliett. Beth Gebhard. Vincent Stanley. Navorn Johnson. Kevin MacDonald. Jill Sansone. Sarah Rucker. Mike Rotondo. Maha Khalil. Jennifer Wiener. Betsy Spigelman. Chisomo Kalinga. Anybody I forgot. Matthew Hellerer. Marvin LaHood. Ann Colley. Donald Rayfield. Carey Harrison. Jack Vernon. Jaimee Colbert. Joe Weil. Ed Taylor. Joanna Yas. Sy Safransky. Andrew Snee. David McLendon. Thom Didato. Dave Eggers. Eli Horowitz. Jordan Bass. Mark Seemueller. Jack Cohen. Charles Polizzi. Scott Giordano. Wayne Stull. Peter Naylon. Steve Dolhon. Dan Schroeder. Jason Peterson. Kristen Case. Maddog Mayer. Mark Andre Singer. Paul Tortorella. Lara McDonnell. Kathryn Morawksi. Christian StomsVik. Lauren Bone. Marianne Chapel. Brian Braiker. Ed Carson. Jeff Oliver. Jane Budge. Tony McGlennon. Michele Melnick. David McCarthy. Dan Biondolillo. Mike Pijanowski. Joe Kennedy. Jamie Hamilton. David Bucci. Tom Chapin. Jason Hurd. Matthew Goulet. Bill, Valeria, Henry and Lilly Walker. Jeff Roda. Mabel

Mackey. Butch Mackey. John Virgolino. Sara Hurley. Jenny Husk. Christian Lopez. Marko Schumacher. Rhona Cadenhead-Hames. Jennifer Lester. Pete Jackson. Micah Wilson. Ed Horton. Mike Johnson. Three other people. Jeremy Insull. Christopher Jamele. Maud Newton. Jason McGuire. Robin Elardo. Angie Pelekidis. Olivia Chadha. Kathy Henion. Kim Vose. Andrea Seastrand. Mark Peterson. Justin Russo. And last but not least, many thanks to the great city of Buffalo, New York.